Praise for Erin Nicholas's *Just My Type*

"Just My Type is a fantastic romance: it is funny and sweet with its big share of steaminess and heartwarming scenes, and it is so much more than a simple romantic story between the hero/heroine: the reader gets to know Sara as a young woman and sees her transformation and blossoming independence and maturity. This series shows friendships and sibling relationships in depth as well, and what I love is the perfect balance between light and funny and deep and heartwarming."

~ *BookLoversInc.*

"Erin Nicholas definitely has a flair when it comes to love, passion and friendship thereby making Just My Type definitely a book reader's will love to read again."

~ *BlackRavensReviews*

Look for these titles by

Erin Nicholas

Now Available:

The Bradfords
Just Right
Just Like That
Just My Type

No Matter What
Anything You Want

Just My Type

Erin Nicholas

Samhain Publishing, Ltd.
11821 Mason Montgomery Rd., 4B
Cincinnati, OH 45249
www.samhainpublishing.com

Just My Type

Print ISBN: 978-1-60928-210-3
Digital ISBN: 978-1-60928-189-2

Editing by Lindsey Faber
Cover by Scott Carpenter

First Samhain Publishing, Ltd. electronic publication: September 2010
First Samhain Publishing, Ltd. print publication: August 2011

Dedication

To Derek. You're going to make some lucky heroine a wonderful hero.

Chapter One

This was exactly why she'd decided not to wear panties tonight.

Sara Bradford's eyes found Mac Gordon sitting where he'd been throughout the wedding reception—lounging back in a chair at the head table, one ankle crossed over the other, tux jacket off, tie hanging loose, a glass of beer in one hand, his other arm draped across the empty chair next to him.

Lord Almighty, he was gorgeous. Just looking at the tuxedo shirt stretched tight over his chest, his thick fingers wrapped around the glass, the half-amused, half-irritated expression on his face and slight curl to one corner of his mouth made her want to cross the room and climb up onto his lap.

Which was exactly what she intended to do.

Mac wouldn't know what to do. None of their friends would know what to do. Her brother and sister wouldn't know what to do. Hell, *she* wasn't entirely sure what to do after that. But they were just gonna have to figure it out. Because Sara wanted Mac and she was going to have him.

As if she'd scripted it, the second cousin of the fourth usher arrived back at her side with a glass of champagne in one hand and a glass of beer in the other.

"Here you go, sweetie," he said, handing her the champagne flute.

She gave him a smile. She hated he was calling her sweetie after only knowing her for a few hours, and not knowing her that well, but she would put up with it for a few more minutes. All she needed from him was an excuse to go to Mac. She had a feeling Doug was about three minutes from being just that excuse.

"Thanks, Doug." She tipped the glass and drained half of the champagne. It was only her second glass, and as she enjoyed the tingles the sweet bubbles gave her, she realized it would have to be her last. She wasn't about to approach Mac tipsy. He'd think that was the reason and use it as an excuse to put her off.

"Sara, I'm so glad we got together tonight. After meeting you last night I can hardly think of anything else," Doug said, leaning close.

"I'm flattered," she said sincerely, leaning back. Which was true. It was always flattering when men found her attractive, sweet, interesting, cute, beautiful, smart, sexy and any of the other adjectives they used. Flattering, but nothing more.

Mac Gordon, on the other hand, had only to walk into a room and she felt such a crush of emotions she sometimes couldn't hide it and would have to find an excuse to leave until she got her composure back. She loved Mac. Plain and simple. What had started out as admiration and gratitude had turned into a crush, which matured into friendship and was now full-blown love. Not to mention the lust. Oh, the lust.

All of which posed a huge problem in her life. Mac thought of her as a little sister. She, on the other hand, compared every man she met to him and found them all lacking.

It had all created a very emotionally—and sexually—frustrating situation.

That was all about to change.

Sara didn't have to check to see if Mac was looking. He'd been watching her all day. It wasn't unusual. He always seemed to know exactly where she was and who she was with.

Like a man in love.

Or an older brother.

Unfortunately.

But today had been different and had been what made her decide now was the time. She'd been waiting for the perfect opportunity to convince Mac they belonged together. The way his eyes had barely left her all day meant tonight was that chance. Her brother's bride, Danika, had chosen gorgeous, sexy dresses for her bridesmaids. The color, a silvery blue, looked good on all of them and the silky material and straight cut was understated but sexy. The backs dipped low, the front came to a V between the breasts and the straight skirt gently caressed the curves of hips, derrieres and thighs before dropping to the floor. It moved with a shimmering elegance and Sara loved it.

She thought perhaps Mac felt the same. The other women's husbands had verbally and tactilely admired the dresses on their wives. As Ben, her brother-in-law, had slid his hands over the silk and said something in her sister's ear that made her blush, Sara had snuck a look at Mac. He'd been staring squarely at her. She'd felt her body flush with heat and had forced herself to stay put and not offer to let him feel the material.

He was watching her now too. Time to put her plan in motion.

She leaned in and hugged Doug, careful to keep space between their bodies. Over his shoulder, she mouthed to Mac, "Help me."

She pulled back and looked at Doug, turning them both so her back was to Mac. "Doug, you're a nice guy."

"Thanks." He moved a little closer, obviously encouraged by her spontaneous hug.

"And I'm sorry."

He hesitated and frowned. "What for?"

"You'll see."

A moment later she felt a big, warm body right behind her. Mac's heavy hand settled on the nape of her neck. "Dance with me."

His deep voice made goose bumps trip up and down her arms. As usual. She loved that.

"See you later, Sara," Doug said, turning away without pause.

She smiled, knowing exactly the glare Mac was giving him. She turned to the big man behind her and intentionally stepped close. "Thanks, Mac."

"You okay?"

That was the way she'd known it would be. He wouldn't hesitate to come with nothing more than *help me* from her. He would do anything for her. At least, he always had. There was one big thing she wanted from him that she wasn't so sure he'd do without question.

"Now I am," she answered truthfully.

"Do I need to hit anybody?" he asked.

She smiled. She knew he was being sarcastic, yet if she said yes, he'd do it. "No. I'm great."

He still had his hand cupping her neck and she felt his thumb stroke up and down the side of her throat. She looked up into his eyes.

His attention dropped to her mouth before his hand fell away.

Dammit.

"I don't want to dance," she said.

"No? Cake?" He glanced in the direction of Sam and Danika's five-tiered white wedding cake with blue and silver accents.

"No. Something else though. From you."

"You're old enough to buy your own drinks, princess."

Sam's friends had called her princess for as long as she could remember. Was she spoiled? Yes. Was she overprotected? Definitely. Did she always get her way? Pretty much. Was it her fault? Not really.

"Yeah, I am. Twenty-five as a matter of fact."

"I remember." He'd been at every birthday party she'd had since she turned thirteen.

"Something else."

"Ride home I can do too. I'm ready to go."

"We can't leave before Sam and Dani," she protested.

He sighed, very put-upon. Sara thought about the ride-home offer. The thing about it was Mac had given her more rides home than her own brother had. No one would think anything of it, least of all Mac himself.

At least up until right now.

"I need you to kiss me."

Several heartbeats passed before he said, "Excuse me?"

"Doug, the guy I was talking to a minute ago, thinks *he's* taking me home. I need you to help me convince him I'm involved with someone."

Mac frowned down at her. "Tell him no."

"He's in town until Tuesday and comes back on business all the time. He'll keep bugging me."

Mac's frown turned to a scowl. "Keep telling him no."

"This is easier," she insisted, moving closer as Mack leaned back slightly. "If he thinks I'm involved, especially with a big, mean-looking guy like you, he'll drop it."

"Mean-looking?"

"When you frown like that." She moved even closer. "Come on. Just a little favor. One kiss."

He'd kissed her cheek, her forehead, the top of her head and her hand before. And once on the lips. New Year's Eve. Two years ago. Which was when the lust had started. She'd never felt like that with even the most passionate kisses from other men and this had been only a New Year's Eve kiss. It hadn't been a peck, but neither had it been carnal by any stretch—it had been full, lips slightly open, up against the full length of his body, lingering for a good minute.

All she'd been able to think after was *wow* and *if he ever really turned it on, I'm a goner.*

"Tell him you're with me," he said with a growl turning back to his chair at the head table. He grabbed her hand just as she thought he was walking away and pulled her along with him. "Stay with me and you won't have to tell him anything at all."

Sara let herself enjoy Mac's hand, big, warm and strong, for a moment before making herself keep up the argument—even though he was right. She wanted that kiss.

"Someone already told him I'm single. He'll think we're just friends sitting together. Even if he doesn't approach me again tonight, he'll probably call tomorrow."

Mac settled down into his chair and pushed the chair next to him out for her. "Want me to stay over and answer the phone until Tuesday?"

She swiveled on her chair seat to look at him, gauging the motivation behind the offer. She knew he didn't mean it like *that.* He'd slept on her couch before.

"Yes," she said simply.

"I will," he told her lifting his glass. "But you have to buy Twinkies."

Mac's favorite food. Normally, she would roll her eyes and joke about his propensity for junk food. But she was in a mood tonight. She leaned over and put her hand on his hard, flat stomach.

"How do you keep these so tight with all those Twinkies?" She rubbed her hand back and forth over the warm, white linen of his shirt.

Mac seemed to freeze. And stop breathing. His eyes were locked on hers and she felt a current zing between them. She'd never touched him like that. They'd held hands, even hugged before, and she'd touched his arms, back, shoulder, even face once, but never his chest, or stomach, or lower.

"Sara?" His voice was definitely hoarse.

"Mac."

"Move your hand."

She slid it downward and Mac shot back, tipping his chair onto its back legs and throwing him off-balance enough that he stumbled to his feet, knocking the chair over.

"Damn, Sara!" he swore. Straightening to his full height and glaring down at her he demanded, "What the hell was that?"

She blinked at him, trying for innocence. "You said..."

"I didn't mean *that*!" he snapped.

"Well, why not? *I* certainly wouldn't mind doing it."

He gaped at her and she almost laughed. She'd never seen Mac flabbergasted like this.

"You wouldn't *mind* doing what exactly?"

Maybe he thought—or hoped—she was talking about something else. She had to make this clear.

"Putting my hand on your..."

"*Okay,*" he interrupted, throwing up his hands. "Enough. You're obviously drunk."

Instead of looking up and arguing his statement, Sara's eyes found the object of conversation almost right in front of her. And *it* looked interested in what she was proposing.

Mac had an erection. Right there. Front and center. Unmistakable.

"You sure you're not interested?" She looked directly at the tent in his pants.

He quickly righted the chair, sat and dropped his napkin in his lap. "Knock it off."

"What? You're telling me you've never thought of it? Ever?"

"Of having your hand down my pants at your brother's wedding? No, I can honestly say I haven't." He wouldn't look at her.

"So when have you thought about having my hand down your pants?"

He opened his mouth, shut it, shifted in his chair, frowned. "Stop it."

She scooted her chair closer. "Mac, honestly. Have you ever thought of us together?"

"Sure. We're together all the time at Sam's, at the center and the hospital." He still wasn't making eye contact.

Sara touched his knee and he nearly jumped out of his chair again. She smiled. She was no dummy. She had a master's degree in psychology and was a licensed social worker in Nebraska. She studied people. She'd watched the two people she knew best—her sister, Jessica, and her brother, Sam—fall in love with their spouses. She'd seen the effect that intense attraction had on people and how they acted until they admitted the attraction and did something about it.

"I'm talking about naked, you and me."

"Of course not," he answered quickly. Too quickly. He was scowling again. "You're a kid, like a sister to me."

He was lying. He had to be lying. Before she could think it out any further and potentially chicken out, Sara slid from her chair to Mac's lap, cupped the back of his head in both hands and kissed him with all she had.

Damn it.

Mac realized he should have seen this coming. But a man could only be expected to be so intelligent when most of his brain cells were saying things like *yes* and *take her* and recalling all of the ways he had imagined her hands on him. And vice versa.

Sara's kiss started off as a point to prove, he knew, but it didn't matter that at first it was only lip to lip. It was the whole thing—the warm, satiny feel of her, the way her butt fit perfectly against his groin, how great she smelled and how delicious she tasted and how incredible she sounded when she sighed, then moaned when his hands went to her hips and his lips opened, deepening the kiss.

He couldn't help it. This was Sara. To hell with the idea she had been like a little sister to him for the past thirteen years, to hell with the fact she was twelve years younger than he was. To hell with the fact he was way too wild for her, to hell with the fact she was his best friend's baby sister and that this was Sam's wedding.

It was that last thought that made him finally use more than four brain cells and pull back.

He held her at arm's length and watched as she pressed her lips together, tried to focus her eyes and sucked in a long pull of air to try to catch her breath.

God, she was beautiful. And *she'd* just kissed *him.*

He'd always been afraid he'd do that before she got herself safely married to someone else. However, doing it at her brother's—his best friend's—wedding was *not* cool.

Son of a bitch.

He stood swiftly and put her on her feet, slowly taking his hands from her, when in actuality he wanted more. Much, much more.

"You need to go...somewhere else."

She blinked at him. "No."

"Yes. Now."

"Doug might find me."

"Well, Sam's about to find *me,* so get scarce."

She glanced over her shoulder and saw her brother coming toward them. "Ladies' room."

"Good choice." Sam couldn't follow her in there.

Neither could Mac. He somehow kept his eyes from following Sara out of the ballroom. It didn't matter. Sam had seen what led up to her exit.

"What the hell, Mac?" were Sam Bradford's first words to his friend.

Mac held up his hands. "Hang on, get the whole story, Sam."

Sam raised both eyebrows. "I'm waiting. About ten seconds."

"She kissed me, Sam. And it was all just a ruse to get that Doug guy to leave her alone."

Sam didn't look convinced. "You couldn't tell him to leave her alone?"

"I did."

"Did it work?"

"Seemed to."

"So what's with the kissing?"

Sam wasn't totally pissed. Mac had seen Sam totally pissed and this wasn't it. He definitely wasn't happy, though. He was giving Mac the benefit of the doubt, but it wouldn't last forever.

It would have been helpful if Mac's brain had been working at full capacity, but a large part of it was still firmly on Sara. How she felt in his arms, how she'd been the aggressor, how good she was with her tongue. And how she'd gotten so good at that.

Damn.

"She thought maybe he'd call her tomorrow or something. I don't know, man. I'm innocent here."

Sam snorted. And it wasn't in amusement. "You haven't been innocent where a woman's concerned since you were fourteen, Mac."

He couldn't argue that and Sam was *not* in the mood to argue, so Mac kept quiet on that point. "I was helping Sara out. I haven't been able to say no to that girl since I met her."

Which was true and damned annoying.

"Where is she?" Sam asked, looking around.

When Sara wanted to avoid her siblings and their ire, she was quite good. Mac let himself quirk a quick smile as Sam looked away, but was fully composed when his friend again turned his attention on him.

"Ladies' room," Mac said. "I think it's time I took her home."

Sam looked at him for a long five seconds. Then said, "I don't think so."

"Excuse me?" Mac was surprised. There had been many occasions when Sam had *asked* Mac to take care of Sara, see her home, take something to her and so on.

"I think she can get home without you tonight, Mac."

There was something serious in his tone and voice. Which sucked. Anytime, but especially on the night when he was getting married, and all should have been happy.

Mac leaned in close and slapped Sam's upper arm. "Pull your head out of your ass, Sam. I'm not doin' anything to your sister. Not now, not ever. Got it?"

Sam stared at him. Then gave him a brief, short nod. "Got it."

To be sure, Mac added, "You have my word."

"Tell her too," Sam said shortly.

"She doesn't..."

"I saw that kiss, Mac. That was..." Sam drew a deep breath and shook his head, "...not something I want to see ever again. Make sure

Sara knows there's nothing going on. Now or ever."

Mac wished he could take such a deep breath, but suddenly he felt like something was pushing in directly over his sternum. "Dammit, Sam. It's fine."

"Make sure."

Mac couldn't quite meet his friend's eyes when he said, "I will."

Sam slapped his shoulder in return. "I trust you."

He might as well have slugged him in the stomach. Yes, Sam could trust him to be sure nothing happened between him and Sara, but Mac already had a ton of thoughts and dreams about Sara to feel plenty guilty about. And that hadn't started tonight.

Oh, boy, this was it.

Sara stared at her reflection in the mirror and oscillated between praying Sam wouldn't hurt Mac and praying that whatever he did he'd hurry up. She wanted to pick right up where they'd left off.

Mac's hands had certainly felt the material of her dress. Specifically the material over her butt and hips, but he hadn't felt as much of her as she'd hoped or wanted. Similarly she'd felt some of him, particularly the magnificent erection that had pressed nicely against her as she sat on his lap.

The woman staring back at her was someone new. This woman looked happy and even a bit triumphant. Sara was a naturally happy and optimistic person. She saw the bright side, looked at glasses as half-full and all of that.

The woman in the mirror was *happy.* A happy that Sara had only seen on other people. Like Jessica and Sam. And their spouses, Ben and Danika. Sara had never been in love before. She'd been in love with Mac for years, but to be truly, fully, utterly in love it had to be reciprocated. Until tonight she hadn't been sure of that part.

Now, she knew. Mac had kissed her back. No question about it. He'd been aroused, he'd wanted her too, he'd done it in spite of his objections to the time and place.

He loved her too.

Her world was complete.

This was perfect movie-love-story stuff.

She pulled open the door to the ladies' room. Whatever Sam had to say to Mac would not take this long. If it did she'd have to rescue Mac. She had much better uses for him.

She stepped back into the reception, immediately searching for Mac. She always did that. In any room, at any event she knew he'd be, the first thing she did was look for him. Even if she didn't immediately go to him, she always knew where he was. This time it felt different. Now she could look for him without hiding it. She could look for him, knowing he wanted her to find him. She could look for him because she was supposed to be *with* him and everyone could know.

The chairs where they'd been sitting were empty, but Mac's jacket was still hung around the back of his. None of the occupied barstools held him. Ben and Jessica sat with Kevin and Dooley—Sam's other groomsmen and Mac's best friends in the world—but no Mac. She even found her brother, dancing with Danika, and rolled her eyes. They were married now. They needed to go home if they were going to act like that. Of course, if Dani was within six feet of him, Sam wouldn't notice a tornado ripping through the building. Then Sara smiled. On Mac's lap she couldn't have cared less about the fact that they were in public or that other people were around and might see. Good for Sam and Danika. They had each other. Their lives were going in a new direction. She was happy for them. She was. Just like she was happy for her sister and Ben. Jessica was six weeks pregnant with their first baby and even though it meant she'd blown lunch off with Sara—a lunch they'd had every Wednesday for the past year—to shop for baby furniture, Sara was happy for her sister. Now Jessica would have someone new to boss around. That could only be a good thing for everyone.

Sara had other things to concentrate on anyway. Like making her own new life. With Mac.

So where was he? She was ready to get started.

Bathroom? Possibly. She knew he hadn't left. For one thing, he would have made sure she got back into the room and with their friends before he left. Then he would have tried to talk her into leaving when he did. Even before *the kiss*, as she had termed it in her mind, Mac was always asking her if she needed a ride, if she needed a drink, if she needed anything. He never left anywhere without making sure she had a ride and knowing who it was with. So he was still here, she was sure.

She decided to wait in the hallway for him. If she could catch him alone, outside of the hotel ballroom she had a better chance of getting another kiss. The fewer eyes and interruptions the better.

The wide hallway had a high ceiling hung with several elaborate chandeliers and evenly spaced enormous mirrors in ornate gold frames on the walls. It was deserted and very quiet. There was another party of some kind going on in the ballroom several doors down, and muted music that increased then decreased as the doors opened and shut came from both that room and Sam's wedding reception, but the plush carpet and padded benches along the walls between the tall potted plants absorbed a lot of the sound.

Sara waited for a few minutes on the bench straight across from the men's room, but finally realized he wasn't coming out. He was either sick, or not in there.

Maybe he had left.

His jacket was still here, but it was a rental. He certainly wasn't in the habit of wearing a jacket, so could have easily forgotten he had one to keep track of. Besides, someone would gather it and return it for him if he left it behind.

Well, she wasn't going back into the reception until she knew he was definitely in there. If one of the others got a hold of her, they wouldn't let her be out here alone for long and they definitely would not let her go out into the parking lot alone to look for his car. But she knew right where it was parked. She'd ridden to the reception in it with Mac, Kevin and Dooley.

It was weird that he might have left. She headed for the front doors of the hotel as she wondered if he had his cell phone. She knew he wanted to continue what they'd started. Unless...

She stopped with her hand on the door leading outside and silently cursed her brother. What had he said to Mac? Had he punched him? Was Mac nursing a broken nose with blood down the front of his tux shirt requiring him to leave immediately? Was he in search of a steak for a black eye? Had Sam simply said *get the hell out and don't come back*? The last was the most likely, but none were impossibilities.

Surely Dooley or Kevin would be with Mac, though, if he'd been hurt or ejected from the party.

Then again, maybe they felt the same way Sam did.

All of them were like big brothers to her. She'd known them since her brother had become a paramedic right after graduating from high school. They were definitely protective. But Mac was one of their own. They wouldn't ostracize him. Especially when *she* was the one who'd started the whole thing.

Dammit. Yes, they would. Not forever, but they would definitely not be happy and would blame Mac. They would think it was all his fault, that he should have known better, that he shouldn't have encouraged her, that he should have seen the signs and put a stop to it all. Stupid as that was. They always expected a lot from Mac. Even looked up to him, in a way.

Mac was older than all of them. He was twelve years her senior and seven years older than Sam. Dooley and Kevin fell somewhere in between. Mac was the unspoken leader of the group. He didn't often exert his authority, but if he did, they would defer to him.

Which meant if they were mad at him, it would be eating him up.

Dammit, again.

Well, they'd all have to get over it. Including Mac.

She headed for his car, to be sure he hadn't left. She needed to find him, and now it seemed even more imperative that it be without an audience of their friends and family.

The car was still there. Sara sighed.

Until she realized there was someone in the car. Two someones, as a matter of fact.

Her heart thudded, then cramped. As did her stomach. She was still a good fifty feet away, but she had a bad feeling about this. She did *not* want to go closer to that car. Yet, she couldn't *not* go closer. She had to be sure it was Mac, for one thing. Kevin would never bring a woman out to the car, but Dooley would. Which would still mean she didn't know where Mac was. For another, her makeup bag and hair supplies from the wedding were on the passenger-side floor. The boys always let her sit in the front.

She was still thirty feet away when she started to get mad. Seriously.

She stomped to the passenger side—*her* side—of the car and yanked the door open. The first thing she saw was a breast. A naked, female breast. Pretty damned close to Mac's face. Which was the second thing she saw. She quickly looked away from both.

She was going to be sick. And pissed off. And a whole bunch of other things she couldn't even name at the moment. But all of that was going to have to wait until later.

Without thinking, she reached into the car and grabbed the woman straddling Mac's lap by the arm and pulled. The woman protested, but Sara's adrenaline overrode the woman's verbal and physical objection. The woman tumbled out, onto her knees beside the car. Sara watched her get up and her blood boiled. She was pretty, young, blond and half-naked. Where Sara had seen only one breast initially, now both were visible and there was a lot to see. It was clear the straps hanging loose had once been tied behind her neck and the bodice of her dress had been pulled down to reveal the goods.

"What the fuck is your problem?" the woman demanded, not even bothering to cover up.

"I need my hairspray," Sara said with a voice that was so far beyond enraged she'd circled back around to calm.

The woman's eyes flickered over Sara's hair.

"I don't have your damned hair spray."

Sara spun back toward the car, determined *not* to look at Mac. So she looked at his hand. Because it was holding the can of hairspray out toward her. She grit her teeth hard and said, "If you have anything hanging out, you'd better put it away."

"I'm good."

His voice sounded weird, but she absolutely could not, would not, look at his face.

"I need the rest of my stuff."

He handed her the little quilted pink bag. "Who's taking you home?"

"None of your damned business. Ever again." She sounded completely composed, much to her surprise. She wanted to do bodily harm to someone. Or a couple of someones.

With the bag clutched tightly to her aching chest, she spun on her heel and practically ran back into the hotel, heading straight to the bathroom. She was grateful for her bag of supplies. She was going to need to repair her makeup after the tears stopped—*if* the tears stopped—and her toothbrush after she vomited.

Chapter Two

"She *what*?" Mac stared at Danika.

"Went to the Caribbean," Danika repeated very slowly, as if talking to someone stupid.

"What the hell for?" he demanded.

It had been six days since the fiasco at Sam's wedding. In those days Mac had realized Sara hadn't told anyone about the scene she'd found in his car. He wasn't sure how to feel about that. It was very strange. None of their friends would have thought anything about it. He was quite often half-naked with women in strange places. Sometimes all-the-way naked. That wouldn't even faze any of them. They also wouldn't expect Sara to be fazed. Or hurt by it. Or devastated, as he feared she really was.

Even though he'd set the whole thing up, to go exactly as it had gone, he still felt like shit. He *never* wanted Sara hurt. By anyone. He knew it had been the right thing to do. She had to be shocked into realizing nothing could happen between them, amazing kiss or not. Had he just tried to tell her that, it wouldn't have worked. She would have tried to talk him out of it. And she would have succeeded.

He wanted her. He wasn't going to lie—to himself, anyway—about that. But he couldn't have her. For a number of reasons. Not the least of which was Sam. And he wasn't going to lie about that either. Sam knew him too well to be okay with Mac being involved with his sister.

But if Sara tried to get her way with some preconceived notion about them having a future together, she would be far too hard to resist. She was just sweet enough, and young and innocent enough, to believe one amazing-shake-the-world kiss was proof they should be together. So he had to convince her she didn't want to be with him.

That he was no good. That their kiss hadn't meant anything to him. There had been only one immediately available and effective way to do that.

Her name was Brandi. And she was...effective.

He hadn't planned it to go quite as far as it had. He hadn't wanted Sara to see Brandi's nipples, for instance. Hell, he hadn't even wanted to see Brandi's nipples. Once he'd asked her to go to the parking lot with him, a place she'd been before—with him—he should have known it would go fast and far.

Dammit.

Still, he certainly hadn't been fighting Sara off since then. In fact, he'd seen her only once, at the Bradford Youth Center she and her siblings had run since their father's death fifteen years before. Sara was the administrator, and all of their friends, including him, put in many volunteer hours. Not that he minded. It was the perfect way to spend time with Sara and not feel guilty about it. Besides, he liked the kids and felt good about the work they all did there.

Now that Sara wasn't speaking to him it wasn't quite the same.

So his plan had worked. Very, very well.

"Vacation," Danika said.

Mac had to blink a few times before he remembered the question he'd asked about why Sara had flown off to a tropical island.

"With who?" Everyone she was close to was still here. He'd seen them all today.

Danika frowned at that. "We're not sure."

"Excuse me?"

Danika frowned at *him*. "Hey, it wasn't my idea and I didn't buy the plane ticket. We got the letter in the mail this morning. She left yesterday. It doesn't say where she is exactly, when she'll be back or who she's with."

"Well, excuse me for worrying."

Danika's eyes widened. "You don't think I'm worried? Besides, I'm living with *Sam*. How wonderful is my life going to be when he reads this thing?"

"He hasn't read it yet?"

"No." Danika sighed. "I don't know what to tell him. He's going to *freak out*, Mac."

Yeah, and Sara definitely knew that too. "Does Jessica know?"

Danika shook her head. "I told Ben. He was bad enough. He started calling airlines and a police detective friend of his. He's acting like she's been kidnapped. He was about to go storming off to find Jess until I made him think it through. He's trying to find some more information out before he tells her so she doesn't lose it."

Mac scrubbed his hand up and down over his face and smooth skull. "Damn it to hell, son of a bitch."

"So what do I do?" Danika twisted the napkin she held into a tight curl. "We just got married, but he's going to want to go storming down to St. Croix. Jessica's only six weeks pregnant—she doesn't need this stress."

"You don't think someone should go after her? Be sure she's all right? For God's sake, Sara's never been farther than Disney World and has never been...well, anywhere...alone."

Danika rolled her eyes. "Well, okay, now don't be ridiculous."

He stared at her across the breakfast bar in her kitchen. "Ridiculous? About what? She's hundreds of miles away, with God knows who, doing God knows what."

"Maybe she's never been that far before but she's..."

He smacked his hand on top of the breakfast bar making Danika jump. "I don't think you understand. Sara literally never goes anywhere alone."

Danika narrowed very suspicious eyes at him. "Nowhere?"

"Rarely."

"Work?"

"Hardly alone. There are fifty kids there with her every day who know her very well."

"What about the drive?"

"Okay, she has thirty minutes alone a day."

"Well, thirty there and back."

Mac grit his teeth. "Okay. Sometimes. Sometimes she gives Kevin a ride home since he lives in the same building. Or one of us goes with her if she decides to give one of the kids a ride home."

Danika thought for a moment. "Grocery store," she said triumphantly.

"Kevin takes her."

"What?" Danika looked at him in obvious disbelief. "You're kidding."

Mac shrugged. "Kevin lives one floor down. They go once a week."

Danika shook her head. "She's twenty-five, Mac. This is crazy."

Mac didn't care. "It works." Sara had never complained and Kevin and the rest of the guys didn't mind helping her out at all.

"Well, maybe she's tired of it. Maybe she's sick of all the pampering and being overprotected."

"So instead of calmly saying, 'Hey, everyone, can we talk about a few things', she gets on a plane and leaves the country?" Mac exclaimed.

"Technically the Virgin Islands are United States territories..."

"I don't give a damn!" Mac yelled.

Danika frowned at him, unimpressed by his outburst. "Look, this isn't *my* fault."

"There has to be a reason." And he had a sick feeling in his stomach that he knew what that reason was. Sara had never rebelled before. She'd also never climbed on his lap and kissed his socks off. Coincidence they both happened within a week of one another? He didn't think so.

"There's no reason in our letter." Danika tossed the folded piece of paper onto the countertop between them. "It says, 'I'm on vacation on St. Croix. I'm fine. I'm not answering my phone or e-mail. I'll call you when I get home'."

"Well, that's a bunch of shit. She had to know we'd be worried," Mac grumbled, rubbing an agitated hand across his head. "Dammit."

"Maybe yours says," Danika said.

"My what?"

"Your letter." She looked at him like he was an imbecile.

His heart hurt. "I didn't get a letter." She hadn't even left *him* a note. Not that she should feel obligated. He wasn't family. But sonofabitch he was just as worried.

"Yeah you did." Danika glanced around. "It came here. I'm guessing she didn't have her address book with her."

"It came here?" Mac repeated stupidly. "A letter?"

Danika rolled her eyes. Again. "Yes, a letter." She moved a catalog and what looked like a bill. "Here." She thrust an envelope at him. It had a hotel insignia on it.

Mac stared at it for a moment. At least she'd stayed in a nice place before she got on the plane. He grabbed the envelope and tore it open, jerking the letter out in one move. He was filled with a mixture of anticipation and trepidation. If Sara was finally going to call him all the names she probably owed him from Sam's wedding night, he wasn't sure he wanted to have it in writing. But if she was going to add in where the hell she was and why, then he needed to know.

Mac, I wasn't going to write to you specifically, knowing that Danika would tell you everything from their letter anyway, it began. Mac felt his chest tighten looking at her handwriting. He glanced at Danika's letter. No hotel logo. So Sara had decided at the last minute to write him. She was thinking about him just before she left. Interesting.

But I finally had to write you too. Because there are things I want you to know that I can't tell anyone else.

That made him feel good. She could confide in him. She could tell him things no one else could know.

I know you are holding yourself back from me because you think I'm a kid. I'm going to show you you're wrong. When I come back, I'm going to be a woman you'll pay attention to. Love, S

Oh, shit.

Mac stared at the *Love, S* at the end and all he could think was *Oh, shit, oh, shit, oh, shit.* He rubbed his hand over his head again. *Oh, shit.*

What did that mean? She had no idea what he thought of her. Or just how much attention he'd been paying. And how guilty he'd been feeling about it.

What did *I'm going to be a woman you'll pay attention to* mean, exactly? Did Sara know what kind of women he generally paid attention to? If she did, how? And how was she going to become one of them? She didn't have nearly enough cleavage for one thing. She also didn't have enough body piercings or tattoos, didn't know enough swear words, hadn't done anything borderline illegal and hadn't spread her legs nearly enough.

Which was what scared the crap out of him.

If she was in St. Croix to catch up with his usual girls he had to get down there *now.* And pray a lot on his way.

"I'm going," he announced, pushing to his feet.

Danika didn't seem surprised. "What do I tell Sam?"

"Don't tell Sam *anything.*" He did not need to deal with his friend's aneurysm right now.

"What about Jessica?"

Mac let out a frustrated sigh. "Tell them she's out of town. Which is true. Shopping. Because I'm sure she's spending money. With a friend. Because I'll be there as soon as I can."

"And do I tell them she's with you?" Danika pressed.

Hell. Did she? Until two weeks ago he wouldn't have hesitated. They would have been relieved she was with him.

Then they'd kissed.

Sam had seen them. Would he believe Mac was going after her out of friendship? *Was* he going after her out of friendship?

He frowned. Of course he was.

Just friendship? The little voice in his head whispered. It was probably his conscience, but he was out of practice listening to it.

Okay, no, not just friendship. However, that didn't mean he shouldn't go. Someone who loved her, who would do something as crazy as going after her, but who wasn't her newly married brother or her pregnant sister should go. After Sam and Jessica, no one loved Sara as much as he did.

"Yes, tell them I went after her. That will keep them from coming too." Sam might kick his ass later, but he wouldn't fly to St. Croix to do it. Sam might worry Mac would kiss her again. Maybe even more. But Sam would also know Sara would be safe from *other* dangers with Mac.

He stomped to the door. He didn't want Sam doubting him. He didn't want Sam to have a reason to doubt him. Sam *wouldn't* have a reason to doubt him. Mac might have some impure thoughts about Sara, he couldn't cut out his frontal lobe after all, but he would not act on those thoughts.

"And whatever you do, keep Jessica from getting on a plane." Lord, he'd have his hands full enough of the younger Bradford girl, he didn't need the older one complicating things even further.

Danika nodded. "You've got it, Mac."

He gave her a quick nod. "Yeah, I do."

"This is a hell of a temper tantrum, princess."

Mac's deep voice vibrated down her spine and through her body, making her sigh. She loved that.

Sara probably should have been surprised, but she realized she wasn't as she took a deep breath and absorbed the fact he was here. She turned to find him nearly right on top of her.

"Hi, Mac."

His eyes narrowed at her casual greeting.

"What the hell are you doing?"

She glanced at the guy she'd been dancing with. His name was Brad and he was very good-looking. Those were the only things about him she knew for sure, besides the fact he wanted to sleep with her. Those were the only things she needed to know.

"Practicing."

His eyes narrowed further and she wondered if he could see anything. "Explain."

"Flirting."

"Apparently you're getting good at it." Mac glared at Brad, who simply continued moving to the music even though his partner had been stopped by another man.

Sara felt her smile grow. "Really?"

Mac's frown came back to her. "Didn't mean it as a compliment."

"Well, it is, since getting good at it is why I came down here."

"We still talking about flirting?"

She grinned at him. "Among other things." She could almost feel his blood pressure rising as she watched him.

"We need to talk."

"I'd rather dance."

"Too bad." He grasped her upper arm and started across the sand toward the fake tiki hut that housed the bar.

She wasn't going to let him boss her around indefinitely, but for the moment she tripped along behind him, simply happy he was there. Sure, she was still humiliated when she thought about the parking lot at her brother's wedding. Sure, she was still disappointed he hadn't been as rocked by their kiss as she had been. But he was here. He'd come to find her on the beach...

"Who came with you?" she asked his wide back.

"No one."

"You came down here alone?" No one in their group did anything alone. Hence, the fact she was no longer on St. Croix alone.

"Yep."

He stopped next to the barstools. Of course, she had dressed as was expected of the tourists on the beaches of St. Croix, which meant a bikini and sarong. Which meant a lot of bare skin. Every inch of which tingled when Mac's big hands went to her waist to lift her onto one of the stools.

The tingling turned into waves of heat the next moment, when he should have let go of her but didn't. His palms rested in the dip of her waist just above her hips and he stood close enough that she could smell his aftershave over the tang of the saltwater. She rested her hands on his forearms, relishing the heat of his skin and the solid muscle under the crisp hair. The hair on his arms was dark, as was the stubble on his jaw in the evening. Those things, along with the thick, dark eyebrows, that were still pulled together in a deep frown, were the only way she knew his hair color. Mac had shaved his head bald for as long as she'd known him. He'd been a swimmer in college and then had kept it up because of the ease. Not only could he pull it off, he made it sexy. She'd been around the hospital for long enough to have heard multiple women comment on how much they liked the look. For a while he'd worn a goatee, which she'd liked, then he'd shaved it and she liked that too. Sara suspected it had a lot more to do with it being Mac than any particular hairstyle—or lack thereof.

The skirt gaped where it wrapped around her hips, baring the leg nearest Mac. His gaze flickered to her thigh, then trailed up over her hips, tummy, breasts, neck and mouth. She was breathing faster when he finally looked her in the eye again.

She pressed her lips together, trying to tamp down the desire to kiss him. She'd had that desire for a long time, but ever since the curl-her-toes kiss at Sam's wedding she wanted it like a bee wanted nectar. What she didn't want, however, was another rejection.

"I can't believe you came alone." She sounded out of breath.

He was still looking at her lips. And holding on to her. "Didn't ask for company."

That surprised her. "You just got on a plane?"

"Took off two hours after I read your damned note."

Wow. He'd reacted quickly. Almost like he cared. It was just after sunset on St. Croix, seven sixteen p.m., which was only one hour ahead of home. "Long trip?"

"Three planes, princess. Three airports. Twelve hours. Very long trip."

And a ticket that had to have cost him over six hundred dollars. Yeah, he definitely cared. She leaned closer and smiled up at him. "I'm glad you came."

"That right?" He didn't smile in return.

"You're not glad you came?"

"I'm not glad that I needed to."

"You didn't *need* to."

"Yeah, I did."

At first, her heart jumped. He'd *needed* to be with her?

Then something in his tone and expression made her frown. It was...resignation. Like she'd gotten herself into trouble and he had to come rescue her in spite of having a hundred other things he'd rather do. He wasn't here because he was worried, exactly. He obviously wasn't here because the idea of a week with her in a tropical paradise was more than he could resist. He was here because he felt obligated. Like a big brother. Since hers was newly married and her sister and brother-in-law were newly pregnant, they sent Mac to watch out for Princess Sara, everybody's little sister.

Terrific.

That realization certainly helped the guilt she'd been feeling over how worried Jessica and Sam had to be.

Mac's thumbs stroked up and down over her skin and she nearly jumped. She wasn't sure he was aware he'd done it. If he was and he was teasing her, it wasn't funny.

She shoved his hands away and pivoted the stool so she faced the bar. She signaled to the bartender, who knew her by name now, and he gave her a thumbs up which meant he'd make her favorite and bring it right over.

"So what? You lost the coin toss?"

He took the stool next to her, scowling at the frothy orange drink with the umbrella in front of her. "Coin toss?" He indicated his need for a beer to the bartender.

"Or did you draw straws since there are three of you?"

"Three?"

She took a long pull on her straw before answering. "Kevin, Dooley and you."

"Kevin and Dooley weren't options."

"They weren't available for the search-and-rescue mission?"

"I came to be sure this doesn't turn into a search-and-rescue mission."

"You came because Sam asked you to."

"Haven't talked to Sam." He took a drink of his beer.

She glanced at him suspiciously. "Text message?"

"No communication at all."

"Jessica?"

"Nope."

She'd always kind of liked Mac's no-nonsense, straight and simple way of talking. Now it was driving her crazy. "Let me guess, Sam and Danika were too physically exhausted to answer the phone and Jessica had to get four more baby-name books from the library."

Mac just looked at her.

"What?" she asked, irritably.

"Feeling a little left out, princess?"

She frowned at her drink. It wasn't that. It wasn't the attention, or the fact that she had always been the center of everyone's attention and now suddenly wasn't. At least it wasn't *only* that. Was she hurt her brother and sister both now had things they'd rather do than talk to and hang out with her? Maybe a little.

But it was more that she missed them. That sounded dumb even in her own head, but their group of friends had always been the center of *her* attention. They were her family. And though she loved Danika and Ben, and would definitely love her niece or nephew, she realized the group was changing. Her rock, her foundation, the heart of her existence was shifting and if Sam and Jessica could change, then anyone could. Especially those who weren't biologically bound to her. And that scared her. That was why now was the time for her to finally let Mac know she wanted him. All of him. Forever.

He was the one part of her life she couldn't—wouldn't—give up in any way.

She had lost Sam to a few dinners and weekends with Dani's family. She was losing Jessica's time and focus to baby and mommy things. Those were good things, things she had to accept because she wanted her siblings to be happy and fulfilled.

But she wasn't losing Mac to anything or anyone. Period.

It was a good thing she was convinced *she* was what could make Mac happy and fulfilled.

"They're so busy with other things it was the perfect time to get away," she finally answered him.

"Uh-huh." He took another pull on the beer bottle.

"So if they didn't send you, you came all on your own?"

"Right."

"Why?" she demanded. He cared about her, dammit, and she was going to make him admit it.

"To make sure you don't do something stupid."

She spun to face him. "For instance?"

"Ending up arrested. Or kidnapped. Or dead."

She puffed out a frustrated breath. Big-brother obligation. That was what this was in his mind. Not I-can't-live-without-you-for-even-a-moment. Instead no-one-else-could-come-so-I'm-here. "Sorry you had to pull your face out from between those breasts."

He grinned and tipped his bottle back. "I forgive you."

She scowled at him. "Well, thanks. And as you can see, I'm not in jail, tied up in a trunk, or six feet under. You can go now."

When she tried to turn back to her drink, Mac's hand went to her elbow and though his hold was firm, it was gentle. The look in his eyes was not.

"I'm not leaving without you."

"Mac, that isn't necessary. I'm going to have a little fun and then..."

"A *little* fun?" he repeated. "I read your note. If you want to keep up with me, there's nothing little about it."

Heat swept over and through her. He was mad, clearly. She wasn't even sure he meant it the way she'd taken it. Still, his words made her want to respond with *prove it.*

"Pretty big talk in your letter, princess."

She made herself lift her chin. "I know. I meant it."

"If you wanna be a woman I pay attention to, you're gonna to have to get into some trouble."

His lazy near-drawl didn't fool her. He was angry about what she'd written. Well, she'd wanted to bait him a bit. She wanted him thinking about her in a new light. It looked like she'd at least gotten his attention.

"I know about your women, Mac." And she did. Too well. She'd been observing Mac, listening to him, learning about him for thirteen years. Even before she'd realized she wanted more from him than the favorite ice cream he would drive out of his way to get for her, she'd been mentally cataloging facts about him.

She'd also, at some point, gotten old enough to understand a lot of the things her brother and his friends talked and joked about...before they'd realized it. She'd heard things she was quite sure they'd all be shocked to know she'd heard and understood.

For instance, Mac liked wild women. A lot of them. Sometimes more than one at a time.

The women that turned his eye were generally toned, dark-skinned—created by regular visits to a tanning bed or by the good Lord, it didn't matter—dark-haired and gorgeous. They also all had an edge.

They were so not the sweet, little-sister type who spent their time in social work.

They were practically the opposite of Sara in every way. Her sister was brunette, but Sara and Sam were blond. Sara's hair fell in natural spiral curls, she had a smattering of freckles across her nose and cheeks, she rarely wore makeup because she didn't need it, and she couldn't walk past a tanning bed without burning. She knew *sweet* was the word most often used to describe her. Up until a few years ago, she'd taken pride in that.

Until she'd realized Mac didn't want sweet.

He wanted wild. Sophisticated. Experienced.

She could be those things. *Would be* those things. With some practice.

"I don't think you know *all* about my women," Mac said.

"I know enough." She took another sip of her drink. She didn't want to think about his women. Except they were all she'd been able to think about since realizing she was going to have to do something drastic to convince Mac she was what he wanted.

"I'm not sure you do." His spun the seat of her stool until she faced him. "You think you know what you're getting into?"

She really didn't. Her sexual experiences thus far had been pretty conventional and not all that amazing. Nothing that gave her tingles thinking about it later. Not like Mac did. They hadn't even had sex, but she could think of him and get warm and tingly just like that.

"Are you going to tell me?" It was the strangest thing, but her heart began racing at the thought of Mac teaching her all the things he liked and wanted. It was fear, in part, along with a healthy dose of excitement.

She didn't know if Mac liked leather or orgies or some other things she hadn't even heard of, but what she did know was that Mac would never do anything that would scare or hurt her.

"Of course not."

She pretty much expected that. "Why not?"

"Sam would kick my ass."

Yeah, probably. But she should be worth it, dammit.

She picked up her half-full glass, considered dumping it on him, and instead removed the umbrella and tipped it back, swallowing the contents in three consecutive swallows. She set the glass back on the bar and swiveled her stool around to face the beach, having to push his knees out of the way. "I guess I'll have to stick with my videos and books. And the Internet, of course." She slid off the stool.

She heard him choke slightly and smiled, refusing to turn. Three seconds later, she felt his hand grab her arm and spin her around.

"Videos?"

She just looked at him.

"What videos, Sara?"

"The videos I'm using to learn about sex."

He grimaced. "Books?"

"And a few magazines."

"Such as?" His voice was gravelly.

She fought a smile. "Most of the books are about understanding men and relationships, but there are a couple about sex too."

"I don't have to ask about the Internet."

She did smile then. "Lots of information there."

"Yeah," he muttered.

"So I'm sure I'm bound to stumble across something you like eventually."

"What the hell is going on, Sara?"

"I'm working on becoming a woman you want."

He cleared his throat. Then he shook his head. "No."

"No?" she repeated. Interesting response. "It's not up for a vote, Mac."

"It, um..." He cleared his throat again. "It won't matter what you learn."

It was her turn to frown at him. "Is that right?"

"Yes."

"Then I guess I'll have to use my new skills on someone else."

"The hell you will," he growled.

Ah-ha. Not as nonchalant as he'd like her to think.

"Tell you what. I'll focus on learning it all right now. We can worry about who else gets to benefit later. I have other things to do too. I've never been drunk, I've never stayed up all night, I've never skinny-dipped..."

He closed his eyes, tipped his head back and pulled a long breath in through his nose.

"I should just throw you on a plane home right now," he said to the sky.

"You're not going to?"

He kept his head back. "No. As damned stupid as that is."

He smelled so good. Sara was momentarily distracted by the scent of his laundry detergent, the Tic Tacs he ate to keep from smoking and the underlying scent that was all Mac. He'd hugged her, sat next to her, even danced with her often enough in the past ten years she would know that scent even in a pitch-black room with fifty other men.

"Why not?"

He frowned down at her. She knew a lot of people found Mac intimidating when he frowned like that. Which was helpful when he was facing down a drunk, angry, abusive husband on a domestic-violence call. With her, it had never worked. Probably because she knew Mac was one of the biggest softies ever made.

"You'd find another way or time of doing...this. And you might not tell me about it next time. Especially if I tell your brother. You want to let loose and be crazy? Go ahead. No problem. I'll be here to be sure you're okay."

It was so not liberated, but she loved the protective tone in his voice and the look in his eyes. "Does that mean cutting in every time I'm dancing with a guy?"

"Depends on the guy."

"You get to be the judge?"

"Yes." He said it in no uncertain terms.

"And what are we looking for in this guy?"

"Someone who keeps his hands to himself, for starters."

She tipped her head and focused on his mouth for a long moment. Then she licked her lips. "That's going to make things difficult."

He tipped her chin up so her eyes were on his. "It will make things easier on my blood pressure."

"It's going to be difficult to have multiple orgasms if he keeps his hands to himself."

The grip on her elbow tightened. "*Excuse me*?"

"I told you I was coming down here to get a little crazy."

"Drinking, dancing, wearing..." his eyes dragged up and down her body, "...almost nothing."

Sara felt her breath hitch as his eyes traveled over the skin exposed by her tiny top and short skirt. "And having sex." Her voice sounded like she had a bad chest cold. "Lots of sex."

"No sex," he said firmly.

"Listen, Mac," she said, tossing her hair over her shoulder. "I'm not going home without trying some of that stuff on the Internet. Period. That leaves us two options."

"Two?" he asked, his scowl deepening. "You willing to entertain the option of experiencing multiple orgasms with another woman?"

She couldn't help it. She smiled. "Would that make it better?"

He growled. Actually growled. A low, deep sound from the back of his throat.

Even though it was a sound of frustration, Sara felt like she'd touched a live wire. Every cell in her body seemed to stand at attention in response to that masculine sound.

"It would be...not better," he managed to grind out between his gritted teeth. "Not much better anyway."

She put her hand on his chest, remembering how she'd touched him at the reception and the kiss that followed.

The kiss that had made her imagine all the other things she wanted Mac to do to her, the kiss that had given her hope.

Now, her hand on his chest felt different. She could feel the pounding of his heart and the rapid rise and fall as he breathed in and out. The hot, firm muscle under the soft cotton. That wide, strong chest made her feel so feminine and small and protected.

"The options are: one, I find a guy here and finally have not-blah sex," she said. "Or two." She stroked her hand over his left pec. "You do it." She let that sink in for a few seconds. "Either way, I'm not leaving here until I've had an orgasm I didn't have to give myself."

Chapter Three

Hell had nothing on standing on the white beach of St. Croix, looking down at Sara dressed in only scraps of material and listening to her talk about having sex. With him.

Since he'd stepped foot on the beach and honed in on Sara, he hadn't been able to truly breathe right. She was barely covered, for God's sake! How was his brain supposed to focus on things like oxygen and carbon dioxide exchange when Sara was practically naked?

She wasn't tight and muscular like he usually liked, nor was she dark or as endowed as he generally preferred. She was blond, soft, pale and less than voluptuous.

And his body was hard and ready to go. Here and now. If he let it.

It seemed he was destined to stay that way for the foreseeable future too. She was talking about learning the things he liked sexually, from videos, books and the Internet.

Thinking about, hearing about, not to mention *watching* her explore the wild world of porn was doing nothing to protect him from needing psych medications, putting his fist through a solid object and *not* doing all of the things to and with her that Sam would—justifiably—kill him for.

There was good reason he'd always ignored his attraction to Sara. Yes, she was younger than him, and his best friend's sister. Even more, she was the opposite of what he liked now. She was one of the sweet girls. The girls he had a horrible track record with. The girls his own grandmother had told him to stay away from. He was no good for a girl who didn't like to get her hands dirty, was always surrounded by friends, liked high heels and manicures and had no idea how great nipple clamps could be.

So now what?

There was no way in hell he could sit here and watch her seduce someone else. Or more than one someone else. A quick glance around the bar ensured him it wouldn't take her much more than a hip swivel and a smile to have five or six young studs begging at her feet.

He couldn't book her on the first flight out of here like he wanted to, for all of the reasons he'd told her earlier, and because he'd promised not to.

That left him only one option at the moment: sit at the bar, drink, cut in when necessary and keep his zipper zipped.

He watched her dance with two guys at one time for about four minutes before stomping across the sand again. Of course, stomping on sand wasn't nearly as satisfying as stomping on firm surfaces.

"Let's both drink," he said.

She spun to face him, still undulating her hips as she looked up at him with a smile. "I already had a drink."

"You need more." His eyes dropped to her mouth. Then lower. He'd never seen her bare stomach, or back, and he was enthralled. To say the least.

Her sarong had slipped down slightly as her hips moved and three silver loops caught his eye.

Without thinking he reached out a hand, inserted the tip of his index finger in the top of the skirt and pulled it lower. His touch effectively stopped her movements. She froze as the pink, yellow and blue flowered material slipped down, revealing an intricate looping design that looked like vines. It spanned from one hip bone to the other just under her belly button and above the top edge of her bikini bottoms. The ink was a silvery color that sparkled in the light of the tiki torches and setting sun.

"What the fuck is that?" he demanded. He was aware the back of his finger rested against the warm, silky skin of her stomach still inside the top edge of the sarong, but he was much more concentrated on the pattern marring that skin.

She stared up at him. "Just for fun."

"Is it a tattoo?" he asked, watching her lick her lips. She seemed nervous. Or something. She was breathing quickly and the only thing moving besides the rapid rise and fall of her chest was that tongue.

"Um...body paint."

He wanted to wipe it away, leave her unmarked. Yet, he also wanted to trace the design. Over and over again. With his tongue. It was sexy as hell. Even as he hated it and the fact someone had applied it to a part of her body he'd never seen, not to mention touched, he was incredibly aroused. Dammit.

"Not permanent?" he asked.

She shook her head and swallowed hard. "I'm still deciding."

"On?"

"The tattoo."

"What are you talking about?"

"I haven't decided what to get. Or where."

"You're getting a tattoo."

"Yes."

"Is that right."

She frowned slightly. "Yes."

"Why?"

"You like tattoos."

"I do?"

"Almost every woman you date has one."

"How do you know?"

"I've seen them. Samantha had that one on the back of her neck, Holly had one on her lower back and Kate had them all over."

"Why did you say almost?" He hadn't realized she'd seen so many of the women he dated. He supposed he hadn't thought she'd care enough to make note of them. Or their names. Or their tattoos.

"I didn't see one on Karen or Anne."

"Doesn't mean they didn't have one," he said. It wasn't a big secret he had seen all of those women naked. It wasn't like he dated them because they sang first soprano in the church choir.

"You're right," Sara agreed, not seeming overly upset to be discussing his sexual exploits and their body art. They could have been discussing how the women wore their hair for as much emotion as she showed. "So I could get it anywhere, I guess."

He knew he shouldn't, but he couldn't help it. He let his eyes drop and travel slowly over her body, mentally making note of all the places he'd love to see a little tattoo. Maybe a butterfly or a lady bug or something else sweet. Better yet, a sparkly princess crown. Because little Miss Sara Bradford was nothing if not a princess, used to always getting her own way, convinced eventually everyone would give her what she wanted. Even if what she thought she wanted was bad for her and the people around her. She thought she wanted him. It was about damned time for Sara to learn not everyone jumped when she said jump.

"You're going to permanently and painfully mark your body because you think that will make me interested?"

She stepped closer and looked up at him with those big green eyes. "No, Mac," she said. "You're already interested. I think a tattoo will help make you willing to act on it."

"Just like that? Magically?" he asked, hating that his body responded to her anyway.

"Well, the tattoo and my new wanton ways."

He coughed, surprised. "Wanton?"

"Last night I spent some time on a website called Wet and Wanton. I took notes."

He was too frickin' old for this. His heart almost stopped beating.

"It isn't going to work," he said, though the voice barely sounded like him. "Girls who are into tattoos and porn are a dime a dozen." He knew that for a fact.

"Right. But in my case the tattoos and porn are icing on the cake, instead of being the whole cake."

That was the perfect princess statement. She was so full of herself. So sure everyone around her was just waiting for a chance to bend over backward for her. So positive there wasn't a chance someone would be able to say no to her. So convinced they would all throw themselves in harm's way for her.

He studied her for a moment, trying to determine if she was bluffing about the tattoo. Was she simply trying to get a reaction from him, to elicit his protective instinct, to prove he had feelings for her? Or was she honestly willing to put ink into her skin because she thought it would turn him on?

"You'll never do it."

"You sure?" she asked.

"You'll see the needle and get light-headed."

"I'm tougher than you think."

He snorted. He'd killed tiny bugs in her bathroom with her nearly gagging in the next room. "Sure you are."

She raised her chin. "I'll do it, Mac. Whatever you want."

Red flags popped up all over. Another girl had told him that, repeatedly, a long time ago. And he'd never recovered. He tried to hide the feeling of a knife stabbing through his chest.

"No problem with me wanting a great big dragon drawn across your sweet ass?" he asked, frowning his meanest frown.

"If that's what gets you goin'," she said. "And thanks for the compliment."

He rolled his eyes and smiled, the dark thoughts dissolving like sugar in coffee. Only she would have taken a compliment out of that. "And more body art. I like this." He drew his finger across the winding vines on her lower stomach.

She sucked in a quick breath, her stomach muscles jumping under his finger.

"Okay," she answered breathlessly.

"You really just gonna let me do whatever I want with you, princess?" he asked huskily. Even though he said it to remind her of how stupid her easy acquiescence was, his imagination ran wild.

"Do you like your women submissive, Mac?" she asked, her own voice pretty husky. "Because I was on a site called Submissive Sweets and I could do that. I also saw a site about female domination. I can't remember the name, but the men on there seemed to be having a good time."

He stared at her, images, ideas, fantasies tripping through his mind as he tried to reconcile the words with the beautiful face he knew so well. The Sara Jo Bradford he knew did *not* know about sexual submission and domination.

"They have free Wi-Fi here?"

"Ten bucks a day." She grinned up at him then. "Totally worth it."

I could do that. She'd actually said that. He still couldn't believe it. She could submit, to him, sexually. That's what she'd said. He had to remember this was Sara. No matter how she was talking. He almost asked what all she'd seen on the site, but decided he would never live through hearing her tell him and he was suddenly quite sure she would tell him. Probably in detail.

Shouldn't she at least be blushing when saying this stuff? Shouldn't that stuff disgust her, or make her nervous, or *something*? Instead, she was talking and meeting his eyes as if she was not only willing, but fully ready to take whatever he could give her.

She had no idea the things he wanted to give her.

"You are so not the submissive type." He didn't go for submissive though. He liked active participation. Very active.

"I'm not?"

"Did Submissive Sweets not define submission?"

"It wasn't necessary," she said dryly. "As they say, a picture is worth a thousand words."

Right. He almost grinned. "Then you figured out it means doing what you're told. No questions or arguments. *Not* your strong trait."

"When does spanking come into the equation?"

Again, he was speechless.

"I haven't looked at any spanking sites. I've seen some listed, though."

Now spanking was something that would do Sara some good. "No spanking." He tried very hard to remember the Christmas he'd given her the kitten. The thing she'd wanted most. Innocent, cute, simple—those were good things. Things he associated with Sara. Kinky sex talk—not as much.

"Okay, no to spanking," she said. "Yes to dragon tattoos."

"Right." He finished off his beer.

"Let's go." She turned, picked up her flip-flop sandals from the sand, slipped her hand in his and started toward the beach condos.

"Where are you going?" he asked, pulling her up short.

"To the tattoo place."

He pulled his hand free of hers. "No. No tattoos. Nothing permanent." Like ruined friendships, for instance.

"I'll sneak out later." She slid close. "Unless you're going to sleep with me. To keep an eye on me. Then I probably couldn't get out without you knowing."

He stared down at her. It was just a big game of chicken, he realized. She didn't think he'd let her do it, so she felt confident talking big, driving him crazy, making him nuts.

There was no way she'd go through with it.

"You're right. Let's go now. This way I know they'll get the dragon right."

He started for the front gate of the resort, Sara in tow.

The cab ride to the shop called, creatively, Body Art, was short.

When they stepped through the doors, Mac finally breathed deep. This was perfect. It was dark, smelled of incense and was wallpapered in various designs for use by the artists. Totally not the kind of place Sara would be comfortable.

Then he frowned at the top of her head as she passed through the door in front of him. She had been here before. She sure didn't seem uncomfortable.

"What do you like?" he asked, gesturing at the designs on the wall.

"You rethinking the dragon on my ass?"

He stifled a chuckle. "Not necessarily. It is smokin'." He dropped his gaze to the object of conversation.

She wiggled it for him as she muttered, "Thanks."

He grinned. He was feeling good again. In control, with a plan that would work.

Sara might have grown up. She might be a woman now. But that didn't mean she was a *woman*. She wasn't ready to play with the big boys. And Mac was a big boy.

"Maybe we should talk about where first," he said. "There's not that much of you, so where we put it might narrow down our choices of what we put there."

She frowned, as if unsure if she would be complimented or offended.

"Here?" She hooked her thumbs in the waistband of her sarong and tugged it low enough to show the dimples just above her buttocks.

Mac stayed resolutely where he stood. Somehow. "No."

"Not lower back?" she asked, looking at him over her shoulder.

"Sam might see it sometime."

"So?" She turned to fully face him, not having pulled the skirt back up. The silvery paint on her lower abdomen glinted in the light.

"Sam isn't going to see your tattoo." That she wasn't going to get. Probably.

Sara propped her hands on her hips. “I’m open to suggestions.”

The tattoo would involve a needle, so there was no way she was getting one.

“Somewhere...else.” Somewhere no one else would ever see it. Ever.

She came toward him, her hips swaying gently, her flat, smooth stomach drawing his attention again. “Maybe here?” She pointed to her right shoulder blade.

“Sam would definitely see that.” So would anyone else who ever looked at her in a tank top. That was not going to work.

“Here?” She bent, pointing at her ankle, but the position drew his eyes to the valley between her breasts shown off by the bikini top.

“Higher.” He wanted it someplace where only he would know about. Very stupid. Totally stupid. But there it was. If Sara was getting a tattoo, it would in be in a place that would only be visible when she was in a thong...or naked.

Of course, she wasn’t getting a tattoo. Then again, if she did...

Somehow he found himself nearly on top of her now, her neck bent back to look up at him. She licked her lips.

“Where do you want it, Mac?” Her voice was husky.

The question wasn’t innocent at all. He knew it. He knew she knew it. He also knew she meant it to be un-innocent.

“Let me surprise you.”

“Okay.”

Something about that made him groan. It was the blatant, unquestioning trust. It was the easy acquiescence to his doing whatever he wanted with her body.

This was so bad.

He was bad. Bad for her.

“It’s gonna be a big needle,” he threw in as one final, albeit weak, attempt to *not* do this.

“Whatever it takes.” She turned and headed for the counter where she rang the bell.

A woman emerged through a curtain behind the counter. She was short, had tight gray curls on her head, wore jeans with a garishly flowered sweatshirt and was chomping on a wad of gum. “What do you need?”

"A tattoo."

Sara said it with confidence, which made Mac roll his eyes. Sara always did whatever she wanted. Usually what she wanted wasn't decided without input from the people in her life—including him. Ultimately, she always got her way because the rest of them made sure any complications were a moot point.

"'Kay." The woman didn't seem concerned. Or any other emotion about it, for that matter. She slid a piece of paper toward Sara. "Sign this."

She did. Without reading it.

"A consent form?" Mac asked, looking at the top of the sheet. "You sure you want to do something that requires a consent form?"

"I get a yearly physical, which requires a consent form, and that's good for me."

Right. Like he was going to win this argument. He wasn't sure why he was even wasting his breath.

"What are you gonna do?" The woman pushed a huge book toward Sara and flipped the cover open. It was a three-ring binder with page after page of designs.

"I know exactly what she needs." Mac pulled the book toward him.

Sara didn't say a word, just leaned her elbow on the countertop and watched.

He flipped several pages but finally got to the smaller, more subtle designs. Still, they didn't have exactly what he was looking for.

"We can do something custom," the woman said around her gum.

"Great."

"Can you draw?"

"Kind of."

She pushed a piece of paper and a pencil toward him.

"You can draw a dragon?" Sara asked.

"Close your eyes," he told her.

Of course he couldn't draw a dragon. But he didn't need to.

He sketched what he wanted quickly and good enough. "There." He shoved it back to the woman.

She looked at it, shrugged and turned. "Meet me behind the curtain."

Sara started for the hot pink and gold striped curtain toward the back of the store. She seemed to know where she was going.

Over her shoulder she asked, "You're coming too, right?"

He wasn't going to miss this. "Of course. If you chicken out, how will I ever know?"

"Where exactly are we putting this thing?"

"Somewhere only I'll ever know." He couldn't help the low growl that intruded into his voice.

She gave him one of those I'm-driving-you-crazy-and-I-know-it female smiles. "Oh."

Of course, the only time he would ever see it would be tonight as it was applied.

"Where?" the tattoo artist, the same woman from the front, asked as Sara climbed up onto the tattoo table and lay back.

"Hike it up," Mac said, looking at Sara's skirt. She wouldn't do this in front of a stranger.

She started to inch the sarong up along her smooth, tan legs.

When it hit mid-thigh—and Mac's gut clenched with the realization she *would* apparently do this in front of a stranger—he stopped her. "Better go from the top." He sounded much gruffer than he meant to.

Sara gave him a knowing smile, which was ridiculous considering she couldn't possibly know all the places his imagination was going.

Her fingers went to the tie at her hip and she pulled before he realized she meant to lose the garment all together. He'd meant she could inch it down. Which he would have explained but he couldn't find his voice once the sarong was spread open, showing off the fact that the bikini bottoms were as skimpy as the top.

He breathed, barely. He blinked not at all.

"Where?" the woman asked, obviously annoyed with how long this whole thing was taking so far.

"There." Mac pointed.

"Here?" The woman pointed next to Sara's belly button.

"No. Lower."

"Where?"

"Lower. Below the paint."

The woman was obviously losing patience. "You wanna show me?"

"Lower." There was no way in hell he was touching Sara. Especially on the inside of her hip bone, just above where the top edge of her bikini bottoms rode.

The woman rolled her eyes and moved her finger down to the top of the bikini. "Here?"

"To the right."

"Here?"

Mac shook his head. "To the right." His gaze flickered up to Sara's.

She smiled and stretched her arms over her head. "Whatever you want, Mac."

Lord. The position, the words, the breathlessness, the way she was looking at him... He was never going to survive this.

The woman moved her finger to the right toward Sara's hip bone and then into the dip on the inside.

"There," Mac said. He looked up at Sara again. "Close your eyes."

She did, with that faint, sexy smile still on her lips.

The needle moved toward her skin and the buzzing noise of the tool started. He wasn't positive he could watch. Sara's breath hissed out as the tip of the tool touched her. Which ensured he couldn't watch. Instead he concentrated on fighting the urge to yank her away from the needle. She was a big girl now, who claimed to want a damned tattoo. If this hurt a little, maybe that would be a good thing. It went against every instinct he had where Sara was concerned, but maybe it would teach her a little something about always thinking she was right. He studied the light fixture and hummed "I Can't Get No Satisfaction".

Thankfully, the tattoo was tiny and took only a few minutes. Mac's jaw still ached from clenching his teeth when it was over.

"All done." The woman pushed back from the table

Sara's eyes flew open. "Already?"

The woman didn't answer as she stripped off the gloves she'd worn and started putting things away.

Sara pushed herself up and peered down at her hip. "You're kidding, right?"

"Nope." He smirked at her. It was the perfect tattoo for her.

"That's it? Where's the dragon?"

"No dragon."

"Not even a dragon king?"

"That," he said, pointing at her hip, "is a princess crown."

She frowned at him.

The tattoo artist ambled back through the curtain—there were a lot of those in this shop—saying, "You can pay up front," over her shoulder as she disappeared.

"Well, if you're going to be stingy on the tattoo," Sara said as soon as the curtain swung back into place, "I have another idea." She leaned toward the shelf to her left and picked up a tiny bottle of paint—body paint to be specific. "I know just where this can go." She didn't move her eyes from his as she unscrewed the lid and tipped her index finger into glittery, hot pink paint. She touched the pad of her finger to her belly button and drew a squiggly line up the middle of her stomach.

Mac faked a yawn as he watched.

Smiling, Sara reached behind her neck and, before Mac realized what she was doing, pulled on the ties holding her bikini in place. The black satin dropped from her breasts and Mac couldn't breathe.

Without a word, she dipped her finger into the paint jar again and circled her right nipple in bright pink.

He was a goner. Just as she'd known he would be.

He couldn't make that matter right then. The threat of negative consequences never had mattered much to him and he apparently sucked at learning from his mistakes.

He took the paint jar from her. "You're doing it wrong."

"Wrong?"

"Lay down."

"Mac, what are you..." Sara started as she lay back on the table.

"Shh," he commanded. "If you talk, then I'll think about this too hard and probably realize what a bad idea it is."

She pressed her lips together.

Mac would have smiled, but the lust coursing through his system had tightened everything, including his mouth. He knew he must look grim as he dipped his index finger into the cool, glittering pink paint. The truth was, he hadn't been this happy in a long, long time.

He touched the pad of his finger against the spot between her breasts and loved the sound of her sharply indrawn breath. He couldn't look at her though. Yes, her bare breasts and nipples were making him crazy, but somehow he knew looking into her face would be worse. He'd want to look into her face and touch her like this over and over and that could absolutely not happen.

Mac drew his finger up and down, watching the line of pink lengthen. Then he traced the curve of her breast above the nipple, curled around and finished off the heart shape. He dipped his finger again, then rubbed it back and forth through the heart he'd drawn, filling it in. Except for the very center. Sara's nipple begged to be touched, but he'd be a goner for sure.

Of course, he'd now seen her naked. Mostly naked anyway. Far more naked than her brother would want him to see her. He'd touched her bare breast. What was the additional harm in touching the nipple too? It was just part of the breast. If he'd touched some of it, why not touch all of it?

When he brushed the tip of his finger over the tight bud, Sara's breath hissed out between her teeth and she arched her back. Without thinking, he glanced at her face. Her eyes were closed, her lips parted. She looked gorgeous.

He brushed the stiff point again, watching her face the whole time. She moaned and then whispered his name. That was his undoing.

He swiped his thumb through the still-wet paint on the curve of her breast, then took the nipple between thumb and first finger, plucking and rolling. She gasped.

"*Yes.*"

Her legs moved restlessly on the table and Mac glanced down her body. Damn, she looked good. Arching and straining, moving under his hands, wanting more.

Looking back at her face, he finally did what he'd been stupidly convincing himself he could avoid forever. He kissed her, with every ounce of lust she'd stirred up within him. She cupped the back of his head in both hands and held him close, kissing him back with abandon and coming off the table as he lifted her then twisted, sitting on the edge of the table and pulling her into his lap. Their lips pressed, their tongues stroked, their breathing grew more labored as he continued to pleasure her breasts until she was practically whimpering.

"Mac, Mac, please," she panted against his mouth.

"I can't, Sara." God, what was he doing? He didn't stop. He did acknowledge the stupidity of what he'd started.

"Let's go..." She gasped as he kissed her neck. "My room..."

"No," he said against the sweet skin behind her ear. "Can't."

"Have to," she managed.

"No."

"But—"

Reluctantly and with more will power than he would have ever given himself credit for, he lifted his head. He looked down at her, hair tousled, lips swollen, eyes glazed, breasts and nipples covered in smudges that had once been pink hearts. His shirt was ruined too, giant splotches of still-wet paint all over the front.

"I shouldn't have started something I can't finish."

She grabbed the front of his shirt, paint and all. "You *can* finish it."

"But I won't."

She stared at him for a moment in obvious disbelief. Then, "Aaarrgh!" She slid off his lap, retied the sarong and reached behind her for the ties of her bikini top as she stomped to the front of the shop.

He was a little slower moving, considering the massive erection he was carrying with him.

"You're an idiot, Mac," Sara informed him when he joined her at the front.

"I know." He extracted a hundred-dollar bill and handed it to Sara's tattoo artist. It was easily twice what he owed. Then he took hold of Sara's elbow and headed for the door.

"A serious idiot," she repeated once out on the sidewalk.

"I know. I should have never started..."

"I want to sleep with you!" she exclaimed, completely disregarding the other people along the sidewalk. "I will do *anything* you want to do. I've been *studying* for this! I know all the sexual terms, I..."

Mac stopped and she plowed into him before she realized she needed to stop too.

"All what sexual terms?"

"I went on this website where they talk to men about sex. Like the best position to give oral sex in and the best way to achieve an orgasm and..."

"What terms?" Mac ground out. Oral sex, orgasms... Exactly the conversation he wanted to be having with Sara.

"Oh. Like..." She smiled at him. "Corkscrew."

That was absolutely, positively his limit.

He wasn't going to last a day, not to mention the four her letter had said she was staying.

He needed her to shut up. And stop standing so close to him. And smelling so good. And everything else. "You need to drink."

"Not that kind of corkscrew, Mac. It's when a man uses his fingers—"

"Shut up, Sara."

She blinked up at him. "*What*?"

"I said shut up. Do not open your mouth again until you're putting liquor in it."

He raised his arm to hail a cab.

"But I—"

"Seriously." It had to have been the tone in his voice. Not commanding, for a change, but pleading.

She shut up.

The orange umbrella drinks were eight dollars apiece, but he'd gladly take out a second mortgage if it meant saving him from Sara's mouth. In every way.

Chapter Four

So this was what a hangover felt like.

Sara groaned and turned over. Why did anyone do this more than once?

Well, she'd wanted to experience being really, really drunk. She wouldn't have done it if Mac hadn't been there to be sure she was safe and got home without incident.

He should have warned her about the jackhammer in her head. She tried to sit up. The *heavy* jackhammer in her head.

She squinted at the clock. Eleven o'clock. She assumed in the morning because sunlight was streaming obnoxiously through her window, but she had no idea what time she'd come back to her condo, how she'd gotten there or...

She quickly glanced down to see what she wore—the same thing from last night—then regretted the rapid movement of her head.

"Ooohhh," she moaned, pulling a pillow across her face and praying for more unconsciousness. In her unconsciousness she didn't have a headache and Mac did all kinds of delicious things to her. Things she hadn't even known about until getting brave enough to type *sex positions* into Google. From there it had been a veritable sexual convention for her. She'd had no idea what she'd been missing all these years...or what Mac had been up to.

A horrible pounding on the door to her condo made her groan anew.

"Time to go, princess."

Normally she loved his voice, and she should have loved that he'd come to her condo rather than getting on the first plane out of here this morning. Last night had been crazy. Great, but crazy. She was thrilled Mac had shown up and not even two hours later she'd been laying on a table in a tattoo parlor, mostly naked, him stroking her breasts with pink paint. Another glance down confirmed there had, indeed, been paint and it had been—and still was—pink.

Mac had touched her breasts.

Things were definitely on track.

She pushed herself up and only thought for a second about throwing up. The urge passed and with it she remembered having thrown up the night before on the way back to the condo. With Mac right beside her.

Yeah, that was sexy.

"Get your sweet ass out of bed, princess. We've got stuff to do."

Hormones apparently worked even when she had a headache. Her body warmed and softened at Mac's words.

"We don't have to get out of bed for the stuff," she said, swinging her door open.

His shoulder was propped against her doorjamb and he looked well rested and not even slightly hungover. In fact, he looked wonderful.

He grinned down at her. "You look like crap."

"I look like I drank way too many orange paradises."

"You did drink too many."

"Your fault."

"You wanted to get really, really drunk."

"I'm crossing that off my to-do list."

"I was going to make you suffer through the hangover. You earned it. But here, this will help." He handed her a bottle of Gatorade. "Take some ibuprofen too. Then we're going for a run."

She blinked up at him.

"Did you hear me?"

"I don't think so." She shook her head. "Thought you said a run."

"I did."

"I don't run."

"What do you mean?"

She blinked five more times. "I mean, I don't run."

His eyes traveled to her toes and back up. She tingled and

clutched the Gatorade against her stomach that was suddenly flipping—in a good way.

"How do you stay in shape?"

She lifted a shoulder. "Good luck, mostly."

He smiled at that. "You don't work out at all?"

"Yoga sometimes."

He wrinkled his nose. "That doesn't count."

"You ever try it?"

"Do you break a sweat?"

She wrinkled her nose this time. "Not if I can help it."

"And you wouldn't want to break a nail," he said dryly.

Sara glanced at her French manicure. Which did look very nice if she did say so herself. "Exactly," she replied without apology.

"Any other physical activity?" he asked with an eye roll.

She opened her mouth and he pinned her with a hard stare.

"It is way too early in the morning for me to deal with you talking about sex, so don't even go there."

She considered that. He was affected by her talking about sex. She could live with that one simple victory for now.

"I like to bike." As soon as she said it, she regretted it. "Sometimes. On occasion. Rarely," she added quickly.

It was too late.

"We'll bike up and down the path that runs along the beach," he said.

"I don't feel good, Mac." She knew she sounded whiny. "You go and I'll meet you later."

"Exercise will make you feel better. You'll sweat out all the junk and get your blood pumping."

"That sounds like one of those stupid things people who like to exercise say."

"You don't like to exercise?"

She raised an eyebrow. "What's to like? You sweat, you breathe hard, you get tired and sore."

Mac shook his head and stepped through the door. She was immediately overcome by the idea Mac was in her bedroom. Mac had never been inside her bedroom. She'd never even been to his apartment. He'd been to her place several times, even slept on her couch twice, though it had been a while since then. They interacted in the homes of their friends, or public places like the youth center and the hospital. It was strange she'd never thought about that before, but now it seemed very intimate having him so near a bed she'd slept in.

She liked it.

"Sara, doesn't it ever bother you to completely live up to every stereotype that has made us call you princess since you were twelve?"

She thought about that for a moment. "I've never taken it as an insult."

He walked to the edge of the still-rumpled bed, stared for a moment, then took a seat in the desk chair. "It was never meant to be an insult," he agreed. "At first it was just funny, then it just stuck. Because it fit."

"Which means you'll totally understand if I say no to the biking. Sweat and I don't get along well, not to mention being out in the sun too long. I burn easily."

His eyes took in how much skin she had showing, even under the pink paint. At that reminder, she felt her heart rate speed up. Suddenly she could think of a few reasons she could get used to sweating.

"You were out—dressed in nearly nothing—yesterday on the beach."

She shook her head. "I didn't go out in the sunlight for more than a few minutes until after dusk."

"Ever heard of sunscreen?"

"Ever heard of skin cancer?"

"Ever heard of wearing clothes that cover...things...up?"

"Ever had a sunburn?"

He paused. "I don't think so. Nothing bad anyway."

"Well, they can hurt like hell. Then they itch and peel. Not to mention the freckles. No thank you."

Mac stretched his legs out and folded his hands on his stomach. "You're pretty mouthy for a girl with a hangover."

"I'm feeling a little better." She realized it was true.

"Drink the Gatorade. Take a shower. Then we're going out."

"I'm not biking. Or running. Or rock climbing," she said on her way to the bathroom.

"How about snorkeling?"

"Ew." She stopped by the vanity and exchanged the Gatorade for a brush. "Seaweed, fish poop, mud."

Mac chuckled. "These are some of the most beautiful waters in the world. You're going to pass up the chance to see coral and fish and..."

"I have the Discovery Channel," she said, trying to brush through a particularly bad knot of hair.

She turned and faced the mirror. And froze. *No*! She was a mess. Her makeup was smudged, her hair was a disaster, the pink paint was smeared all over, and her eyes were bloodshot. This was a fantastic way to entice Mac into bed. Puke on him and then greet him the morning after looking like the undead.

She *never* saw anyone without being put together. She wasn't high maintenance— She stopped. Okay, she was. But she didn't spend hours getting ready— Again, she paused. Okay, it took her over an hour on even the most casual day.

The thing was, it wasn't vanity. She just liked that stuff. It was fun. It was her hobby. She loved messing with her hair. She kept it long because of all the style options it gave her. It wasn't unusual for her to try two or three completely different hairstyles in one morning before deciding on how to leave the house. She also loved makeup and nail polish and stick-ons and body lotions and sprays and gels. She loved the colors, the textures, the smells. She liked clothes and shoes too, finding it fun to have a variety of styles and needs from casual sweatpants to fun jeans to fancy dresses. But it was the before-the-clothes-go-on stuff she liked best.

"I read there are some historic shipwreck sites and..."

"So go," she said, suddenly irritable. She tossed the brush down. She was going to have to find a salon. She was going to have to dazzle Mac later to make up for this disaster. "I came down here to vacation alone anyway."

Mac didn't say anything for a moment.

She avoided looking at him. He was either looking at her like she was nuts, or like she'd hurt his feelings. Either one would make her feel bad.

"Fine. I'd love to snorkel."

"Great. I'll find plenty to do."

"Like?" he said

"I have a long to-do list," she informed him. Which was a lie. She'd come down here to do three things—go far away from home by herself, get drunk for the first time ever and figure out what was so damned great about sex anyway. In that order, for the most part.

She only had one thing left to do.

And now that Mac was here, the chances of her doing it were looking pretty slim. She couldn't do it with someone else. Not when the man she was madly in love with was right here. And that man was certainly not cooperating. Yet.

"Give me an example," he said, stretching to his feet.

She finally faced him, horribly self-conscious about her streaked mascara. "Shopping."

He'd clearly been expecting something more risqué because it took him a moment to repeat, "Shopping?"

"Yes." She flipped her terribly tangled hair over her shoulder. "There is some amazing local jewelry and there's this shop that makes handmade soaps and lotions I want to check out."

Mac sighed as if very put-upon. "Fine, let's go."

He wasn't invited. In addition to lotions and jewelry, she had to find a salon to help her do something great to surprise him with later. "You snorkel, I'll shop. We can meet later."

"I can shop." He said it like he was saying, *I can push that heavy boulder up that steep mountain over and over again.*

"Why would you shop?" she asked, annoyed. Why couldn't he just leave something alone for a change? "I don't want to snorkel, so I shouldn't have to snorkel. You don't want to shop, so you shouldn't have to shop."

"I don't have to shop. I choose to shop."

Sara looked at him, then pointed to the front door of the condo. "Snorkel. I mean it. If you come shopping with me, I swear all I'm going to look at—and try on—is unbelievably skimpy swimming suits and lingerie and I'm going to show you every single one and ask your opinion."

He opened him mouth. Then shut it. Then spun on his heel and left the condo without looking back.

"Four o'clock. Right here," he said simply, before the door shut behind him.

Sara quickly showered and then dressed in a simple white sundress and sandals. With her hair still wet, she grabbed a taxi—or more accurately, had the concierge call a taxi for her—to take her into Christiansted to what he promised was the best spa on the island.

When Sara emerged two hours later, having been wrapped, masked, colored, trimmed, massaged and generally pampered, her headache was gone—as were her natural curls. She'd let the woman straighten her hair, cut two inches off the length and color the light natural blond with chestnut streaks. It was time for a change, time for everyone outside of her to realize she was serious about being a new woman, so maybe they needed to see the outside of her differently. She was even able to ignore the slight stinging of her new tattoo.

She walked right past Mac, turning to watch him stalk toward the front doors of the spa with barely a glance in her direction. Amused, she watched him enter the spa and leaned back against the warm stone wall of the building to wait for him.

Less than two minutes later, he was on the sidewalk glancing in each direction with a deep frown.

"You come here often?" she said, in a false, husky voice.

He turned toward her voice and then stopped. "What happened to you?"

She propped a hand on her hip. She knew she looked good. She also smelled good. She'd asked about the local shop that made their own soaps and one of the girls had offered to run over and get Sara whatever she wanted. Upon their recommendation, she now owned, and smelled like, a tangy pineapple-and-mint combination. Which Mac would like if he got close enough to catch a whiff.

"I shopped and got my hair cut."

He looked from her to the front of the spa, which was quite obviously geared toward the tourists with some money to spend, then back to her. "That takes two hours and fourteen minutes?"

"You were timing me?"

"I snorkeled for an hour. Then waited. And waited."

"You said four o'clock."

"I'm hungry."

"So go eat something."

He shrugged and, if she wasn't mistaken—which she surely was—looked a little sheepish.

"Figured you needed to eat too."

"They served me fruit and rum while I was getting my pedicure."

Instead of admiring her toes he looked at her with a frown. "Rum?"

She laughed. "It's a local staple, Mac, they had to at least offer. I did turn it down. I ate the fruit, though."

"Yeah, this looks like an authentic island hangout," he said sarcastically. "It was probably here when Columbus landed."

"Well, whatever, it's not your job to make sure I eat. I'm perfectly capable of knowing when I'm hungry." She pushed away from the wall. She wanted him ogling her in her sundress and complimenting her hair and wanting to kiss her as badly as she wanted to kiss him, not being, well, how he was being.

"Fruit is a side dish," he said, falling into step beside her. "You have to eat more than that."

"Such as?"

"A burger, a steak, chicken," he said.

She shrugged. "I don't eat a lot of meat."

He sighed. "I know. You're damn picky."

"It's not picky, it's..." She thought about the fact that a lot of food either didn't appeal to her or upset her stomach. She didn't eat anything too spicy, too greasy, too heavy, too sweet... "Okay, maybe I'm picky."

Jessica had raised Sara since she was twelve and their father had died. She'd read probably twenty parenting books and had taken the healthy eating and nutrition stuff to heart, since it was something she could control—unlike the nightmares that plagued Sara at least four nights a week for the first eight months.

Sara hadn't had soda, candy bars, potato chips or any other junk food. She hadn't even tasted a Cheeto until she was twenty. She ate pizza on occasion and liked ice cream, but she simply hadn't developed a taste for snack foods. She wasn't all that crazy about eating, period. She ate because she got hungry, but rarely had a craving and didn't know of a food she couldn't live without.

"This is the Caribbean. The fish here has to be phenomenal," Mac suggested as they walked.

She didn't understand his obsession with whether she ate, but she liked shellfish. "I could probably eat scallops or something."

"You will eat scallops or something," he said firmly. "You need to eat and I don't think I've ever seen you eat a burger."

"You probably haven't."

"That's weird. Who doesn't like cheeseburgers?"

Sara shuddered. "Me."

"Maybe you just haven't had a good one."

"I don't want one. Maybe I'll try scallops."

"You order them or I'll order them for you."

Mac often got bossy with her but never surly. She hoped the uncharacteristic behavior was due to sexual tension. If it wasn't now, it would be.

"Sure, let's go eat," she said, with a big smile. "Scallops sound good. Thanks, Mac."

He looked suspicious—she just couldn't win—as he escorted her down two more blocks and then around the corner. "The cabby said this place has great food." Mac held the door open for her.

She looked at the front of the dilapidated building off the main street. "The cabby? Why don't I go back to the spa and ask them..."

Mac took her elbow and steered her through the doorway of the tiny restaurant that held ten empty tables. "Because I want to eat real food that comes in a proportion that might have a chance at filling me up and won't cost me a month's pay."

Sara pulled her bottom lip between her teeth. She'd never thought about finances where Mac was concerned. He was a single guy with no major expenses as far as she knew. Truthfully, she didn't know much about Mac's lifestyle outside of what he did for a living. Since her brother did the same thing she knew quite a bit about it and how much it paid. She knew about the time he spent with his friends since all of those people were also her friends. Oh, and of course she knew about his *romantic* liaisons. Or, at least she knew what she overheard and inferred.

She knew his parents had been killed in a car accident when he was in college. She suspected that was part of his bond with Sam since he was the only one of Mac's friends who had also lost both parents. But she didn't know about his hobbies, or if he had investments, or if he was paying off college loans or out-of-control credit cards, or if he had siblings.

"Do you have brothers and sisters?" she blurted as Mac steered her to a small corner table and held her chair out. She didn't sit, but stood watching him process her question.

He shook his head. "Only child."

"Welcome! Please sit." A young boy, of fifteen or sixteen, approached from the general direction of the kitchen. He laid menus on the table, but Sara barely noticed him. She continued to stand, staring at Mac, feeling she couldn't let this moment slip away.

There were things about him that she wanted to know. She'd never met any of his family or any other friends besides the guys that were as much a part of her life as his.

"Do you have grandparents, aunts and uncles, cousins..."

"Grandparents are gone. Yeah, a few of the others. But my family is the guys, and you and Jess, and Danika now."

For some reason, Sara felt her throat tighten and her eyes sting. She'd known it, of course. Everyone in their group felt the same way. They were all closer than a typical set of siblings and any one of them would do anything for the others. But hearing him say it, with the look he had in his eyes and that tone in his voice, made her homesick suddenly. She loved all of those people so much.

The waiter continued to hover near the table, clearly confused about why they weren't sitting.

"We're going to need a minute," he told the boy. The waiter moved off, but neither Mac or Sara even blinked.

"You don't really think of me as a sister, do you, Mac?" she asked in a whisper. No teasing, no flirting, she just needed to know.

"I did. For a long, long time, princess."

"I know. But now..."

"It's been a while since it was that simple."

Sara would have thought that admission from him would make her heart leap and cause little cupids to begin dancing on the tabletop.

Instead, she felt relieved.

"So," Mac said, after the silence had stretched several long moments. "Now what?"

Now what? She looked at him. That face that she loved, that body that she wanted, that character she needed.

"I know what you want me to say," she told him. "But I don't want to go back to the way it's always been. Not with the way I feel about you."

He looked angry. "You're going to keep on trying to seduce me and making me turn you down?"

"You'll eventually say yes."

He glared down at her. "God, I wish..."

"That you'd done more last night?"

Heat, which could have been anger or lust, flared in his eyes. "That you would have had even one person, ever in your life, say no to you."

"Ready to order?" The waiter had returned.

"No." Mac's tone was enough to send the man quickly back to the kitchen.

Sara felt much braver than she probably should. But not having Mac in her life forever was simply not an acceptable option and she refused to even let him consider it.

"I think you know what's going to happen," she told him.

He stepped closer, shoving the chair between them out of the way. The scrape of the wood leg against the wood floor grated. He glared down at her. "You think if we have a fling you'll get over me and these feelings and *then* we can go back to how things need to be?"

Sara closed the remaining inches between them and risked touching his chest. He did not pull away from her hand and she found her courage and optimism bolstered. "Mac, I know for a fact once we make love, nothing will ever be the same."

He pulled in and let out a long breath. "Dammit, Sara," he swore. "What the hell do you think you want here? You want to fuck me? I can maybe live with that. You want to date me? That's stupid. You want to move in, spend every waking moment together, be the only woman I ever look at again? You've *got* to know that isn't going to happen."

She didn't flinch, she didn't blink. "Yes. I want all of that."

"And it's that easy in your mind?"

"Yes."

"Your brother will kill me if he even finds out I've seen you half-naked. If we sleep together, he'll...never forgive me."

Sara stood strong, but she had to dig her fingernails into her palm. She saw the pain it caused Mac to think of disappointing—or betraying and losing—his best friend. But she believed Sam wanted her to be happy. Once he understood that Mac was the answer to that, he'd come around.

"Sam wouldn't kill the man I love."

Something flashed in Mac's eyes and he leaned toward her. Just when she was sure he was going to kiss her, he pulled back. His eyes narrowed. "You have this happy little picture in your mind of how this is going to go. We date. Everyone is overjoyed for us, no problems, no resentments. I buy you flowers and candy. You cook candlelight dinners. We walk on the beach at sunset. Blah, blah, blah."

Other than the fact she didn't cook and there wasn't a beach within a hundred miles of Omaha, the whole thing sounded pretty good.

"This is so typical." He pointed his finger at the tip of her nose. "You're thinking about you. What about everyone else? Our friends have feelings you know. They need our group too. And if we change anything it changes everything. For everyone."

She knew that. She was living it with her brother and sister. It was inevitable things were going to change—she'd accepted that—but she was going to be sure any change with Mac was in *her* favor. Typical? Maybe. Selfish? Maybe. Still her plan no matter what? Absolutely.

"I love them too," she said softly.

"Do you? This could hurt them. Badly."

"It doesn't have to."

"What about when we break up?" he asked.

"What do you mean?"

"I mean, if we date and everyone is as great with it as you seem to think they will be, when we break up *that* will mess up the whole group."

"The group is already messed up!" she exclaimed.

Her reaction surprised him enough that Mac didn't respond right away.

"Do you think I haven't thought of all of this?" She frowned up at him. "I'm not stupid. At least this change I'm a part of and in some control of."

His eyebrows shot up. "I see."

"No you don't." Although she was pretty sure he did. "Things have already changed. Ben, Danika, the baby. Us changing it more won't make a difference. It will be even better because it's us, the two of us, still there—just together."

He shook his head, exasperated. "Lord, princess, you're a pain in the ass. I am definitely going to break up with you after we sleep together."

She smiled in spite of his words. She was winning, slowly but surely. "No, we'll stay together. It will be much easier on the group."

"Stay together until they're all dead and can't care?"

"We'll stay together period. We can have it all."

His eyes narrowed slowly. "You think I'm going to *marry* you?"

She lifted a shoulder, ignoring the way her heart thudded at the word *marry* and that Mac seemed quite clearly appalled by the idea.

"Might as well. We're going to be sleeping together for the rest of our lives anyway."

"And that's all marriage is," Mac said, his words dripping in sarcasm.

"You think I'm that naïve?" she asked, getting a bit irritated by this whole being-with-you-is-such-a-horrible-idea thing. Being with her was *not* a horrible idea. She was great. She was especially great for Mac. He should be *thrilled* she wanted to marry him.

And she did. She wanted to marry him.

"I know marriage is more than sex," she said.

"Yeah, it's also *compromise.* Not always getting your way, giving in once in a while," Mac said, leaning in and trying to look mean. "Can you even spell compromise, Sara?"

"Can I get you some water?" The waiter was back, probably sent out again by the restaurant owner to attempt to get *something* for the crazy American tourists.

"No." Mac slipped a twenty from his pocket and handed it to the boy. "We'll tell you when we're ready."

"For someone who lectures me about always expecting to get my way, you sure don't mind having everyone do what you want them to," Sara commented. "You're even willing to pay for it."

"You want me to *pay* you to forget all this craziness and leave it alone?" he asked. "I will. Thousands, Sara. Cash."

She shook her head. "Never. I know what I want and money won't help me get it."

"How about sacrifice? That's a good marriage word too. Heard that term before, princess?" he asked dryly. "How about putting what's best for someone else ahead of what you want and need?"

"I'm thinking of you and your needs right now."

"You think I *need* you?"

She met his eyes evenly and prayed to God she was right. "Yes. I do."

He ground his back teeth together, then said, "You think highly of yourself."

"Because you've been telling me how wonderful I am for years."

That stumped him for a moment. "Maybe I should start insulting you."

"Go ahead." She stepped back and spread her arms. Mac adored her. She knew he cared. He loved her. He didn't know, maybe, that he was also *in love* with her, but he thought she was great. A huge headache sometimes, but great.

He looked at her for a long moment. Then said, "I like your hair curly better."

It wasn't even a true insult. She smiled.

"You're a brat sometimes," he added.

She shrugged. She *was* a brat sometimes. Just like he could be a jerk. In spite of which, she still loved him desperately.

"You give me all kinds of headaches." He'd moved closer again and they were an inch away from being belly to belly. His voice had lost the angry edge.

"I know."

"You're spoiled."

"You helped with that too."

"You're sexy as hell."

The sudden shift caught her by surprise and she sucked in a quick breath.

"You know what you do to me, don't you?" he asked, lifting his hand to her face. "You're so sure of all of this because you know you make me hard just by breathing." He slid his hand from her cheek to the back of her head. His fingers tangled deep in her hair, warm against her skull. "You know I think of you when I'm jerking off in the shower."

Her eyes widened and liquid heat flowed through her veins, touching every cell.

He pulled her closer. "You know I'll never sleep well at night until I know what you sound like when you come." His next words were whispered against her lips. "And you're using it against me."

Before she could reply he'd covered her lips with his, immediately stroking into her mouth with his tongue, not letting her move or even think. He held her firmly and made sweet love to her mouth.

She loved every second of it and simply gave in. It was what he demanded, though she figured he would not have been surprised if she'd fought him. Then again, why would she fight when he was giving her exactly what she wanted?

He gave up for the moment. How could he fight Sara giving him exactly what he wanted? *Her.*

He was only a man.

Hearing her say she loved him, that he needed her, that she wanted him to make love to her for the rest of her life had been slowly chipping away at his resolve. He wanted her. God knew how he wanted her. And he did love her.

Hell, he'd been feeling guilty about that for a couple of years now.

He just couldn't have her.

And he sure as hell was *not* going to marry her. But Sara couldn't define the word no.

There might be only one way out of this and it wasn't going to be easy—on either of them.

He couldn't insult her and he couldn't be mean to her. This was Sara after all. He could not break her heart.

He could, however, ruin her illusion of him—of them. All he had to do was reveal the side of him he'd carefully hidden all these years.

Simply put, he wasn't a nice-boyfriend type of guy.

He was a good friend, a great paramedic, a really good time. But he wasn't romantic or noble or selfless with women. He'd learned, the hard way, to find the right women for what he wanted. He liked his sex raw and dirty and was never going to live with guilt over that again.

The best advice he'd gotten on the subject had been from his grandmother. Of all people. She hadn't used the word sex or tramp or slut, of course. But after one particularly bad breakup with a very nice girl, she'd told him that even though parrots and whales were both beautiful creatures, he needed to decide if he wanted to fly or swim and quit expecting the parrots to be okay with the waves he made.

Even then he'd thought it was a pretty clever metaphor, but being a smart ass he'd asked if she thought girls would appreciate being called whales. She'd smacked him on the side of his head and told him bluntly that he should stay away from nice girls. He'd taken the advice to heart. It was unfortunate it hadn't come until after the third parrot.

Sara was a nice girl. A parrot, for sure.

A *stubborn* parrot.

Convincing her *she* did not want *him* was the only way this was going to work out without anyone getting hurt. And was probably going to be easier than convincing her he didn't want her.

He pulled his mouth from hers, loving how she followed him with her lips for a moment, not wanting to let him go.

"I want to see you naked. Now."

She nodded, looking slightly dazed. "Let's go to my condo."

He shook his head. "Now." He watched her look around the empty restaurant. It was past lunch and before dinner, so there wasn't a crowd—or an audience—but there was no way sweet Sara would get naked in public.

"Here?" she asked.

He crossed his arms and tried to look disappointed. "I like a streak of exhibitionism," he said. He did too. He'd had sex in more than one public restroom and in two storage rooms he could think of. And there had been a couple of times in his car in public parking lots. And an elevator. They hadn't had sex, but he'd gotten an eyeful between the twenty-second floor and the lobby.

Definitely not nice-boyfriend material.

The idea of taking Sara up against the wall of a toilet stall didn't sound appealing. Sara was too good for that. But she would remind him of that and it would be a moot point.

"Okay."

Belatedly he recalled the tattoo parlor from the night before and the way she'd stripped her bikini top off without a second thought.

She started in the direction of the ladies' room and then turned to look over her shoulder. She slid the strap of her dress down and as she stepped into the enclosed hallway the dress slipped down off of her left breast.

Mac went from hard to granite in less than a second. Dammit. This was already backfiring.

He tossed another twenty on the table, stalked over and grabbed her hand and headed out of the restaurant, swearing under his breath. He was obviously going to have to go a lot further to convince her she didn't want a part of his games, his sex life, or his...life.

The sick feeling in his gut at that thought was probably because he was still hungry.

It was going to take an actual demonstration to give Sara a full picture of what she did *not* want for as long as they both should live.

A cab was stopped along the curb a half block away and Mac headed after it, giving a sharp whistle to catch the cabby's attention. Fortunately, Sara had pulled her dress back up to cover herself.

Once they were settled in the backseat, he once more did as Sara had accused him and used money to get what he wanted. He handed the cab driver thirty bucks and said, "Take the long way back, mind your own business and don't look in the rearview mirror."

When the man nodded his consent and pocketed the money, they pulled away from the curb and Mac said to Sara, "Do you have panties on?"

He didn't look at her, but in his periphery saw her pivot to face him.

"Yes. Well, a thong."

Damn. He wasn't sure this game was such a great idea. Still, he had to keep going. He had to push her into discomfort in order to push her away.

"Take it off."

She sat and stared at his profile for several seconds. Then, without a word, she lifted her butt off the leather seat, reached up under the skirt of her sundress and pulled the underwear off.

He couldn't help but look then. The thong was white. Virginal white. And tiny.

He held out his hand and she put the warm silk in his palm. He cupped his fingers around it and then slipped it into his front pants pocket.

"Now come here."

Without hesitation, she slid across the seat. He wrapped his arm around her waist and pulled her into his lap, one knee on each side of his thighs, making her straddle him. Without panties. Mac took a moment to compose himself so his voice wouldn't come out as a squeak. The backseat of a cab wasn't new to him either, but he'd never felt this wound up before.

"Let me see your nipples," he told her, finally letting himself look at her face.

She was flushed, breathing hard, her lips slightly parted and her eyes full of heat, surprise and anticipation. She reached up and pushed the straps of her dress off her shoulders, then peeled the straps down, taking the upper portion of the bodice down as well.

Her breasts bared, her nipples prominent, she sat on his lap, waiting for his next move.

"Put one in my mouth."

He kept his hands firmly around her thighs, just above the knees, not daring to even twitch a finger for fear his hands would never stop until Sara was naked and begging him to take her hard, right there in the cab.

What made him nearly lose it, still in his boxers and blue jeans, was that Sara didn't hesitate to respond to his commands. She pushed up slightly off his lap, her hands going to his shoulders, to put her right breast in front of his mouth, then leaned forward, offering the tip.

Mac's tongue tasted it first. He flicked over the hardened nipple, causing her to moan. Then he closed his lips around it, kissing gently, before he sucked, once soft, then harder, making Sara squirm on his lap and her fingers tighten on his shoulders.

"Mac," she whispered. "More."

He sucked again, willing his own fingers to lessen their grip on her thighs as he fought the wave of lust. He licked, sucked and licked again. Then switched to the other side with only a slight turn of his head. She knew what he wanted—and what she wanted—and she shifted to give him access to the left breast as well.

Several delicious minutes later, he gave her the next order. "Touch yourself."

Finally, a hesitation.

"What do you mean?"

"Squeeze your nipple." He figured they could start slow.

She lifted her hand to her right breast and took the tip between her thumb and forefinger. She tugged gently and sighed with pleasure.

Mac was amazed at his willpower. Everything in him screamed at him to take her, but he was still clothed and his hands hadn't left her thighs. Impressive. Or stupid. Still, he was going to congratulate himself for what he could, because in the next few hours, maybe days, he wasn't going to be the nicest guy in the world.

A minute later, God proved His existence—and that Mac wasn't completely off His list—and they arrived in front of the resort.

"Cover up," Mac told her. When she was slow to respond to his instruction, Mac slipped the straps of the dress back up to her shoulders as the cab stopped.

He threw thirty more dollars into the front seat and slid from the cab putting Sara on her feet first and then nudging her along in front of him.

Without a word, they walked toward her condo, not touching but overwhelmed with awareness of one another. He needed to shock her, he needed to push her sexually, he needed to turn her off, but everything he did she kept right up with.

Dammit. He'd been here before. And regretted it. He wasn't doing that again. Guilt was not something he lived with well. He hadn't forgiven himself for the past, and he hadn't forgotten, but he was strict about his reparation, which made him feel better.

He'd made himself choose between women who wanted meaningful relationships and women who could match his sexual preferences, understanding that, for him, they didn't mix. In his life there were no women who might fall in love with him, no women who might require him to remember anniversaries, no women who batted an eye at having their hands tied during sex.

And now there was Sara. She couldn't fit into his life either, but she was the first in a very, very long time that he wanted to. He had to get to Sara's no-way-in-hell limit damned quick.

He needed to get creative.

She fumbled at the door with the key so Mac took it from her, calling upon his nerves as a paramedic to control the adrenaline coursing through his body and keep his own hand steady. He got the door unlocked, pushed her through and shut and locked it behind them.

Sara came at him, obviously intent on kissing him. He held her off with a hand. "Bed. Strip on your way."

Mac didn't watch her walk across the suite toward the bed. He turned away, braced his hands on the doorway and hung his head, breathing deep, trying to gain some control.

He was absolutely not going to have sex with Sam's little sister.

Okay, so some people would say they'd already been pretty intimate. He wasn't going to promise it wasn't going to go a little further. It had to in order for him to show her he was way too wild for her. He just wasn't going to kiss her. Not unless it was absolutely necessary. He wasn't going to touch her any more than that. At least, he was going to try not to touch her. He *definitely* wasn't going to bury himself as deep as he could go, over and over and over.

Yeah, that one he wasn't going to do.

He turned around a moment later, feeling as in control as he was likely going to get with the knowledge he was going to see every beautiful, naked inch of Sara Bradford before he left that condo.

She hadn't had much to remove. Just her dress, since he had her thong in his pocket. She still hadn't listened to him. She was lying on her back, propped up on her elbows, her smooth tanned legs dangling over the edge of the bed, mostly covered. At least as much as she'd been covered since being on St. Croix. He stopped in front of her and looked down at her.

On a bed. Like a wet dream come true.

Even if he hadn't seen in the cab that she wasn't wearing a bra, there was obviously nothing between her breasts and the thin white satin of her top—the hard points of her nipples were evident.

He'd wanted women. He'd felt heat and passion. He'd never felt burned alive from the inside like he did now. He knew, even as he gazed down at her, once he saw her, saw every inch of flesh on this woman, he would never want another. Ever.

This had the potential of making him a very lonely, sexually frustrated person from here on.

Still he said, "Take it off."

Her eyes widened. "I'd rather you did it."

He frowned. She was going to be difficult even now? "Sara, take it off."

She reached her hand behind her neck and pulled on the end of the tie that held the top up. The material gave and the front slipped down to reveal the smooth peach-colored skin of her chest and upper swells of her breasts. Not far enough.

"More," he said hoarsely.

She grasped the satiny material between her thumb and first finger just above her belly button and tugged. The fabric slipped down, tortuously slow, until her beautiful breasts and hard nipples were fully revealed.

His mouth went dry as if it was the first time he'd seen her. Somehow, this felt different. This was premeditated. This wasn't a spontaneous painting or an attempt to shock her in a public place. This was a private showing. All for him.

She was tiny all over. She wasn't more than an A cup and he'd heard her bemoan that fact in the past. Right now, though, she didn't look upset. About anything. And he sure as hell wasn't complaining.

"Now what?" A mischievous smile teased the corner of her mouth.

"All the way. Off." He was already beyond the ability to make full sentences.

She lifted her hips off the mattress. She looked at him expectantly as if waiting for him to pull the skirt down. There was no way he was touching her.

Being by a bed with her was a bad idea.

Watching her undress was a terrible idea.

Thinking about all of the things he wanted to do to her was a horrible idea.

But touching her? Putting his hands on the woman he'd been comparing every other woman to for five years? Running his palms over the curves and silkiness of the woman he'd been depriving himself of, purposefully, for five years?

No way in hell. That would be out of control.

He'd had bad, terrible and horrible ideas before and survived them. He'd always been in control.

"Take it off."

She wouldn't leave him alone. If he didn't do this, do *something,* she would not leave it alone. He couldn't take it. He couldn't take having her flirt and tease and try to seduce him. So he was going for the shock factor to shut her up. At least long enough to get her back to Omaha, dump her back on her siblings and then disappear for a while to get over her. Shouldn't take more than a decade or two.

She shrugged, like it didn't matter to her one way or another, and lay back, grabbing some material in her fingers at each hip and tugging it down, shimmying as she did it. The motion caused her breasts to bounce a little.

Mac bit back a soft curse and closed his eyes.

"What's wrong?"

"Nothing," he said tightly.

"You're not going to look?"

He shook his head. He couldn't. Not right now. Maybe ever.

He'd already seen her. Twice. In the tattoo parlor and the cab he'd had the environment and the knowledge he was *not* going to make love to Sara like that, to keep him in check. Now they were alone. In a private condo, with a locked door, on the island, thousands of miles from anyone they knew. There was nothing to keep him in check—except him.

He'd been beat up, shot at and hung over. Never could he remember feeling this sharp, hot, acute pain before. His body strained to go to her. His mind strained to run in the opposite direction. He felt, literally, pulled in two by equal and opposite forces.

"You want to look, Mac."

He did. He really, really did. He'd caught just a glimpse in the car. Not damned near enough. He groaned in resignation and opened one eye.

"Holy sh..." The words trailed off as his breath left and his other eye opened as well. Wide. "You're supposed to be sweet and innocent."

He felt, and sounded, like he was strangling.

"I am. No thanks to you. I'm hoping to be thanking you for more than that tonight."

He groaned again. "What the hell am I supposed to say to that?"

"Just say 'yes, Sara, I fully intend to make love to you until neither of us can walk'."

"God," he growled. "This is ridiculous."

"Mac," she said, shifting her legs against the sheet, the motion drawing his eyes. "I want you. I know you want me too."

He shoved a hand through his hair. "I can't, Sara. Why don't you get that?"

"You've already crossed a line," she said. She slid her hands, palms down, over her hips and around to the front of her thighs where he was resolutely not looking. "You've seen me naked now. It's not like the rest is much of a jump."

He gave a humorless laugh. "Right. Naked is pretty much the same thing as sex."

"Good, so we agree."

"I haven't even touched you."

"I know. I wish you would correct that oversight."

He was being punished. There was a rather long list of things he might be punished for, so that wasn't the important part. The important thing was realizing if this was cosmic discipline, then getting out of it was probably not an option.

"I'm not going to touch you, Sara," he said.

"I want you to give me my first orgasm without a vibrator, Mac."

Lord, when had Sara turned into the sexy, brazen siren that was now naked in front of him? Had he known she would talk like this, his control over the past five years would have been tested even harder.

He finally let his eyes roam over her body. He was trying to be a good guy, but there was a limit. The Pope himself couldn't stand here for this long and not look.

Sara was the epitome of petite. Her tiny breasts would fit twice in his palm and his fingers would nearly touch if he circled her waist with his hands. She made him feel gigantic, manly, protective. And nearly crazed with lust.

Her hips flared only slightly from her waist and her legs were slender. She was short, but her legs seemed to go on forever. At the apex of her thighs was the prettiest thatch of blond hair, trimmed into a perfect V. Otherwise she was perfectly smooth.

"You wa..." Mac coughed and tried again. "You waxed."

"Hurt too. For all that trouble you could be a bit more accommodating," she said with a little pout.

He wanted to kiss it better. With everything in him, he wanted to lick across the now-smooth skin and appreciate her work.

"You wouldn't have to," he said, his tongue feeling twice its usual size. "You're gorgeous."

All the blood rushed from his head as she shifted her thighs apart. "You mean it?"

Sara lay on the top of the white linen comforter, her hair hanging free, her cheeks flushed, her lips parted. She was still propped on her elbows, jutting her breasts forward, the nipples begging to be touched. One leg hung over the edge of the bed, the other was bent slightly at the knee, showing the dewy pink folds of her sex, ready and hot. For him.

Mac drew in a long, ragged breath.

He couldn't touch her. She was offering him her heart. He knew that. Which he could not—would not—take. She was offering something else as well; something he could perhaps take without guilt. Or at least without as much.

Her innocence.

"You want an orgasm, right now, in this room, with me?" he asked. He reached down and adjusted the front of his pants, the erection behind his zipper hard and nearly painful.

Her eyes followed his hand and she licked her lips. She nodded. "Definitely."

"You trust me, princess?"

She met his eyes. "Absolutely."

"I have more experience."

"I know." She frowned slightly, as if not liking the reminder of other women.

"So you should do whatever I say, right?"

"Okay."

"Touch your right nipple."

Chapter Five

Sara hesitated. He'd just told her to touch herself, like in the cab. Not exactly what she'd been expecting, but then again, she hadn't exactly expected to have Mac in her room right now. She'd hoped, planned, imagined, sure. Expected…no.

She lifted her right hand and cupped it over her breast. She shivered at the contact and let her eyes slide shut, wanting more than anything for the hand to be Mac's.

"The nipple, Sara," he said. "Touch it."

She ran the pad of her index finger over the firm point. And sighed. It felt good. Having Mac watch her do it felt even better. Naughty. And wonderful.

"Harder."

Her eyes flew open. She barely recognized his voice. She had never even imagined the look on his face. It made everything in her feel hot and tingly and on edge.

She took her nipple between her thumb and first finger and squeezed gently. Her breath escaped between her teeth in a hiss.

"Now lower," he said roughly.

She focused on him. His thumb was hooked in the waistband of his khaki shorts. She could see the hard press of his erection behind the fly and knew he wanted her, no matter how hard, or why, he resisted.

"Lower?" she asked, sliding her other hand down over her ribs and stomach. She stopped short of where she knew Mac wanted to see her hand.

"Between your legs, princess."

She spread her legs a bit more. "I want to see you too," she said as his eyes focused between her legs.

"No."

"Yes." She slid her legs together again.

His eyes lifted to hers. "What do you mean?"

"Unzip, Mac," she said. She couldn't help her smile. He was the man she'd known, trusted and loved for years now. Today he was the man who was making her so hot she could barely breathe.

His eyes blazed for a moment as his fingers paused over the button on the front of his shorts. "You sure?"

"Completely." She lifted her hand to her breast again and tugged on her nipple.

He groaned and undid the button, then dragged the zipper down over his impressive erection. A moment later his shorts dropped.

"I knew you'd wear boxers," she said absently, looking at the hard length evident behind the soft blue cotton.

"You've imagined me in my underwear?" he asked, an eyebrow cocked.

"And stripping you out of them," she said, meeting his eyes directly.

"It's a day for fantasies to come true, I guess." His eyes dropped to the area between her legs again. He hooked his hand in the elastic at his waist and pushed the boxers down to drop in a pool at his feet.

She couldn't have, at that point, remembered the color of said underwear. She was completely and totally focused on the almost-intimidating erection rearing up in front of her. He was huge. Not that she had personal experience to compare to, but she had been on a number of websites lately. Once she'd gotten past the initial shock, she'd moved quickly to curiosity.

"Whoa."

"Thanks," he said dryly.

"My imagination didn't do you justice."

"Thanks." He sounded hoarse.

"Neither did the Internet."

"Okay." His voice was strained now.

"I mean, seriously, Mac—"

"Okay, okay." He reached down and covered the sight with his hand. "Knock it off."

"What? I'm loving this."

"You act like you've never seen a penis before."

"I haven't. In person."

He squeezed his eyes shut. "Shit."

"That's romantic."

"Sorry." He opened his eyes and gave her a half grin. "I wasn't exactly going for romantic, though."

She smiled back. That grin was Mac. It reminded her of every single reason why she'd waited for him to be the one in this room with her at this moment.

"Go for hot. And amazing."

"I'm there, honey. Honest."

"Can I touch you?" He'd said *he* wouldn't touch *her* ...

"Hell no." He looked appalled at the idea.

She frowned. "I'll be gentle." She sat up.

He stepped back. "No, Sara." He started to bend over. "We have to get dressed, this is crazy."

She fell back and spread her legs. "What do you want me to do?"

He froze, half bent, his eyes immediately zeroing in on her hand on top of her curls.

Slowly, he straightened. And licked his lips. She felt a wave of heat wash over her at the look on his face.

He swallowed with some difficulty. "Touch yourself."

"If I can pretend it's you touching me."

"Please."

Her fingers went lower, brushing over her most sensitive spot, making her suck in her breath.

"More."

Her middle finger found her clitoris and she pressed, her breath hitching as she watched him watch her. The heat in his eyes was the most stimulating thing she'd ever imagined.

"Now you," she said.

His eyes met hers and he took his cock in hand. He stroked to the base and back up, shuddering as he did it.

"More," he demanded.

She circled her clitoris with her finger, then stroked lower, touching the hot wetness below. She pulled the liquid heat up and over the sensitive nerve endings, breathing faster. Her other hand cupped and squeezed her breast, tugging on her nipple.

Mac stood watching, stroking himself as well, palming the shaft and squeezing as she longed to do. The sight made her inner muscles tighten further and she was suddenly on the brink of climax.

"Mac," she breathed, needing to say his name at this moment.

"Yeah, honey."

"I need you, Mac." She felt the building tension, also somehow aware she couldn't do this without him.

"Go deeper," he ground out. He'd moved closer to the bed, his knee bumping against hers.

The feel of his skin against hers was almost enough to send her over the edge. Almost. She couldn't believe she was doing it, even as her middle finger moved lower and slipped inside the silky heat. She closed her eyes. Though she didn't want to miss the sight of Mac, for a moment she couldn't help it. The pleasure was intense. Almost more than she could take.

"God," Mac choked out. "I can't believe this."

She moaned and opened her eyes. "Please, Mac."

He stepped closer and put his knee on the bed, dipping the mattress.

"Oh, yes." He was going to touch her finally. Her own hand withdrew.

"No." He grabbed her wrist. "Keep going." His eyes were hot on hers. "Please." The last word was a quiet plea and there was enough emotion to make her return her hand.

She circled over her clitoris, moaning, more at the look in Mac's eyes as he watched than at the amazing sensations. "I need you," she whispered, begging him to help her to the summit.

Mac stroked himself, then leaned onto one arm, elbow locked. His erection pressed against her hip and she cried out.

"Keep going," he said through gritted teeth.

Then he slipped two long, thick fingers into her and she cried out again.

She gasped. "Oh, yes."

He pressed his hips forward, his hard, hot shaft against her hip, burning her skin. "Sara," he groaned.

She lifted her pelvis and tried to turn, encouraging him to slide into her truly. He continued with his fingers only. Still, that seemed to be enough.

She felt the tension coiling tighter and hotter. *This* was what she had been waiting for. *This* was what she knew, somehow, only Mac could give her.

"Sara." His breath was hot against her cheek.

"Mac." And suddenly she was there. Amazingly. Everything came together and then shattered. She arched against his hand.

A moment later, she felt him shudder and the sensation of fluid heat against her hip.

He collapsed beside her and she turned into him immediately. Her sigh was deep and full.

Two minutes, which felt like two seconds, passed before Mac swore softly near her ear and pushed himself swiftly up off the bed. He didn't look at her. Instead, he continued muttering under his breath as he swept up his clothes and stalked to the door.

She pushed herself up onto one elbow, watching him, waiting for him to look at her.

He jerked his pants up, yanked the door open, stomped out and slammed it behind him.

Well, *that* was definitely not romantic.

Nice one, Mac. He had been berating himself throughout showering and changing clothes. *You sure shocked the hell out of her.* Even when he was chewing himself out he chose sarcasm. *She hated every second. She's never going to want to do* that *again. Good going.* Ha.

On the contrary, Sara had been with him—and more—the whole time. She'd been excited by what he'd wanted her to do and she'd done it.

Had she ever.

Okay, so he needed a new plan. Or not a new plan, maybe he

needed to step up the current plan. He had to solve this problem before they got home. Or before he lost his mind.

He jerked his door open, determined to go and find her, tell her all the nasty things he was into—in a public place, with both of them fully dressed—and then hustle her pretty little scandalized butt onto the next plane out of here.

He nearly plowed her over.

Sara was standing outside of his condo, looking as if she'd been about to knock. Startled for a moment, she didn't immediately smile or speak. When she did, the smile shot straight to his gut and brought back every memory of every centimeter of skin and every little sound she'd made.

"What are you doing?" He scowled down at her.

"Seeing if you're ready."

He was a smart man. Experienced, able to learn from his mistakes. He was *not* going to give her seductive openings with questions like "ready for what?".

"We're going to go have dinner," he told her firmly.

"That's why I'm here."

"It is?"

"Yeah, I'm starving. I worked up an appetite."

Stupid, stupid. He'd asked a question. He should have known better.

"We're eating in public."

"Okay." She shrugged.

"And you're changing clothes."

Sara looked down at the turquoise tank top and khaki shorts she wore. They were pretty conservative, especially compared to what she had been wearing, but it showed too damned much skin for him. *Any* of Sara's skin was enough to remind him of how she smelled, felt, tasted...sounded.

"This is the most covered up I can be out of my suitcase," she told him, obviously reading his mind about the reason for his protest.

That didn't make him any happier. She already knew how much he wanted her. Knowing he was completely tied up in knots whenever she was around was not going to be a good thing. Sara was sweet, but she'd proved she was not above using *every* weapon in her arsenal when she wanted something. Or someone.

"I'll buy you something." He headed for the main building on the resort, approximately two blocks from his condo. There were two or three shops there and he was convinced he'd find her something there that would at least allow him to make it through dinner. Sara sighed and followed behind him.

"Sweatshirt and sweatpants or kimono?" he asked five minutes later.

Sara looked at him like he'd just asked if she wanted to be flogged or burned at the stake. "It's eighty-one degrees out! I'm not wearing sweatshirts and pants!"

"Okay, kimono it is." He pulled the smallest one—which was still going to be huge on her—in bright peacock blue, from the rack and started for the register.

"You've got to be kidding."

He wasn't and he was growing tired of her not listening to anything he said.

"I'm not kidding. You're wearing this, or you're staying in your room."

"If you're there..."

"Alone. Completely alone."

"Maybe *you* should be the one to stay completely alone in his room. You seem to be the one with the problem," she said crossly.

"I am, Sara," he snapped. "I'm totally the one with the problem."

"Because you're unsatisfied. If you would have just..."

He turned on her, suddenly furious. He was trying to be a good guy! A good friend to her brother. A decent human being. A keep-everything-in-his-pants non-pervert. She'd been pushing and tempting and teasing since he'd gotten here and he was at the end of his rope.

He had intended to have this *conversation* over dinner, but now was just fine with him.

She appeared startled when she looked into his eyes and Mac knew all of his frustration and end-of-the-rope showed. He came forward, which made her wisely back up, until she came up against the wall. He didn't stop at a comfortable distance. He got as close as he could, totally invading her space, slapped a hand on either side of her next to her shoulders and leaned in.

"Listen, princess, here's the situation. The final decision. No more discussion. All you get to do is say 'okay' when I'm done."

Her hands were flat against the wall behind her and she looked like she might have realized she'd pushed him too far.

"The bottom line is you can't keep up with me sexually, Sara, and that's a deal-breaker for me. There are sixteen sexual positions that I like and you'd have to start a stretching program to accomplish at least seven of them. I want handcuffs, nipple clamps, toys and at least one other woman."

She opened her mouth.

"I'm not done."

She closed her mouth.

He wasn't lying to her. He loved toys and had definitely enjoyed more than one woman at a time on occasion. Of course, this was Sara. He didn't need much more than her smile to get going.

For now.

That was the kicker. He wanted Sara. More than he'd ever wanted another woman. More than he'd ever want another again, he was sure.

But he'd never ever wanted a woman indefinitely.

It had taken him a while to figure out why that was. When he had it made sense. He liked pushing boundaries, he liked teaching women new things, seeing how far they'd go for—and with—him. As egotistical as that was. Which was why he stuck with more experienced women. Now. Women who knew their limits and weren't shy about letting him know. Even the experienced ones, though, ultimately got to their limit. Then he was ready for something new.

It wasn't kinky. At least not all the time. It wasn't crazy. All the time. Sometimes pushing a woman's limits simply met introducing them to sexy lingerie or a new position or two.

Whatever it was, it eventually came time to move on. Until then it was fun. It was sex. There were no drugs, no pain, no disrespect. When they said stop, he stopped. When they said more, he gave more. It was harmless.

He made sure of that. First, do no harm. Just like the frickin' doctors.

In the past, he'd thought he could have amazing sex with women who loved him. What he hadn't realized was that loving him meant they wouldn't say no or stop, even when they wanted to.

He would not make that mistake again. Not with Sara. Especially not with Sara. He knew Sara thought he walked on water. Much more than any other woman ever had. Most women met him and liked him based on his looks and a few minutes of conversation. Sara was basing her draw to him on much more.

Which meant she trusted him. Which meant when he screwed it up it would be all the more devastating. Not only would it ruin his connection to her, but the entire group, their family, would be disrupted. He couldn't let that happen. *Wouldn't* let that happen.

"I appreciate the fact you think I'm worthy of your affections, but the truth is, I'm not the warm-and-fuzzy type of guy. Where women are concerned, I want down and dirty, wild and raunchy. And, princess, you're not it."

He pushed back from the wall, his stomach cramping as he watched her absorb his words.

"You want me," she said, quietly. "I know you do."

"I do," he admitted. "For now."

She thought about that. "How long?"

Now the feeling in his stomach was less regret and more a definite *uh-oh.*

Time for one of those questions he'd likely end up regretting. "How long what?"

"How long do you want me for?"

Damn. Great question. One that he couldn't answer. He never knew when the excitement would wear off. That's why he hung out with women who didn't expect a lot of notice.

Yeah, this was just terrific.

He said the only thing he could. "I've already had you."

She tipped her chin up and took a deep breath in through her nose. "So you're done with me?"

"Yep." He couldn't meet her eyes, though.

"As of right now?"

He just knew she was going to somehow make him sorry. He said, "Yes," anyway.

"Okay. Then as of right now, you step aside."

He moved toward her again, making her look up at him. "Define step aside."

"You give up the right to give me advice, to interfere, to even be informed of what's going on in my life."

"Bullshit," he said with deadly calm. That was simply never gonna happen.

She looked him right in the eye. "You're not my brother, you're not my father, my guardian, my power of attorney, my husband... You're just a guy who I fell in love with, offered everything to and who turned me down."

He wasn't breathing and he couldn't seem to change that.

Fell in love with.

Everything.

Turned me down.

Her words wouldn't stop echoing in his mind. Love. She'd said it before. For some reason this time was the first he truly believed her. He could have everything she was, everything she had. He didn't deserve it, but he wanted it. With a desire that almost brought him to his knees. And he'd turned it down. She was right. He was a damned idiot, but she was right. He wasn't going to take what she was offering. Couldn't. For her sake.

Now she wanted him out of her life? No fucking way.

"Bullshit," he repeated firmly, reaching for her. He grasped her upper arm, needing to touch her, needing to hold on to her somehow. "I'm your friend. That doesn't change."

"I can't control how you feel any more than I can control how I feel," she said to the neckline of his shirt. "I also can't control what you do. But I can control what *I* do."

"What does that mean?" he asked, his throat tight.

"It means I won't be spending time with you, I won't be calling you, I won't be confiding in you, I won't be...needing you."

"So that's it?" he asked, trying to suppress the anger, and panic, building in his chest.

"Yes. This isn't a buffet. You don't get to come through and pick and choose what parts of my life you want to be involved in and what parts you don't want."

"All or nothing?" he demanded.

"Yes."

"You're going to tear our group apart because you want to get laid?" he demanded, feeling the anger and panic increase. He couldn't lose her.

She raised her eyes to his then. Slowly she shook her head. "Not laid, Mac. Loved. I want to be loved. By you."

She yanked her arm free of his grasp and stepped around him. She almost slid out of her flip-flop. She paused and shoved her foot into it more securely, then headed for the door.

Un-fucking-believable. Mac was still staring after her.

This thing just kept getting better and better.

He'd come down here to keep her sober and safe. He'd ended up getting her drunk, helping her get tattooed and nearly making sure she tried every sexual position he knew.

Now they'd broken up when they hadn't even been a couple.

How had this gotten so screwed up so fast?

He headed for the beach bar where he'd first seen Sara when he arrived on the island. He needed to drink. Heavily.

As he tossed back the shot of rum, then took a long drink of beer, he contemplated the situation.

He was in deep shit.

Somehow he'd contributed, unintentionally, to Sara seeking a sexual revolution. Now she was a loaded weapon. She had the looks, the motivation and just enough knowledge to be dangerous in her search for orgasmic perfection.

He couldn't sleep with her. He also couldn't—or at least shouldn't—do any more of what they'd done in her condo. But he also couldn't just let her go off on her own.

He'd tried rejecting her at the wedding and look what had happened. She'd taken off for an island. Alone. With hardly any clothing. She was determined to go wild and used to getting her way. A recipe for disaster.

The scumbags and man-whores would be all over a sweet young thing like Sara, and she'd be in too deep before she knew what was happening. It wasn't like she was demonstrating incredibly responsible decision-making. She's chosen *him* as the object of her affections, for instance, and he was far from the upstanding nice guy she deserved.

Of course, the idea of Sara with *any* other guy made him want to put a fist through a wall. Prior to their kiss at the wedding he was able, and willing, to ignore it all. It wasn't easy, but it was possible.

Now he'd had a taste of her—and then some—and there was no way in hell he was going to be able to ignore *that.* The kiss had been bad enough. After thas afternoon in her condo... Well, he was never going to fully recover.

She was going to go wild and now he knew what that looked like.

He shifted on the barstool, suddenly less comfortable in his jeans.

At least a thousand men would be lined up within an hour, and there wasn't a damned thing he could do about it short of literally locking her up or beating them off with a stick. Also literally. Which he'd enjoy to some extent.

She was doing all of this to get his attention—and to torture him since he'd said no to her. Heaven forbid someone tell Sara something she didn't want to hear.

She'd said that she wasn't going to be talking to, calling or seeing him. But she would find ways to make him miserable. She knew him. The more outrageous she was—like jumping on a plane to St. Croix out of the blue—the more worried he'd be, the closer he'd want to stick, the more of his attention she would monopolize.

The more attention he gave to her, the harder it would be to forget that he wanted her more than he'd ever wanted anything. For the rest of his life he was sure that whenever he was within ten feet of her he'd be remembering what it felt like to almost have her.

Basically, he was screwed.

God only knew what she—or the men around her—would do if he tried to just walk away.

But he was *not* the right guy for her. Even if he wanted to be. He wasn't and he'd never risk hurting Sara the way he'd hurt...

He stopped that thought before he could complete it. It was good to remember that he couldn't be with nice girls, but he couldn't quite bring himself to remember the details of why. None of that would *ever* happen to Sara. Period.

Even if the man he had to protect her from was him.

The question was how in the hell was he going to do that?

He couldn't reject her. He couldn't keep her. He couldn't convince her this was a bad idea. Once Sara got something in her head the only person who could change her mind was her.

But what could convince her that she was wrong about this? Sara's entire life had been about getting her way. She had no reason to believe that things wouldn't happen the way she planned or that any of her ideas were less than perfect.

What she didn't realize was that things turned out for her because there were always people to bail her out, to smooth things over, to soften the landing.

He would be sleeping much more comfortably if Sara, just once in her life, had been allowed to fail miserably and live with some regret and disappointment about even one choice she'd made.

And suddenly Mac had his answer. He thunked his bottle down on the bar and sat up straighter.

It was actually quite brilliant. And simple.

He couldn't tell her she was wrong. He couldn't insist she was wrong. He had to *show* her she was wrong.

By giving her exactly what she thought she wanted.

It was time for Sara to figure out that she wasn't always right.

"Ask me to marry you."

"Are you drunk?" Sara stood in her pajamas in the doorway to her condo and stared at the man she loved and hated equally at the moment. Mac had just said the word "marry" to her and it didn't have the word "not" or "never" with it.

"I had a couple drinks," Mac admitted. "But I'm not drunk."

"You must be," she said. "You just told me you're done with me, you've had what fun you wanted and I'm not enough for you. Now you're telling me we should get married."

Mac had his hand shoved deep in his pockets and he looked tired, but lucid. The faint scent of rum had met her as he'd leaned in close and kissed her cheek when she opened the door, but he did seem to have all of his faculties functioning at adequate levels.

"You have to ask me, though. Everyone knows that you always get your way. You ask, eventually I say yes. Been that way for twelve years. Why stop now?"

She crossed her arms. "I've been asking you to have sex with me. You've said no to that."

He sighed. "Yeah. So far."

In spite of the grim look on his face, her heart flipped. Then her eyes narrowed. "Is that why we have to get married? To assuage your guilt when we have sex?"

He sighed again. "Something like that. Sam's going to be pissed no matter what, but I can't sleep with you and have you move in with me if we're not married. That would be worse. At least this way he won't think this is...like all the other women."

"Am I different, Mac?" she asked quietly.

"You know you are."

She shook her head at that. "Not sure. Hopeful."

He put a hand against her cheek. "You are. Very different."

Her heart squeezed in her chest and she tried very hard to suppress the squeal that climbed in her throat. "So marry me," she said calmly.

Something in his eyes made her catch her breath. A tenderness, a concern.

"Okay," he said simply.

She stared at him, not trusting her emotions at the moment. The confrontation in the resort shop had shaken her. Now this. She wasn't sure what to feel. Except for relief.

She couldn't deny it. Mac was going to be hers forever. No matter who else came along, what else changed or shifted in her family, she would have Mac. Sam and Dani could shop for furniture, have their private, only-them dinners, and Jessica and Ben could go to baby classes and buy their condo in Aspen.

She could get her own furniture, her own dinners and condos. With Mac.

The fact that Mac had agreed to it so absolutely, though, gave her pause. His friends were the center of his life. He'd do anything to keep their little family intact. So in his mind, this was a major sacrifice on his part.

Or was it simply a surrender?

In the end it didn't matter. She was getting what she wanted and if he didn't want it for the right reasons yet, he would. She'd make sure she was the best thing to ever happen to him.

"When?" she asked.

He raised an eyebrow, but simply said, "Tomorrow morning. Before we leave."

"We're eloping?"

"Yes."

"We're leaving them out of all of it?"

"They might try to stop it, or talk us out of it."

She acknowledged her brother would very likely try. It scared her to think he might succeed. "You're right. We should do it tonight."

"Why the big hurry? We'll get it done before we get home." He sounded like he was talking about a root canal.

She stepped out of her condo and onto the little porch with Mac. "Because the sooner we have the wedding, the sooner we can have the honeymoon."

He backed up a big step. "Tomorrow morning. Ten a.m. Down on the beach. It's all set up. You have a spa appointment at eight. They'll deliver your dress there."

She grinned up at him. He'd thought of everything. "That's amazing, Mac."

"Yeah." He said it gruffly.

She noticed he was staring at her mouth.

She licked her lips. "How about a night-before kiss?" she asked.

He took a half step backward again, then paused and swore under his breath. He stepped forward, grasped the back of her neck in one big hand and pulled her forward into his kiss.

Within a few seconds she was on tiptoe, her hands fisted in the front of his shirt, straining to get closer. The heat of his kiss quickly started a fire burning along the path of her veins and nerves, spreading rapidly throughout her body. Wedding schmedding. They should start the honeymoon right now.

He let her go just as quickly as he'd grabbed her and she stumbled slightly as he stepped back, away from her.

"See you tomorrow," he said and turned and disappeared down the lamp-lit walk toward his own condo.

She pressed her lips together, still tingling from the combination of the kiss and the knowledge Mac had just accepted her proposal and arranged their wedding.

Their *wedding.*

She carefully stepped through the door into the condo, softly shut the door and clicked the locks into place and walked calmly to the bed. Then she let out a loud *whoop,* jumped up onto the mattress and started bouncing up and down squealing and laughing.

This thing just kept getting better and better.

They were married by ten thirty-nine. It was fortunate that St. Croix was a very popular wedding—including elopement—destination and no one had even blinked when asked to throw a ceremony together in twelve hours.

It would have taken thousands of dollars, months of time and still not yielded results as beautiful as standing on a white beach by the deep blue of the ocean, a gentle breeze blowing, surrounded by tropical flowers.

Their witnesses were two native girls who worked at the resort, a tourist couple from Indiana that Sara had met at the spa and assorted other people enjoying the beach at the same time.

Sara didn't care a bit. She was sure their friends and her sister would insist on a reception, or perhaps, a repeating of the vows since they weren't there. Their absence on the biggest day of her life was the only dark spot in the day, but the elopement made sense and...she wanted it.

Mac was hers now. Her lawfully wedded husband.

She was ecstatic.

He'd looked directly into her eyes when he'd recited his vows, he'd held her hands as she repeated hers and then he'd kissed her so sweetly and tenderly she'd gotten tears in her eyes. Just as she had when she'd stood at the end of the makeshift linen aisle laying on top of the sand and met his eyes for the first time since donning her wedding dress. He looked wonderful, dressed in white linen pants, a white silk-blend shirt open at the collar and barefoot, standing on the sand waiting for her with an easy smile.

He'd looked stunned for a moment upon seeing her in the simple white silk dress. The bodice was a halter, bordered by pearls that tied behind her neck. Another sash wrapped around her waist and tied just below her shoulder blades, leaving the back of the dress to plunge low, making a bra impossible. The hem ended just below the knees and she padded barefoot onto the beach. His daze didn't last. His eyes heated as they followed her down the aisle and by the time she'd joined him in front of the officiate he was looking at her with a smile she would definitely term loving.

It had been wonderful.

They'd toasted with champagne, and eaten amazing rum cake, an island specialty.

It wasn't until the limo pulled up in front of the airport and the driver unloaded her bag from the trunk—the bag she hadn't packed and certainly hadn't brought with her to the wedding—that Sara realized her wedding night was not going to be spent in St. Croix.

"We're going home?" She turned accusatory eyes on Mac. "Now. Just like that?"

He nodded, without looking at her, and got out of the car.

"We won't be to Omaha until midnight," she pointed out.

"Twelve nineteen," Mac said, shouldering his bag and pulling the handle out on her rolling suitcase. He headed for the sliding doors leading to the check-in desk for their flight.

Fine, he wanted to be high-handed and just do everything his way, then she could follow his lead. As they stood in line, Sara flipped open her cell phone and dialed.

When the operator answered she said, "I need the number for the Hilton Hotel, downtown Omaha, Nebraska."

Mac turned to look at her, but didn't say a word. Sara chose to fuss with the collar of his shirt while she waited to be connected.

"I am returning tonight, after midnight, and need to book the honeymoon suite," she told the woman who answered at the hotel.

"How many nights?"

"One." She gave the woman her name, address and phone number, then reached into Mac's front pants pocket and withdrew his wallet. He made no move to stop her as she removed his credit card and read the necessary information into the phone.

As she disconnected, she looked up. He was watching her with mild amusement.

"You live in Omaha."

"Yes."

"You missed some rent payments?"

"No."

"Rat problem?"

"No."

"Sold your bed to pay for groceries?"

"No."

"So nothing wrong with your place that would keep you from sleeping there?"

"No."

"Yet, I'm paying three hundred dollars to sleep in a hotel for just a few hours."

"No."

He raised an eyebrow. "I'm not invited?"

"I didn't say that." She moved close and smiled up at him. "I was saying no to the sleeping part of your sentence."

He held her gaze for a long moment, then his attention dropped to her mouth. He sighed. "I guess I'd better rest on the plane. I'm an old man, you know."

She rolled her eyes. "Don't give me that. You've been keeping up with two women at a time and using positions that could cause injury."

She had to laugh it off. His recitation of his sexual preferences in the resort shop the other day had been like being punched repeatedly in the gut. She'd known, for a long time, about Mac's reputation. She just hadn't allowed herself to think about it. It was strange how she'd been able to separate the things she knew and the things she'd found on the Internet from Mac and real women. Then after he'd talked about the things he wanted, that she couldn't provide, she'd let herself think about Mac having sex with other women. And she'd hated every single second of it.

He didn't laugh it off, however. Instead, he just stood looking at her.

"Sir?" A voice interrupted their stare down. "Sir, please move ahead in line."

Mac checked them in—she wasn't surprised to find he'd somehow managed to get them on the same plane on the way home—and then took her hand as they walked to their gate. Nothing more was said about his sexual past, or their sexual future.

They drew attention as they walked. Not Mac as much, maybe, but she did in her white wedding dress and the pink and white flowers still threaded through her hair. She wasn't about to remove them, though. She wanted the whole world to know she was married and if Mac didn't want to make a spectacle out of them, then he should have taken her back to the condo before heading to the airport.

The condo with a bed. Which she knew was part, if not all, of the reason they *hadn't* gone back.

What a chicken.

She pulled out her reading material as they settled into two seats in the gate area. Which got Mac's attention.

"What the hell is that?" he whispered.

"A catalog."

"So I see." He glanced around. "Is that appropriate for reading in public?"

"Everyone else here is reading for pleasure or work. This is a little of both for me," she whispered back.

"What have I done to deserve this?" he groaned.

"I think most men would be jealous of you having a wife who is studying a sex-toy catalog," Sara told him. "It's not all raunchy. I mean look at this: cotton-candy-flavored body powder. *Great for licking.* I'm so getting that."

Mac tipped his head back, covered his eyes with his hand and groaned again. "Please don't."

"Oh, I am," she told him. "And these chocolate body pens. You use them to write on each other...then lick it off."

"Yeah, you could have stopped with chocolate body pens. It's kind of self-explanatory."

Mac shifted in his seat and Sara hid a smile. He'd been getting his way all day—and last night when he'd gone back to his condo—if she felt like torturing him a little, she would.

"Do you like piña colada flavor?" she asked.

"No. Not at all."

She smiled. "Well, there's lots of choices. How about lemon meringue?"

"No."

"Bubble gum?"

"Definitely not."

"Beer flavor?"

That opened his eyes. "What do they have in beer flavor?"

"Nothing that I've seen yet. I was just making sure that if I find something I can order it without hesitation."

He sighed. "What are you looking at?"

"Edible massage lotion."

"What's with all the edible stuff?"

"That's just the catalog section I'm in."

"I'm not interested."

A quick glance at his lap told a different story. "Then I'll flip to a section you are interested in. Oh, look, the nipple-clamp section."

Mac surged to his feet. "I'm going to get something to drink."

Sara felt a surge of satisfaction. She was getting to him. Which was exactly what she wanted. He was *not* going to ignore her and he *was* going to be thinking about their wedding night. And all the nights after that. Maybe even some daytimes.

Sara crossed her legs, settled back in her chair and smiled up at him sweetly. "I'll be waiting right here for you. Honey."

Chapter Six

Finding a drink was a weak, but usable excuse to get away from his sexy, sweet-smelling, seductive wife. Mac felt a shiver trickle down his spine. His *wife*.

In the morning light, with a decreased blood alcohol level, an almost restful night of sleep and not seeing Sara for several consecutive hours, he was pretty sure he'd overreacted with the whole marriage idea.

Marrying her was a rash decision, over-the-top, ridiculous really.

He hadn't stopped the ceremony though. Once he'd seen her standing at the end of the aisle he decided that while he was showing Sara what a mistake she'd made, he could also enjoy having her for as long as it was possible.

Which was almost worse than never having her at all. After all, how could an addicted gambler be expected to only play one hand of cards and then get up and walk away from the table?

Having her and *having* her were two different things, of course. He couldn't sleep with her. For one, that was what she wanted. She'd gotten him this far with her manipulations, but things were about to change for Princess Sara. She was going to learn that Mac didn't give in. If he was on the losing end of a game, he simply changed the game.

Secondly, he couldn't sleep with her and then give her up.

So he was going to take it one step at a time. For the time being, he had to avoid the Hilton's honeymoon suite. And there was only one way to do that.

He sent a text message to Danika. *We're landing at 12:19.*

The minute Sam and Jessica heard Sara was back, they'd be there no matter what time it was.

Mac decided to enjoy the walk down the hallway of the airport while Sam still liked and trusted him. Because he knew the first thing out of Sara's mouth when they landed would be...

"We got married!"

They'd just passed the security gate and were heading up the hallway toward the baggage claim when Sara saw her sister, brother and in-laws. She ran toward them, the lightweight white dress she'd worn for the past fourteen hours flowing behind her.

She was so beautiful. The smile on her face positively glowed. Her hair was escaping the elaborate twist the spa had done for her that morning and she'd been asleep against his shoulder for the past four hours, but she was gorgeous. And for just a moment, Mac stopped walking and simply watched her hug her siblings and tell them her big news.

When four pairs of shocked eyes and one pair that was ecstatically happy turned to look at him he made his feet move again.

"What do you mean you're *married*?" Danika demanded.

The other three seemed too stunned to speak.

Sara danced to his side, sliding her arm through his, and cuddled up next to him.

"I'm dead," he muttered to the top of her head.

"I'll protect you," she whispered back.

"What the *fuck*?" Sam's sudden exclamation echoed down the airport hallway and everyone streaming through toward the baggage claim stopped to stare.

Danika moved closer and took his hand. "Easy," she said softly, still looking at Mac and Sara.

"What'd you do, you son of a bitch? Get so drunk you didn't know what you were doing?"

"Hey!" Sara said, stepping toward her brother. "What the *fuck* is that supposed to mean?"

Jessica stared at her. "Sara!"

"What? That's the only reason he'd marry me? If he was too drunk to know any better?"

Sam was glaring at Mac. "Drunk or dying. And if you're dying it better be in the next twenty-four hours."

"Sam, calm down," Mac said in a low, steady voice, squeezing Sara's elbow against his side. "Let us explain."

"Is it true?" Sam demanded. "Start with that."

Mac sighed. This was going about how he expected. He wasn't bruised yet, so he thought that was a good thing. He just wasn't sure it would last. "Yes, it's true. We got married this morning."

"Without us?" Jessica asked, looking confused and hurt.

"Well, it had to be behind *my* back," Sam said. "That's the only way in hell it would happen!"

"I'm a grown woman, Sam!" Sara shot back. "You don't have a say."

"The hell if I don't..."

He took a step forward and Ben stepped in front of him.

"Take it easy, Sam. This isn't the way to handle this."

"You're right," Sam said, staring at Mac. "I don't want to pay to get the blood out of the airport's carpet. Let's go out to the sidewalk."

"Did it ever occur to you that I did it this way because I knew you'd be a jerk about it?" Sara asked her brother. "Did it ever occur to you I might be just as hurt by this as you, because I would *want* you at my wedding but couldn't ask you because you'd act like this?"

Everyone, including Mac, looked at her with surprise. Sara never talked to anyone like that, most of all her siblings.

"Sara," Jessica started. "You have to understand why we're upset."

"I'm happy, Jessica," Sara said, her voice calmer. "I would think that would be enough to make you happy too."

"But we're—"

"Upset because you didn't make this decision," Sara cut in. "You're not sure how to react because every other major thing in my life has been laid out by you."

Mac felt a vibration of unease rumble through his gut. No, he thought a moment later, this couldn't be just about proving she was able to make her own decisions. She'd gone to St. Croix to prove to *him* she was a grown woman. But surely she hadn't said yes to getting married just to prove a point to her siblings.

Had she?

She was in love with him. She'd said so. She had to mean it, dammit.

"Sara, I just don't think—"

Sam cut his older sister off. "We'll get it annulled."

Sara glared at him. "What are you going to do? Throw me over your shoulder and carry me down to the courthouse? You'll make me sign my name or, what, you'll ground me?"

Mac almost laughed at the ridiculousness of the statement. Sam had never grounded Sara. He'd never disciplined her at all. No one had. That was part of the reason Mac was currently in this situation.

"I'll..." Sam clearly didn't have an answer. So he resorted to more scowling. "Dammit, Sara, this is stupid. You can't just run off without telling anyone anything and then come back married. For God's sake! What did you think we were going to do?"

"It is possible, Sam, that this isn't about you at all." Sara crossed her arms and stared at her brother.

"You're my sister!"

"And this isn't a college tuition you can pay for me or a job you can make up or an apartment you can rent. Who I spend my life with is up to me."

Oh, shit.

The unease in Mac's gut increased. Especially when Sam said, "You actually thought we would arrange a marriage for you?"

"Not exactly, but you have a pretty good idea in your mind about what the guy should be like."

"I..." Sam swallowed. "Of course. I would want you to be with a good guy."

"And I am."

Son of a bitch.

Mac knew then that this was about a lot more than a misplaced crush or a spontaneous temper tantrum. The whole trip to St. Croix hadn't been just for his benefit after all. The elopement hadn't been planned, but Sara was certainly smart enough to take advantage of an opportunity. It was clear now that Sara had gone on the trip—and then married him—to show her siblings she could make a good decision without their help. He was the most obvious choice because they knew and liked him and well, because he'd been there. Hell, it had even been his idea.

Sam didn't answer at first, but finally he said, "You don't care if we're upset?"

Sara lifted her chin. "You'll get over it. I'm an adult. I can take care of myself."

Sam's jaw was tight, his arms crossed, as he looked from Sara to Mac and back. "Bullshit. You haven't ever taken care of yourself."

Sara flinched and Mac clenched a fist, but simply cocked an eyebrow at his friend. "A little harsh, Sam?"

"Shut up, Mac."

"Don't you mean brother?" Mac asked, definitely taking a risk.

"You want to do this here?" Sam asked.

"What I want to do is have you back off of Sara a little bit." Mac drew himself up to his full height and mimicked Sam's stance.

"Is that right?" Sam asked, also standing tall. "Feeling protective of your new wife?"

"Yeah." He was. He wasn't sure he wanted to, especially suspicious of her motives as he was, but if anyone got to be mad about this situation, it should be him.

"Fine, I'll leave Sara alone," Sam agreed. "Why don't you tell us about *your* plans, Mac."

Mac looked at his friend and saw everything he didn't want to see: anger, hurt, uncertainty and, worst of all, genuine worry. Because of him. The strain on his friendships had already started. Unfortunately, he had to deal with Sara before he could make the rest right. Sara wanted to prove she'd made a good decision? Well, it wasn't going to work that way. He was going to make her admit she'd messed this up. She thought she wanted to play house with Mac. He knew exactly how to show her what that meant.

"Sara's giving up her apartment and moving to my house with me."

Sam was the only one in the group who'd ever been to his house. He was the one staring at him with the most incredulity. Everyone else probably just thought having Sara move to his house was normal. Which it would have been if his house was just a normal house and Sara was just a normal girl. None of them knew that in this case it meant moving Sam's spoiled sister, who had regular manicures, wore skirts and dresses almost exclusively and depended on her Blackberry like she did water, to a rural Nebraska town with no stoplights and nothing that was open past ten p.m.

"Away from us," Sam summarized.

He didn't get it. Mac shouldn't have assumed he would, especially in the mental and emotional state Sam was in at the moment, but he'd hoped Sam would get what he was trying to do.

"To my house," Mac repeated.

"In Oscar?"

"Yes."

"It's an hour away."

"Forty-five minutes."

"She won't know anyone there," Sam said.

"She'll know me."

Which wasn't enough. Mac knew that. Not for Sara. She was social, loved people, loved helping people and being involved and being busy. Oscar, the small town where all six hundred and twenty people knew everything about one another and didn't welcome anyone who hadn't been born there, was going to be tough on Sara.

And she was going to be away from her family. That would be the worst part. For her.

Which was the point. Painful as it might be for him to put her through.

Like a half-naked Brandi in the front seat of his car, he had to use drastic measures to shake Sara up and out of this daze and make *her* be the one to end it.

"Your house is a hundred years old." This Sam said looking directly at Sara.

Mac, on the other hand, did *not* look at Sara. "One hundred and six."

Sam would understand later, after he thought about it. All of the reasons he was giving for Sara to hate moving to his family's homestead were the reasons that this was a great idea. A great idea Sam would catch on to. Eventually. Hopefully.

"Sara, say the word," Sam said, returning to glaring at Mac. "You don't have to go with him."

Mac held his breath. He wanted her to say she did not want to go to his house. He did. It was best.

"Of course I'm going with him. It's my home now too."

Mac's breath whooshed out in what felt, strangely, like relief.

Not good.

"You'll hate it there. It doesn't even have running water."

Mac rolled his eyes. "If you're going to scare her, at least do it accurately," he said. "The water was a temporary problem."

"I'm going no matter what," Sara said stubbornly, pressing closer to Mac's side.

"What about your job?"

Everyone turned and looked at Jessica.

Sara took a deep breath. "I'm—"

"She'll just take a break while we get settled," Mac said. Sara's job was so much more than a job. The David Bradford Youth Center was more than a charity too. It was truly the center of the Bradford siblings' lives, it was a huge part of what pulled and kept them together. So Sara couldn't go to work right now. He needed her to focus on his life and being his wife so she could be properly horrified without any life preserver. And the sooner the better, so she would end it quickly.

"A break?" Jessica asked.

"Or I could quit."

Everyone turned and looked at Sara this time, like a slow-motion tennis match.

"Quit?" Jess repeated.

"Time for changes," Sara said, squaring her shoulders. "I'm married to the guy I picked, moving in to a house that you had nothing to do with, maybe it's time for a career choice my sister didn't invent for me."

Jessica stared at her. Sam glared. "You don't have to be a brat, Sara."

Sara sighed. "I didn't mean it like that. It's just...we all know the Center doesn't need a full-time administrator. We all know Jess and you set it up for me to keep me close. Which is great, but you have plenty of volunteers to run the place. Heck, you and Dani and Jess and Ben spend as much time there as I do most weeks. So—" she took a deep breath, "—I quit."

Mac, for his part, couldn't help the admiration he felt. Sara was right about her siblings setting everything in her life up for her, including her job. Their intentions were good, but it was okay for her to start doing some things on her own. He still wasn't thrilled about being one of the rebellions, but he couldn't deny it was a good thing for her. Besides, he didn't expect his part in it to last past Sara finding out he had cows in his backyard.

"I can definitely support her if she wants to stay at home and wait on me hand and foot," Mac added, helpfully.

Sara gave him a raised eyebrow.

Jessica looked worried.

Sam just stared at both of them for a moment. Then said, "Fine. Whatever. Do whatever you want."

He turned and stalked off. Danika leaned in and gave Sara a quick hug, then put her hand against Mac's cheek. "I hope you know what you're doing," she said softly. Then she turned and followed her husband.

"I don't know what to say," Jessica told them, her eyes watery with tears.

Ben slipped his arm around his wife's shoulders. "Just don't make us choose, Mac."

Mac wanted to say, *What do you mean?* or *Sam's making you choose* but neither was true. He knew it. He felt it. This was all his fault.

So he was going to fix it.

"I know you love her," Mac said. "I do too." That much he could say for sure. He loved her. And them.

Those were the reasons that this was the most difficult situation he could imagine.

"Figure this out," Ben ordered. Then he kissed the top of Sara's head and stood back while Jessica faced them.

"I've always just wanted to do the right thing for you," she told Sara.

Mac finally looked down at his wife. She was tearing up too as she hugged her sister and guardian from the time she was ten. "I know that, Jess."

"I want to hear from you. All the time. I mean it."

"You will." Sara wiped her cheeks and laughed. "I'm moving to Oscar, not China, Jessica."

"I know. But you're usually right here. I see you every day..."

Mac felt his gut knot as he watched the sisters hug one last time.

Jessica said nothing to him, just looked into his eyes, then hugged him as well.

Mac watched Ben turn her to leave and watched as they walked away.

This sucked.

Because everything was going to change. At least until Sara realized that she wanted her old life back. And he knew that after all of this, even when things were back to normal, he'd never be the same again.

Sara awoke when Mac killed the engine. She hadn't meant to sleep. She hadn't wanted to sleep. And it became apparent, as she looked around at the dark yard lit only by the tall light on the one corner, that as she'd slept Mac had taken it upon himself to bypass the Hilton and go straight to his place in Oscar.

She yawned as Mac got out and went to the trunk of the car. Oscar, Nebraska. She knew he was from a little town outside of Omaha where he still had a house, but he also had an apartment in Omaha because of his long, odd work shifts, so she hadn't thought much of his hometown. She'd certainly never been to Oscar and couldn't have told anyone even what direction it was from Omaha.

Still, after Mac's surprise announcement that they would be living in Oscar, she had to admit that having some distance and time from her family and friends seemed a great idea. Especially after the fiasco in the airport.

She wasn't going to think about that.

Pushing the door open and getting out to stretch, Sara looked around. Wow, it was really dark out here. Not it's-nighttime-so-of-course-it's-dark dark, but we-are-in-the-middle-of-nowhere dark. She turned in a full circle. Yep, she was right. Dark all the way around. Really, really dark.

The next light was the tall yard light like Mac's and it looked to be about a half a mile away.

There was only one place it was this dark and things were half a mile apart.

Holy cow.

Mac lived in the country.

Not just a small town, he didn't just have a big yard. He *lived in the country.*

A cow mooed softly somewhere off to her right and she almost laughed. Holy cow, indeed.

"This way." Mac slammed the trunk shut and picked up their suitcases. Well, *her* suitcases. He'd come to St. Croix with one duffle bag, which he slung easily over one shoulder. She, on the other hand, had two suitcases and her hard-sided makeup case. He handled them easily too, but it was obviously more awkward.

She started across the yard toward the house, searching the ground for a sidewalk. All she found, with her eyes and her four-inch heels, was grass, dirt and rocks. Wobbling dangerously as she picked her way across the yard between the car and the house, she finally reached the bottom of the steps leading to the front door, without seriously spraining her ankle.

Mac was standing, holding the door open, the suitcases just inside. He'd turned on the porch light as she hit the first step and she smiled up at him gratefully.

She stopped with one foot on the ground and one on the first step. With the light on she took in more of the front of the house. It was made of good old red brick. At least the front, original part was. It was a two-story with a pointed roof in three sections where add-ons had obviously been done over the years. The steps were made of stone as were the wide balustrades on either side. Five steps led up to the heavy wooden front door with an old-fashioned gold door knocker. On either side of the steps were huge picture windows partially covered by the lilac bushes that grew up in front of them.

It was too late and she was too groggy to take note of many other details of the house. But she had all the time in the world. This was her home now.

"You need me to carry you up here, princess?" Mac asked lazily from above her.

Moths circled the light over Mac's head and looking at him,

standing in the doorway, waiting for her, she was filled with a crazy sense of rightness and felt a little choked up. She was about to walk into her home with her husband. It was perfect. It was probably the late hour, the jumble of emotions from facing her family and the lack of sleep.

She climbed the steps. "How about across the threshold?"

Mac stepped forward, facing her squarely. Then he dipped his knees, wrapped his arms around her and stood up straight. They were body to body, full length, her feet dangling several inches from the ground. His eyes locked on hers, he turned toward the house and stepped through the doorway, carrying her across the threshold.

"Kind of like that?" he asked huskily, still holding her.

"Yeah," she said breathlessly. "A lot like that."

Then he was kissing her. The craziness was not the late hour or the emotional toil of the day. The whirling emotions, the hot want, the wild giddiness was all about Mac.

She wrapped her arms around his neck and arched even closer. She had very little leverage in this position, but she wiggled against him, making him moan, which further heated her blood. It was a fully hot, wet, possessive kiss. Mac's lips moved on hers, urging her to open to him, then stroking boldly when she allowed it. When she licked along the inside of his lower lip, he groaned and turned to back her against the wall just inside the door. Here he could press more fully against her, grinding his hips against hers. Sara reached down, pulled her skirt up so she could bend her knees and wrap her legs around his waist. Mac's erection fit perfectly against the heat between her legs and as he thrust against her, she felt as if she was melting all over and being wound tighter and tighter at the same time.

He pulled his mouth from hers, breathing hard, not moving his hips or the rest of his body a millimeter. "I haven't kissed you since we said our vows," he said raggedly.

"I know." It seemed both three seconds ago and a million years ago.

"That's too damned long." He muttered it like he wasn't real happy about it.

She smiled. "I know."

Suddenly she found herself standing on her own two feet. He bent and picked up her makeup case, shoving it into her hand. "Bedroom is up the stairs, down the hall, take a right."

She blinked at him. "You want me to go on up?"

"Yep." He nudged her, not that gently, in the direction of the staircase off to her left.

"Okay," she said slowly.

"I've been gone. Need to check the house," he said, already moving down the hallway. "Go on."

Fine. She'd meet him up there.

She climbed the wide sixteen steps to the second level and found the master bedroom and for a moment just stood in the middle of the room, amazed. It was huge. The bed was a king-sized, four-poster made of heavy, solid wood. Two matching dressers occupied one wall, while the wall directly across from the bed was made entirely of windows. With no curtains. Of course, clear out here, who was going to see in?

There was a door that led into a bathroom, another that opened into a walk-in closet only a quarter full of clothes—mostly denim and plaid, which made her smile because it was so stereotypical—and another that led to a sun porch. An actual sun porch.

It was on the upper corner of the house and both walls held windows that started at about thigh-high on her and went to the ceiling. It was floored with hardwood and held white wicker furniture. She was sure it was gorgeous with the sun shining in and couldn't believe Mac hadn't put a thousand plants out here. But the night sky, bedazzled with a million stars, was breathtaking.

It might be a hundred and six years old, but she loved this house.

She quickly stripped out of her dress. She didn't have her suitcase up here, so couldn't grab either of her sexy nightgowns, but it was stuffy in the house, since it had been shut up while Mac was gone, so she decided to just stick with the silky white thong she wore. Besides, any covering, even a negligee, was counterproductive to her plans for the next hour. Or so. She washed her face, brushed out her hair and headed for the bed.

Mac still hadn't joined her on the second floor, so she pulled back the quilt that covered the bed—again, stereotypically in her mind—and slid between the cool sheets.

The next thing she knew, she was awakening to a bright slash of sunlight warming her face.

In bed. Alone.

It was easy to tell Mac had never come to bed and her first thought was worry. He'd been checking things over. Had something happened? To him? Or was there a problem with the house he'd stayed up all night fixing?

Pulling the sheet from the bed, she wrapped it around her body toga-style and went looking for her husband. The other doors on the second level led to two more bedrooms—fully furnished though a little dusty—and a bathroom that was bare of towels, soap or any other hint people ever used it. The last door opened to a staircase leading to the attic. A real, old-fashioned attic that ran the length of the original part of the house. It was filled, as it should have been, with boxes and trunks, old furniture, a rack with several long dresses and coats and other odds and ends. She loved it and intended to explore it fully later.

Heading to the first floor, Sara found a living room, fully furnished with somewhat outdated pieces and lots of dust, but with a huge fireplace she hoped worked. There was also a formal dining room with a gigantic dining table that would easily seat twelve, along with a built-in buffet displaying a gorgeous set of china. She suspected somewhere within the drawers she would find the family silver as well.

The woodwork throughout the house was beautiful, but wood polish hadn't touched it in some time and Sara made a mental note to find out if someone in town cleaned houses. She had no idea how to clean real wood and upholstery and draperies and a fireplace and all the other things this house had that her tiny apartment didn't. She didn't want to ruin anything, but she also couldn't live in a dirty, neglected house.

She moved into the kitchen next. Again, a huge room, but she was less overwhelmed by the size, having come to expect high ceilings and a lot of space when she walked through the door. There was a large center island, seemingly endless glass-front cupboards and the most recent updates of the house, it seemed. While an old-fashioned wood cook stove would have looked right at home, the appliances were very modern, from the stove to the microwave to the fridge. Sara was relieved at that. She wasn't much of a cook and would struggle enough with a recipe not to mention having to figure out some old stove that needed lighting versus just turning the burner on.

There was a back porch all along the back width of the house. There was a deep freeze back there, as well as several hooks hung with jackets and overalls, with boots of various kinds on the floor. It seemed to be a general storage area as well, with some boxes and crates stacked on one end. The porch led out to the yard that went on for several yards of lush green grass and tall, well-established trees. There was even a swing, hung from one thick branch, and she caught a glimpse of wooden slats in a far tree that could have easily been the wall of a tree house. In the distance she saw what was likely a garden and then rolling hills, more trees and wild grass that went seemingly for miles.

Sara turned back to the house with a mixture of emotions. This was isolated. She hadn't even seen another house in that direction. Of course, the town of Oscar was obviously around here somewhere, but it was really quiet out here. And she had yet to find Mac. She was definitely alone.

The pantry—which was stocked with breakfast cereal, several canned fruits and vegetables and some pasta—and another bathroom were off the kitchen. That was where she found the damp towels, the faint smell of soap and the smudge of toothpaste on the counter that indicated Mac had been in there within the last hour or so. Continuing her search led her to a family room with a huge sectional couch, a big screen television, a stereo and other electronics that confirmed *this* room was used by her husband.

There weren't many touches of Mac. Or anyone. It was like he kept to the bedroom, the lower-level bathroom and the TV room. She assumed he ate here, though there wasn't much food to prove it. The fridge was bare except for a half-gallon of milk, a carton of eggs with only three eggs left, ketchup, a package of hotdogs and some apples. The freezer had three ice-cube trays, and four frozen burritos. She couldn't even find hotdog buns.

Finally she stopped in the doorway between the TV room and the kitchen and accepted the truth she couldn't quite believe. Mac wasn't here.

She headed for the front of the house, opened the heavy front door and confirmed what she'd already started to accept. Mac's car was gone. He wasn't here. He'd left.

Surely just to go to town, though, she told herself. He was probably getting groceries. After all, she'd just realized how bare the kitchen was. Yes, that had to be it.

A rumble on the road signaled someone coming toward their

driveway and she stayed in the doorway, waiting to see Mac's car turn in.

Instead, a shiny red pickup with an extended cab rolled by. The driver was a young guy. He was too far away to see his face, or any detail beyond the baseball cap on his head, but he'd lifted his hand to wave and it just froze there as his speed went from a full twenty miles an hour down to ten.

Sara started to return his wave, then realized she was still draped in only a sheet. She went ahead and waggled her fingers at him, then quickly backed up and slammed the door.

Great. What a way to meet the new neighbors.

She stood in front of the door, staring at the wood, listening to the ticking of the grandfather clock and the quiet around it. It was never this quiet in Omaha. She didn't remember the last time she'd experienced quiet like this.

It was weird.

She turned and looked around the foyer of Mac's house. *Her* house, she corrected. She liked the house, but it was... not hers. Not really. She had nothing here that belonged to her. Not even her husband.

She shook her head. He was just in town. He probably ran into some people and was chatting. Maybe having coffee at the café. That was what people in small towns did. So she assumed. Probably because of something she'd seen on TV since she didn't really know anyone else who lived in a small town.

He'd be back soon.

Then they'd discuss having some of her stuff moved to the house.

When he got back.

Soon.

Sometimes having friends just wasn't worth it, Mac thought.

Sam walked by on his way to the soda machine and Dooley started humming "Here Comes The Bride". He'd been doing it all damned day. And it wasn't because he was unaware of the tension between Sam and Mac or the reason for the tension.

News of Mac and Sara's wedding had reached Dooley and Kevin, the two other members of the best paramedic team in the city and Mac and Sam's other two best friends. Mac suspected Jessica or Ben had told them. It wasn't like it was supposed to be a secret. But these guys didn't tread lightly on sensitive subjects. Not that Sam or Mac ever had either. It was just weird that the sensitive subject *was* Sam and Mac.

Sam said nothing, however, to the "Here Comes the Bride" rendition, and Mac was too far away to kick Dooley this time.

"Knock that shit off," he muttered as the door swung shut behind Sam. "You want him to kill me, is that what this is?"

"Not until you pay me the fifty bucks you owe me," Dooley said, not even looking up from the sports magazine he was reading.

"I don't owe you fifty bucks," Mac said.

"Then I don't want him to kill you until I have a chance to win fifty bucks from you and get paid," Dooley said.

Mac *hated* watching what he said and did around Sam. They'd been friends for so long there was almost nothing off-limits between them. They told each other everything, told the other exactly how they felt about things, could say *quit being a jackass* to the other and it would be taken only as *I must be acting like a jackass today* rather than with any true offense.

Mac was about at the end of his rope today. The tension was thick, obvious and juvenile. Hell, he'd almost prefer to have Sam break his nose and get it over with. If it would mean things would go back to normal, he'd gladly do it. The problem was, he wasn't so sure things would *ever* go back to normal. And that made him nearly sick to his stomach.

Things had been great. His life had been just fine. Why did Sara have to come along and have feelings for him? He'd been okay with wanting her from a distance. Kind of.

Things were complicated now. Things had been easy before. He had everything he needed: good friends, enough money, a job he liked and was good at, a place to call home. Hell, that was more than most people had. He'd been happy. Content. Fine.

Now it was a mess.

All because of one tiny blonde.

Dammit.

"I don't think I should have to give you a wedding present," Kevin said from where he was playing solitaire at the coffee table.

"Okay," Mac said.

Then he realized Kevin had spoken because Sam was back in the room. There was no talk about weddings, beach vacations, bikinis, honeymoons, or anything related unless Sam was within hearing.

They were trying to start a fight.

Mac knew why too. The tense silence between Mac and Sam, the two leaders, was as hard on Dooley and Kevin as it was on Mac and Sam. It affected the team. Which was bad for a team like theirs. They literally had life-and-death situations thrown at them on a daily basis. If the team wasn't functioning, those lives were in more danger. The team had to communicate, trust each other, work together.

The kind of bullshit that was going on was a threat to all of them and anyone out there who was going to need them tonight.

Dooley and Kevin were trying to get everything out in the open and dealt with before they had a call...or the two of them went nuts.

"Seriously. I would have gotten you something nice too," Kevin said. "Now I don't think I'm obligated."

Mac just concentrated on flipping a penny into the paper cup in front of him.

"Trust me when I say you want a gift from me," Dooley said. "Right, Sam? I give good gifts."

"Shut up, Dooley," Sam said sullenly.

"No way. Not until I hear you say that you appreciated my wedding gift to you." He turned a huge grin on Mac. "It's a game. That you play in the bedroom. You roll the two dice and one gives you an action, the other one gives you a body part. So you roll and get *lick* and..."

A wadded up fast-food restaurant bag hit Dooley in the head.

"Do *not* say even one body part. This is my sister we're talking about for Chrissake."

Sam was glowering at Dooley and Mac sighed. This was just perfect.

"I was not," Dooley said, grinning. "I was talking about your wife."

Kevin shook his head. "You have a death wish."

"Anyway," Dooley went on, clearly not caring. "I might get you something. I'm not gift-wrapping anything since I wasn't there, though."

"Fine," Mac said.

It wasn't like Mac to be the quiet one. He was one of the leaders, the first to give somebody trouble if they were in a funk or acting like a jerk. But he just couldn't bring himself to poke at Sam. It was his fault the crew was tense. It was his fault his friendship was on the rocks.

"I bet Sara looked hot in her wedding dress," Kevin said. "Of course, she always looks hot. There's just something about a woman in virginal white that gets me."

Mac couldn't help the smile as Dooley laughed at that. Kevin was a born-again Christian who was hardly shy about proclaiming his beliefs. Every once in a while, though, he said something like the old Kevin, the one they'd all known before his religious awakening six years ago, and it always sounded funny.

"Yeah, Sara is a honey," Dooley agreed. "She's so young and sweet that I try hard to keep my thoughts pure, but no man could have missed that she's turned into a gorgeous woman."

Mac grit his teeth and concentrated on gently flicking a penny at the Styrofoam cup. Dooley was simply telling the truth. He was also trying to get a rise. It was nothing Mac should react to. He should take it as a compliment. He'd married that sweet, gorgeous woman after all. But he *hated* thinking about other men looking at her like that.

"You think this is the way you want to take this conversation?" Sam asked.

"It isn't gonna kill you to know that men find your sister attractive. You're either great at the whole denial thing, or you're stupid, if you didn't think that was happening," Kevin said.

Mac raised an eyebrow and kept his mouth shut. Kevin was generally the peacemaker, the voice of reason, not the antagonist. And he never called people stupid.

"Is that right?" Sam asked, leaning back in his chair. "So I should just let you all talk about my sister however you want to? It shouldn't bother me?"

Kevin shrugged. "None of us are saying anything bad about her. And if you think your sister was going to her grave a virgin, without ever having anyone lick any of her body parts, you're stupid."

The silence in the room was several agonizing seconds long. Everyone stared at Kevin, first, because he was *not* the one to talk about body parts in any context and second, because he'd dared to *really* put the situation out on the table.

Kevin put three cards down in front of him, studying the game rather than his friends. “Besides, if Sara wants Mac to be the one to lick her, then it should be Mac,” he said decisively.

Well, there was no ignoring the issue now.

Dooley finally recovered enough to laugh and then clap his hands. “I totally agree, Kev,” he said. “Totally. And I’m getting you dice after all,” he said to Mac. “Because there’s also *kiss*, *stroke* and, my personal favorite, *suck*.”

They all jumped when Sam’s hand slammed down on the tabletop. “And that’s all there is, right?” Sam said. “Marrying her means Mac gets to fuck her, right? That’s what it’s all about?”

“You would rather he’d slept with her without marrying her?” Kevin asked calmly.

“No!” Sam shouted. “No! I don’t want him touching her!”

“Why not?” Kevin asked. “At least you know he knows what he’s doing.”

And suddenly they were at the root of the problem. Just like that.

“Is it so wrong for me to want my sister to be with someone who might appreciate more about her than her ass?” Sam demanded.

That was what Mac had been waiting for. He was out of his chair and around the edge of the table, the front of Sam’s shirt in his fist, Sam on his feet, in seconds. “Now who’s being the son of a bitch?” he snapped. “You can say whatever you want about me, but it better by God be true.”

“You’re going to stand there and tell me you’re in love with her?” Sam asked, glaring right back, unconcerned about Mac’s hold on him.

“Is that so hard to believe?” Mac asked, shaking him. “It’s Sara. She’s...amazing.”

“And young and innocent and thinks you walk on water,” Sam nearly spat at him. “That and being exactly your type—it’s not too hard to love that, huh?”

Mac shoved Sam away from him before he put his fist in Sam’s face. “You don’t know what you’re talking about.”

“Like you haven’t known she’s seen you as a hero for years,” Sam said, advancing on Mac again. “Like you haven’t loved knowing she thinks you can do no wrong. No matter what you screw up, or who you screw over, you can always count on Sara to think you're perfect."

Mac squeezed his fists tightly, fighting to hold onto his temper. "Are you sure you're not just jealous?" he asked. "You should have been her hero, Sam. You should have been the man she looked up to. You didn't want that. Now you're pissed because someone else is important to her."

"And you want to keep it that way," Sam shot back. "Talk about jealous. You realized Sara had grown up and realized she was going to eventually fall in love and you hated the idea she might call someone else for a ride home, or to ask advice, or to take her to some party. So you convinced her she was in love with you."

Mac stared at his friend. He hadn't consciously wanted Sara to fall in love with him, but yeah, he hated the idea she would need someone more than she needed him.

Fuck.

"She started this," Mac said, his voice calmer. "She came to me first."

"You should have said no."

"I did."

"That's what you told me at the wedding. Then you go to St. Croix with her..."

"*After* her," Mac corrected.

"And come back married," Sam went on. "You told me you were going to tell her nothing was going to happen. Ever. How is marrying her telling her that?"

Mac looked at his friend, decided that if Sam was going to punch him he would have already done it and asked, "Are you going to listen to what I'm going to say?"

"Am I going to like it?"

Mac thought about that. "Hell, I don't know," he said honestly.

"I swear to God, Mac, if you say anything about licking or sucking..."

"Shut up," Mac said bluntly. "We haven't even slept in the same bed."

That seemed to surprise Sam enough he did stop talking. For a few seconds. "Yeah, well, you forget how well I know you and how many stories you've told about your women," Sam said. "I know you're not even all that fond of sex in a bed."

It was true. Mac preferred more unconventional sex. Beds seemed so clichéd. "I'm trying to tell you..." He couldn't honestly say that he hadn't touched her. "We haven't had sex." Probably more information than Sara wanted her brother and his friends to know, but that was too damned bad.

Sam looked skeptical as he gave one nod. "You gonna tell me why, I suppose?"

"Because..." He sighed. Because he wouldn't be able to do the right thing and get her to break things off if he made love to her. He'd be completely addicted then and his selfish nature wouldn't let him leave her alone. "I can't break her heart and I know I can't be married to her."

Kind of true. He liked the idea of having Sara all to himself for the rest of his life in many ways. But he wasn't what Sara wanted...or deserved. So okay, he'd known she looked at him with stars in her eyes and yeah, okay, he'd liked that. Having a woman like Sara think he was great was good for his ego. He'd had plenty of women think he was great. Then again, he made a habit of spending time with women who had low standards.

"Being married to her has already been that bad?" Sam asked.

Mac could see the tension in Sam's shoulders had eased somewhat. "I suppose you're going to be pissed at me if I say yes?"

Sam seemed to have to think about that. "Maybe. Hell, I'm so messed up about all of this I don't even know."

"We've barely *been* married. We've spent our married life so far on an airplane and in my car with her asleep the whole time."

"And last night," Dooley piped up.

Mac didn't take his eyes from Sam. "I slept on the couch." He held up a hand quickly as he saw Sam about to respond—probably with a *bullshit*. "Sara went to bed and I slept on the couch no matter what you want to believe."

"Why?" Sam said simply.

"Yeah, *why*?" Dooley echoed.

"I know I'm not good for her, Sam," Mac said, feeling his gut clench as he admitted it. "I know I'm not going to be able to give her the life she wants. Or deserves. Okay? I might be a lot of things, including an asshole at times and a dog when it comes to women, but I know Sara and I know my lifestyle is not going to be right for her. I'm too damned old, cynical and stubborn to change."

Sam crossed his arms and watched Mac with a strange expression. "You gonna explain to me how all of that equals you marrying her? Because so far, that sounds pretty damned stupid."

"She thinks she's in love with me, Sam," Mac said. "And I can't break her heart. For one, she won't listen. For another, I just...can't. I can't hurt her. So I need to show her she doesn't want to be with me. Make her be the one to break things off."

"You had to *marry* her for that? You couldn't just date her or something?"

Mac knew a wedding seemed—okay, *was*—a little over the top. With anyone else he would never have gone to such extremes. But this was Sara. He'd always gone to extremes for and about her.

She had to walk away from him and this was a guaranteed way of making that happen. He couldn't go through it more than once so it had to be extreme and *effective* the first, and only, time.

"She thinks she wants it all, and she'll never let go of that if I don't show her what that really means. She has to move to Oscar and be a part of my life before she'll realize she doesn't want it. I can't move her to my hometown, to live with me, without marrying her, Sam."

Sam sighed and nodded. He understood that part.

"I'm just not going to...make it any more real than it has to be." Mac wasn't about to admit to Sam that *not* sleeping with Sara was the hardest thing he'd ever done and he was avoiding it more for his sake than hers. He was just going to keep telling himself she couldn't truly satisfy his needs anyway.

Sam looked at Mac's shoulder instead of meeting his eyes as he said, "She's not quite the...speed...you typically like."

Meaning Mac generally went for flashy and easy. Sam had too, until he met Danika.

"I've never gone for inexperience," Mac said. Which was true. Didn't make Sara any less desirable to him, but *that* was definitely more than Sam wanted to know.

"I, um, appreciate you're trying to protect Sara," Sam said, still focusing only on Mac's shoulder.

Mac chuckled. "She's not a victim, Sam. She blackmailed me, more or less, into the marriage."

"How's that?" Sam asked, finally looking at Mac directly.

"She told me I couldn't be a part of her life anymore unless it was like this."

All three men looked surprised.

"What about when you get divorced, or annulled, or whatever?" Dooley asked.

"She'll just admit this isn't what she wants and that we rushed into it and I'll tell her I understand and we'll agree we're better as friends. Then things will go back to how they've always been."

Dooley shrugged, Sam looked skeptical and Kevin looked concerned.

"When are you moving her out to Oscar?" Dooley asked. "We can help."

Mac appreciated the offer, but said, "She's already there. I'll just have Jessica or Dani get some clothes and stuff for her, but no sense in getting any furniture or anything. I'm going to keep paying her rent. She'll need her place back after we break up."

"She's already there?" Sam repeated. "Right now?"

Mac nodded. "We drove out last night."

"She's out there alone?"

"Yes." Mac straightened. He knew Sam wouldn't like Sara being alone so far away, but it was important.

"Why wouldn't you have her stay with you at your apartment in the city on the days you're working?" Kevin asked.

"She'd be too comfortable there," Mac said. "Oscar is my home. That's where she's going to have to be okay."

"Alone."

"When I work, yes." And he worked twelve-hour shifts, three days in a row, then four days off, then four days on and three days off. As they all knew, since they did the same thing.

"What's she gonna do there all by herself?" Dooley asked.

Mac didn't know. If she was bored or pissed about it, it would just speed the breaking-up thing along.

Which was a good thing. Or so he kept telling himself.

Chapter Seven

It took Sara a total of an hour and ten minutes to realize Mac wasn't just in downtown Oscar running errands. That was when she found the note taped to the mirror in the master bedroom that said, *Going to work, see you tomorrow.*

The crew worked seven p.m. to seven a.m. She would be alone almost every night. Here, in this house. Alone.

She'd thought about calling him and telling him what she thought of his sneaking out and going to work right after getting married, then decided he was probably expecting her to call and be upset and that she was going to surprise him by acting completely fine with being abandoned in a town she didn't know. Or several miles outside of the town she didn't know.

Then she decided she was going to surprise them both by actually *being* completely fine with it.

She was the one who wanted a new life, a life that her siblings had not planned for her, a life that proved she wasn't the spoiled princess everyone assumed she was. What better place to prove that than on an honest-to-goodness farm? What princess lived on a farm?

Not that she knew what living on a farm entailed. Farms brought to mind images of animals she'd never seen in person and being outside a lot. She was more of an inside girl and wasn't sure if the cows she'd heard the night before were Mac's. Surely at some point in thirteen years he would have mentioned owning cows, right? Of course, she'd never realized he lived far outside of Omaha on a farm, so a detail like being responsible for livestock could have been missed as well, she supposed.

She was going to need further instruction before tending crops or caring for animals, so she decided to get on her laptop and check her e-mail.

But there was no wireless Internet access and she couldn't find a computer in Mac's house, not to mention a hookup to the Internet.

She checked her cell phone. Very weak signal strength.

Terrific.

The television had only the basic channels. The package didn't include the Food Network, or the Home Decorating channel, or any of the other channels she checked out.

It was Wednesday, so she did find a couple of soap operas. She watched one, simply because she wanted to hear another human voice. She was not an introvert. Not by any stretch. She couldn't go without talking for more than five minutes and she loved people.

It occurred to her that she was very rarely alone. Really only when she was in her apartment at night and that was usually late. She had dinner with her family almost every night, at one of their houses. She also often stayed late at the Youth Center when there were kids who couldn't or didn't want to go home and then caught a ride home with Mac or Kevin. The center wasn't in a great neighborhood and they refused to let her stay there without one of them. Weekends she spent with the group as well, often sleeping at Ben and Jessica's Saturday night rather than driving home only to turn around and come back to their place for Sunday brunch.

Of course, their guest room was going to be turned into a nursery soon. Yes, they'd probably eventually convert part of their basement into a guest room, but it was just as well Sara now had her Saturdays covered. She was a married woman. She had a husband. She had *Mac.* She was so good with that.

As long as he was here.

She pushed to her feet. She was *not* going to sit around this house and do nothing, waiting on Mac to come home. For one thing, it was pathetic. For another, he wouldn't be back until the next day. She'd be a stark raving lunatic by then.

Fully dressed this time—in one of the only things she had with her, a sundress she'd taken to St. Croix—Sara opened the front door. Around the left corner of the house was the large front yard, part grass and part crushed white rock where they'd parked last night. There was no garage, but there was a red barn. Of course there was. This was a farm. There was denim and plaid hanging in the closet and a patchwork quilt on the bed. How could there not be a barn?

She'd never been inside a barn. Or even seen one up close and personal. Naturally, she started in that direction.

It was relatively anticlimactic when she pushed the big doors open. It was empty except for an old blue pickup truck that hadn't seen a road, or a car wash, in a long time. Not a tractor or a combine or a horse saddle in sight.

Her eyes scanned the dirty floor, the horse stalls, the cobwebs, then returned to the pickup. She got a little closer. She'd never driven a pickup. It did, however, have wheels. She just hoped it had an engine. Checking on that was probably possible. Just not for her. It was under the hood she knew, but opening said hood and then identifying the engine, was a bit beyond her.

There was another way of knowing if it had an engine though.

She pulled on the driver's side door. It wouldn't budge. It wasn't locked, she could plainly see. Dammit, it was broken or rusted shut or something. She rounded the front of the truck and pulled on the passenger-side door. It swung open with a little muscle and a loud, protesting creak. She climbed up in the cab and slid across the cracked leather seat to sit behind the wheel, pleased to see that the keys hung in the ignition. The key turned and the engine stuttered. It didn't stay running, but it brought a huge smile to Sara's face. She glanced side to side. The truck should fit down the center aisle, but she wasn't sure she could make it around the edge of the stall she was parked in. She turned the key again and the engine stuttered, then stopped. The third try, Sara noticed the stick shift. And the extra pedal on the floor.

Crap.

A stick shift.

She didn't know how to drive a stick.

Getting out, she slammed the door as hard as she could. The rusty hinge kept that from being as satisfying as it should have been. Stomping across the farm yard was also less than effective in high heels. Especially when she turned her ankle.

Dammit.

That she was fine stranded on Mac's farm, alone, was harder to pull off than she'd expected.

Stomping got easier when she got up on the wooden floor of the back porch. She suspected Mac knew everyone in Oscar and probably didn't need a phone book, but she hoped his house had one anyway, even if it was just holding something up.

It was, surprisingly, in the top drawer of the table that held the phone. Seemed too easy. She flipped to Oscar. Or tried to anyway. She turned past the four pages for Oscar three times before finding them. Good grief. Four pages?

Running her finger down the columns, she was looking for cab services, but was open to anything that might be of assistance with her quest to find a working mode of transportation, or groceries, or decent shoes. Oscar City Hall was where she finally settled. If anyone would know what was in town, it had to be city hall, right?

"City hall."

Another human being's voice. Sara sighed. "Hi."

"Hello?" An impatient human being's voice. "Can I help you?"

"I hope so," Sara said with feeling. "I don't suppose you have the number to a cab service?"

There was a long pause. Then a chuckle. "Who is this? Very funny."

"This is Sara Bradford." Gordon. Crap. She wasn't used to that yet.

"Well, no, Miss Bradford, I'm afraid we don't have a cab service. Or a limo service." The woman chortled.

Okay, so she was stuck. And hungry. "Is there any place in town that delivers food?"

The woman got a big kick out of that one.

"No, honey, sorry." The woman was still chuckling. "Seeing as how you can walk anyplace in town in less than four minutes, not much need for cabs and delivery and stuff."

Right. Less than four minutes. Great.

She was stuck with frozen burritos.

"Anything else I can help you with, hon? I've got people in here."

"Oh, no, nothing. Thanks."

Sara disconnected and stared at the freezer. She'd never had a frozen burrito before. She'd never had an un-frozen one either. Then again, she'd never lived on a farm or been inside a barn. Looked like it was going to be a day of firsts.

Ten minutes later, the burrito cut open on a microwave-safe plate, Sara just couldn't do it. She was starving, but after the first bean she knew she'd rather drink the out-dated milk in the fridge.

Instead, she opened a can of peaches from the pantry and ate every last one straight from the can.

Then she decided to be resourceful. If there was something Sara Bradford Gordon knew how to do, it was get people to do what she wanted and needed them to. Oscar, Nebraska was going to be no different. She was independent, intelligent and charming. Those ingredients could surely be turned into a full stomach.

Sara headed for her makeup case. She needed a ride to town. Which meant she needed new appliqués for her toenails, more lip gloss and a clip for her hair.

He had to go home. For something. Toothpaste. Sure, toothpaste. A guy had to have toothpaste.

Didn't matter that there were probably a thousand stores in Omaha that sold toothpaste. He liked *his* toothpaste.

"You're going home?" Kevin asked. "Like Oscar home?"

"Yeah." Mac shifted on the bench of the booth, trying to get comfortable. "So?"

"So you have to be back here in like..." Kevin glanced at his watch. "Five hours."

"Yeah." He knew that. Going to Oscar was stupid. He worked twelve hours, seven p.m. to seven a.m. It took about an hour to unwind before he could sleep for six to eight hours. Then he got up, worked out, ate and had about an hour to kill with a movie, book or errands before he had to report back to the hospital. It just wasn't worth driving back and forth.

But he'd done something stupid. Unable to stop thinking about Sara and knowing he'd be unable to sleep after his shift the night before, he'd stopped by Sara's apartment. It wasn't like he broke in. He had a key. He and Kevin both did. They were her stand-ins if Sam and Jessica weren't around. Sam and Jessica were *always* around, but he and Kevin still had keys. Just in case. Which was how Sam and Jessica did everything in regards to Sara.

He'd intended to stop by and grab her a few things. Some books, for instance. Maybe some CDs, movies, something to pass the time. She was sure to be bored. Plus she needed some clothes that weren't bikinis and sundresses, which was all she had in her suitcase. *He* needed her to have some clothes that weren't bikinis and sundresses. He knew she mostly owned dresses, but she had dresses that covered...more. He would have most certainly noticed and remembered horribly skimpy dresses. Surely she had some sweatpants or something. And she had to have some underwear that wasn't a thong. If she didn't, he'd stop at Walmart and buy her some.

He'd also decided to be thoughtful and pick up her mail, water her plants, stuff like that. She was going to be coming back here to live in a few days. A couple weeks, tops.

It was the mail thing that had screwed him.

Not that looking through her underwear drawer—which had ended up yielding some not-thong offerings after all—or gathering the shampoo and body wash that was so *Sara* hadn't affected him. But he'd been holding it together until he went to get her mail. The bills were nothing. He fully intended to pay and send them off without her even seeing them. The woman's magazine that proclaimed *Have the best orgasms of your life!* caught his attention, but he was able to put it in the flowered blue and yellow bag he'd snagged from her closet without incident. It was the white and pink box that tripped him up.

Apparently Scandalous Somethings did not promise their patrons that they would be discreet in shipping. Not only was their name written in large, bright pink script across the front, their logo was a cartoon phallic shape thrust through a pink heart. Really understated. Whether Sara had missed checking the box that said "plain wrapper requested" or not, she'd apparently found the Rush Delivery box. The words were also bright and big across the front.

There was no way he was leaving that box unopened.

Inside he'd found the flavored body powder she'd mentioned to him. In two flavors.

He happened to like both cotton candy and banana splits. A lot.

Then there were the pasties. Three different designs. That would look incredibly hot on Sara.

Of course, anything would look incredibly hot on Sara. Just as nothing at all looked incredibly...

Hell. He should have never opened the box.

Now that bright pink tissue paper was spread across her sofa cushions, he couldn't stop. The box was too big to not promise more than pasties and powder.

So he found the wedge. The pink, fur-covered wedge. In case he didn't know what it was for, there was a picture on the label. Of a naked couple quite pleased with the positions afforded by the wedge. All four of the positions depicted. Then there were the words "and many more" under the pictures.

Many more. Three more came to mind right away.

Damn.

He almost dreaded digging further into the box. He did it anyway. Because he was a masochist.

There were four silk ties. One for each wrist and ankle. In—big surprise—pink. Along with two mini-vibrators "for tongue, fingers or anywhere else your imagination can think of". Finally, he found the big vibrator. Full-sized. At least. It was also pink.

He turned the end, which switched it on. It came with batteries. They worked great.

He was going home. To Oscar. Right now.

"I'll be back in time to start the shift," he told Kevin.

Kevin pushed his now-empty plate away and took a slug of coffee. "You sure?"

"Of course. I'm just going to check on Sara."

"Has she called?"

"No." Which was making him nervous. When she'd realized she was alone, with no car, poor cell reception, no Internet, he'd expected her to be on the kitchen phone to him.

What was she doing?

There wasn't much she could get into on the farm. One of the reasons it was a good place to keep her.

Still, he was going to check on her. And deliver her package.

"I can come back and pick you up in about an hour. I have to go over and pick up my dad's order at the lumberyard. I'll take it home and then I'll come back for you."

Sean was her neighbor, as it turned out. He was seventeen and lived with his mom and dad on the farm just down the road from Mac. He was also the one who had driven past in his red pickup when she'd been standing on the front step in only a bedsheet.

Sara had sat on the front steps of the house, leafing through an old newspaper, the Oscar Reporter, for about fifteen minutes before Sean drove by again. She'd waved to him as he'd, predictably, slowed by her driveway. Being a friendly, small-town boy, he'd waved back and then turned into the driveway when she motioned him in.

After explaining her dilemma, he'd been more than happy to help. He was going in to town anyway, it was no bother.

"That would be great."

What she was going to do for an hour in downtown Oscar, she didn't know, but she couldn't impose on him any further. His dad had sent him to town on an errand and she didn't want him to get into trouble. He explained that school started for the year on Monday and he was hurrying to help his dad finish some projects before he was in class all day. He was a senior at Riverside Community Schools, the consolidated school the kids from Oscar and two neighboring towns attended.

So far she knew there was a grocery store, where Sean dropped her off, a city hall and a bakery. Oh, and the lumberyard, of course. She needed the grocery store, but wasn't going to carry perishables around for an hour. Other than that, she wasn't sure Oscar had anything she needed.

Until she came to Style With A Smile. Quite obviously a beauty salon. Suddenly Sara felt right at home. *This* was universal, this was where she could feel right at home, this was...

Nothing like Omaha.

When the bell above the door tinkled as she walked in, every eye in the place turned toward her. There were three stylist chairs, all full. Three stylists, all at least twenty years older than Sara. Five chairs in the waiting area, also full. And Elvis singing from the stereo speakers.

Every eye not only took notice of her, but traveled from the top of her high- and low-lighted blond hair, over the turquoise sundress that dipped low in back and rode high on her thighs, to the three-inch turquoise open-toed shoes, to the tips of her French manicured toes with the carefully applied turquoise swirls.

"Honey, you lost?" asked the woman nearest the door, scissors still poised over the head of the woman who sat in the chair before her.

"N-no." Sara put on her best smile. She wasn't used to being eyed so critically. Goodness, most of the time people commented positively on her clothes, hair and makeup.

The teens she worked with were not well off at all, yet instead of wanting her to dress down to fit in, they loved living vicariously through her fashions and styles. She'd learned early that they wanted to see her in the newest trends, wearing and buying the things they couldn't have. Of course, her hand-me-downs made it to the center long before they were truly ready to be taken from her closet. And once a month the students at the local cosmetology academy came by to give free manicures and pedicures to the girls. She loved helping the girls find new hairstyles or earrings—also handed down from her own collection or from her sister, sister-in-law or even Danika's sisters—that made the girls feel pretty and more confident.

She knew the focus on pampering and beauty tips reinforced Mac and the gang's idea of her as a princess, but she knew the truth: everyone, even at-risk teens—maybe *especially* at-risk teens—deserved to feel special and frivolous at times. Those kids didn't have enough frivolous in their lives.

Jessica and Ben gave free medical care, Sam and Mac and the rest, including Danika, taught the kids practical things like car care, cooking, plumbing and wiring. How to dress up a pair of jeans and how to make homemade lip gloss were Sara's contributions. They were important too. The girls loved the things she taught them.

On the contrary, these women made her feel like she'd just told a raunchy joke in the middle of a tea party.

Giving people money was always a good way to get on their good side. "I'm hoping to get a manicure." She held her hands up and wiggled her fingers. She didn't *need* one but she wouldn't mind a color change and it would kill some time. It would also allow her to meet some locals.

Some locals who acted as though she'd just spoken Swahili to them.

The not-answering-just-staring-at-her went on for several seconds.

Finally, the redhead rolling the white hair of the woman in the middle chair said, "We don't do manicures on Tuesdays."

Sara blinked at her. "Today is Wednesday."

"Or Wednesdays," the woman washing hair in the farthest chair said.

Uh-huh. Right. Okay.

She was perky and sweet, not slow.

"Then I'll have to come back tomorrow," Sara said, with fake brightness. The five women sitting in the waiting area were still staring at her. She just gave them a big smile of their own. "You're obviously very busy."

The only woman in the chairs to even attempt a smile said, "Oh, only Helen's waiting." She gestured at the frail-looking woman with stark-white hair. "The rest of us are just chatting."

Upon closer observation, the rest of the group all had coffee cups in various states of full in hand. "I see," Sara said politely. "I'm sorry to interrupt."

"Oh, it's great you came in."

Sara was surprised and almost replied to the friendly comment. Then the woman continued.

"You've just given us something new to talk about for the next week. At least."

Sara wasn't sure what to say to that, but conversation seemed expected. "I don't suppose any of you ladies would know someone who cleans houses?"

Again there were several seconds of silence following her words. Did they need an interpreter? Or subtitles? Sign language?

Finally, one of the women in the chairs looked around at the others. "Someone who cleans houses?"

"Yes." Sara smiled a smile even these strangers would know was phony. "The house is in need of a floor-to-ceiling spruce up." She looked around at the faces that were either frowning or looking confused.

"*The* house?" one woman asked.

"M-my house." She did not stutter.

"We know a few women who clean houses," another said.

"Oh. Well..." What she was about to say seemed like the wrong thing to say even before she said it out loud. "That's...exactly what I need." Sara wondered why she felt like she had just waded into a shark tank.

"Yeah. All of us clean." A few snickers met the woman's comment. "*Our own* houses."

That was why.

"The cleaning supplies are in aisle four at the store. You might want to start there."

Sara took a breath in and then let it out, trying once more for a smile. She *never* had trouble smiling, and she was getting ticked about the difficulty presented here. She wasn't asking anyone for a kidney, nor had she announced that these women all had ugly children. Yet, they were still treating her...like this.

"I'm sorry I bothered you." It was time for a gracious exit.

"Which house is your house?" someone asked before she could escape.

Could she get away with just leaving without answering? She looked around at the twenty-two eyes intent upon her.

Probably not.

"It's...um..." There was that damned *um* again. "Mac Gordon's house," she said.

"I thought you said *your* house."

"Yes. My house. Mine and Mac's."

"Mac?"

She was a patient person. She hung out with teenagers most of the time. And her siblings. And Dooley and Kevin. And, well, Mac. She had to be patient to maintain a healthy blood pressure.

"Yes. Mac."

"Do you mean *Jason*?"

She was either going to stop speaking, or carry cue cards so she didn't have to worry about if she was being understood.

"No. Mac. Mac Gordon. Very tall, broad shoulders, shaves his head."

"Right. *Jason*."

She'd never heard anyone call him Jason. The minister in St. Croix hadn't called him Jason. She hadn't looked closely at his signature on the marriage license but surely she would have noticed him signing Jason. Wouldn't she? Okay, she hadn't really been paying attention to those details.

How, in all the years she'd known him, had she missed that his real name was Jason, though? She thought she knew a lot about him. She thought she knew *him.* And all this time she hadn't even known his name. That felt weird and the obvious next question was, what else didn't she know about her husband?

The women were all looking at her waiting for a response. "I've never heard him tell anyone his name is Jason," she said truthfully.

"I heard they called him Mac in college," one of the coffee drinkers commented, addressing the other women instead of Sara.

"His middle name is MacDonald," the woman having her hair set supplied.

"His mother was a MacDonald," someone else said.

"My sister married a MacDonald. The first time," another commented.

Sara started to inch toward the door.

"You're *living* with Jason Gordon?"

Once again the spotlight shone brightly.

"Um." She had the feeling the sharks were circling for more. "Yes. Just got here last night."

"Really." The woman trimming hair nearest the door paused and put her scissors down. "Where's Jason?"

"In Omaha," Sara said, knowing *she* would have been thinking what the hell is he doing in Omaha while she's here? "Working."

"Did you get kicked out of your apartment?"

Sara blinked at the woman who had asked. The question was so ridiculous she wasn't sure how to answer. "No. Of course not."

"Did your house burn down?"

She frowned. "No. Nothing like that."

"So you're just here for..."

Sara raised an eyebrow at the impertinent question. "For good," she said. Then she went for the shock value. "After all, this is where my husband lives. Where else would I live?"

The long silence was much more satisfying this time.

"Your husband?"

"Yes."

"Jason?"

"Yes."

"You're married to Jason?"

"Yes."

There wasn't even a creak of a chair spring.

"Since when?" someone finally asked.

"Since Tuesday."

"We haven't heard a thing about it."

"I'm sorry." Though she wasn't. At all.

"Was it one of those drunken Vegas weddings?"

Now she was getting irritated. "No. We were completely sober. It was on a beautiful beach on St. Croix."

"Is that Mexico?"

"The Virgin Islands," she replied easily.

"Are you pregnant?"

She was expecting that one. "No, I'm not." She smoothed her dress over her flat stomach. It was catty and she thoroughly enjoyed it. She'd probably feel bad about it later, but for now she was able to give an actual smile.

"So you just...eloped?"

"Yes." She wished she didn't feel the need, but she said, "Mac and I have known each other for thirteen years. We're very close and have an amazing chemistry. It may come as a surprise to you all, but it was quite inevitable to us."

She believed that. She really did.

"Thirteen years?" a woman repeated. "Good Lord, you look good for your age."

Sara just took the words as a compliment and did not comment further. "I should get down to the store," she said, moving purposely for the door this time. "It was nice meeting you all." A small lie for the sake of being polite.

"Aisle four," someone called after her.

She heard the group's laughter as the door swung shut.

She was so damned beautiful, Mac couldn't breathe for a moment when he stepped through the back door into the kitchen.

He'd been looking at her—and thinking she was beautiful—for years. Why the oxygen suddenly deserted his body now, he couldn't understand.

And even stranger was that it wasn't the short, skimpy dress she was wearing, or that her hair hung loose and sexy, or that he was carrying a box full of sex toys and accessories.

It was because she was standing in *his* kitchen, in her bare feet, muttering under her breath, chopping something on a cutting board—which was more food preparation than he could remember ever seeing her do—and it hit him, like a hand upside the head, that she was *his*.

Even if it was temporary. Even if her brother hated it. Even if he, himself, had resisted it. She was his, right now, in this moment.

That made him harder than seeing her spread open naked on the bed in St. Croix.

Well, okay, *as* hard.

He overheard something about "horrible manicures anyway" as she turned to dump something into a bowl sitting next to the sink.

"What are you doing?"

She jumped and spun toward him, something red running through her fingers.

"You scared me!" She said. She gave him a huge smile the next second. "You're home."

She looked thrilled to see him. Which resulted in even more heat and want and need.

Her smiling. At him. In his kitchen. *That* was making him hard.

He was losing it.

"I'm home," he repeated, feeling a strange tenderness. He went farther into the kitchen.

"I'm glad." She stood just looking at him, smiling that smile.

"You're dripping."

Her eyes widened. "I'm...what?"

"Dripping. On the floor." He looked down at the linoleum. "What is that?"

She looked down and then started. She swung toward the bowl. "Strawberries."

He looked at the counter as he came toward her. Blueberries, more strawberries, bananas and a cantaloupe awaited her knife. "What are you doing?"

"Cutting up fruit." She giggled. "That isn't obvious?"

Bananas. Like banana splits. Like the body powder in the box. Mac shifted and cleared his throat. He set the box on the kitchen table and decided to ignore it. "I don't think I've ever seen you actually make food."

She laughed again. "Not sure this counts as making food."

He loved her laugh. Loved it more when he caused it. It had certainly happened before but even that felt different now. Now that they were married. Then he frowned. "Where'd you get the fruit?"

She looked at him and rolled her eyes. "The grocery store. It's so *small.* Not a lot of choices."

He nodded at that absently. "So you went to town?"

"Yes."

"How?"

She narrowed her eyes as she looked at him. "You thought I was stranded."

"I *knew* you were stranded."

"That wasn't very nice."

"I had to work." And he'd wanted her stranded. Bored, hating the farm, hating her new life and out of his sight—so he wouldn't feel guilty about the whole thing—and out of his reach, so he wouldn't make things worse. Not to mention Oscar was her punishment for using him to mess with her siblings.

"Well, I made friends with the neighbors."

Of course she had. Sara made friends everywhere she went. "Which neighbors?" It would be either the Wesleys or the Carvers...

"Sean."

"Sean Carver?"

She shrugged. "Is there more than one Sean?"

No. That wasn't the point. "You didn't even ask him his last name?"

She shook her head and put a strawberry in her mouth.

"You know better than that, Sara," Mac said. The truth was, she was usually very careful and sensible about stuff like that.

"He lives up the road. I assumed you'd known him all his life."

"I have," Mac admitted. "*You* haven't."

"Well, I was starving and he had a truck and was willing to give me a ride. If you don't want me talking to strangers, you need to stock more in this house for food than frozen burritos, or bring my car out here."

The frozen burritos were one of his favorite things. If she didn't like them, she should divorce him and move back to Omaha. "How do you expect me to drive both cars out here?"

"Take me to Omaha with you when you go back and I'll drive my car out."

It made complete sense. But he wanted her here, where she would be bored and alone and learn to hate it quickly and want her old life back. Hell, if she had her car she'd drive farther than downtown Oscar. She could easily go to Omaha anytime she wanted and not have to live with the inconvenience and lack of selection and less-than-top-of-the-line that simply went along with living in a small town. On the other hand, there was more fresh air, friendly smiles and peace and quiet in Oscar. It was a trade-off.

Then he looked at her again. The turquoise sundress, the high heels lying next to the stove. A few things clicked for him. "You went downtown dressed like that?"

She raised an eyebrow. "This is one of five outfits I have here with me. It was the least wrinkled."

Right. She hadn't maybe chosen the dress, exactly. Still she looked...not like the women in Oscar.

"Did you go anywhere besides the grocery store?" Gus, the grocer, would hardly mind having Sara show up looking like this. And he wouldn't have tolerated anyone saying or doing anything that made her uncomfortable.

"The beauty shop," she said with a little frown. "I like the grocery store better."

Mac almost groaned. Style With A Smile. Well, the entire town of Oscar now officially knew Sara was here.

"Did they ask who you are?" Of course they had.

"Yes. And they told me your real name is Jason." She looked a bit put-out to have not known that.

Mac smiled. "Around here I'm Jason. There was another Jason in my anatomy lab in college. They used Mac for me to keep us apart."

She smiled and tipped her head, watching him. "Jason, huh? I don't know."

"You don't have to call me Jason."

"It might get confusing if I don't. No one here knows you as Mac."

She would hopefully not be here long enough for her to have many conversations about him with anyone. Mac just shrugged. "It doesn't matter. I answer to both."

"I could call you Sugar Cakes or something, I suppose," she teased, sliding closer and smiling up at him.

He chuckled at that. "I don't think I can pull Sugar Cakes off."

"How about Stud Muffin?" she slipped her arms around his waist.

He felt the press of her breasts against his stomach and wanted to return the embrace. And then some. "No baked goods," he said, trying to step back.

"Maybe Big Guy."

She wiggled against his big guy and Mac quickly pulled her arms free and put a foot of space between them. There was no way she could have missed his erection, but he turned the conversation stubbornly.

"You can't go into Oscar dressed like that, Sara," he said. He bent to grab the plastic bag he'd brought in with her box.

"Like what?" She looked down. "I know this is a little short, but..."

"But it's not that different for you." He thrust the bag toward her. "You always look like...that." He gestured toward her, indicating everything from her hair to her toenails. "You have to tone it down a bit."

She frowned, looking down again. "Tone what down?"

"Sara," he said. "You know what I mean." And if she hated it, then...good. One more thing for her to hate about life here.

"I don't."

"You look like you've spent two hours in a salon wherever you go. You look like a million bucks. You could have stepped out of a magazine."

The dazzle of her smile distracted him. "Wow, thanks, Mac." She stepped close again. "I don't think you've ever said anything like that to me before."

Because it would have given him away. He couldn't comment to her, or anyone else, how stunning he found her. Or how intelligent, interesting, funny, sweet... He simply avoided talking about her altogether for fear it would have been all too obvious how he felt about her.

"You know you're gorgeous, Sara. You have men following you like puppies."

She laughed. "I don't know about that. Okay," she added when he started to argue. "I know there have been men who find me attractive."

Mac rolled his eyes at the understatement.

"But," she continued. "*You've* never acted attracted."

He was a hell of an actor then. "I've worked very hard at that," he told her gently.

She looked into his eyes for a few seconds, then nodded. "Well, you certainly don't have to do that anymore. I think it's more than acceptable to be attracted to your wife."

Wife. The word sucked the air from his lungs again. She was his. Legally bound to him. He could do all the things he'd spent so long trying not to even imagine. It was expected even. He could see her every day. He could listen to her laugh without worrying that he was staring like a lovesick teenager. He could talk to her all night long and not worry about it being an inappropriate hour for two people who were just friends to be alone.

He stepped close. Thankfully the plastic bag she held rustled as his thighs met it, reminding him he could do none of those things. He had to work at making her *not* his wife, not bound, not accessible to him. They had to go back to how it was before. When they didn't talk all night, didn't do any of the things he thought he might die from not doing.

"The women in Oscar are...less...flashy, Sara," he told her. "Not that they aren't beautiful and sexy, they just don't...go to such lengths."

That sounded stupid even to him.

"What lengths?" she asked, glancing down at the bag.

"They're just more conservative here." That was true enough. People were much less concerned here about labels and styles and trends.

"How do you suggest I tone it down?" she asked, now looking at the bag as if he might have put a smelly diaper in it.

"Just...less. Less elaborate hairstyles, less jewelry, less skin, less heel," he said flicking a glance toward her shoes again.

Finally she stuck her hand into the plastic bag, felt around and withdrew the gray cotton. She dropped the bag and held the garment up with both hands.

"What is this?" she asked.

"Sweatpants."

She looked at him. "Sweatpants? It's August, Mac. It's eighty-eight degrees during the day."

She had to cover up. He didn't care how she did it, but at her apartment he'd been unable to find anything baggy. "You can turn the air-conditioning up."

"You want me to wear sweatpants?"

"Yes. Or jeans. Or these." He squatted and dug in the bag to pull out the black workout pants with the white stripe running up the side of either leg. "They go with this." He pulled out the zip-up jacket that matched.

"Great. At least it's a coordinated look," she said dryly.

He sighed and stretched to his feet. "You can't walk around Oscar in those sundresses."

"I bought these for St. Croix. I have other dresses."

"I brought some of them," he said. "They're in the car. They're still pretty..."

"Flashy?" she asked, seeming amused.

"Not all of them." Though there were plenty of silky, sleeveless numbers in her closet. "They're just obviously expensive. More expensive than you'll see around here day to day. These women shop at the mall, not at boutiques."

"I don't shop at boutiques," Sara protested. "All the time," she amended when he arched an eyebrow. "Only when they have sales."

"Still..."

"I spend way more money on my hair and makeup than on clothes," she tried to defend. "I'm not that into labels. I just like the way the more expensive fabrics lay and they last longer and..."

He crossed his arms and waited. She finally sighed. "Okay, I can try toning it down."

"You won't be able to get massages and manicures and spray-on tans and facials and all of that either," he told her. "They don't have it here and if you drive to Omaha for it, they'll think you're stuck up."

"Yeah, I kind of figured that out," she muttered.

That got his attention. She'd been in the beauty shop. "What do you mean?"

"I asked about manicures today."

"Uh-huh," he said, motioning for her to go on.

"They said they don't do them on Tuesdays or Wednesdays. So I'm going back tomorrow. I'm guessing they'll say they don't do them Thursdays either."

Interesting. "Did you ask about anything else? Massages?"

"Just cleaning ladies."

"What?"

"Someone to come in and clean the house."

Oh, boy. Mac shook his head. "How'd that go?"

"I think I offended them."

"You're new."

"No one here cleans houses for a living? That's not an unusual request. And it's not like I asked if any of them were exotic dancers or something." Her temper made her eyes flash.

"You're an outsider, Sara. They don't know you and the first thing you say is that you're looking for someone to clean your house."

"So?"

"So they might have taken it to mean you were too good to clean your own house and you're looking for a local to do the dirty work for you."

She stared at him. "I have no idea how to clean a house. I can wipe a sink or dust a living room, but I don't know anything about curtains and woodwork and windows and..."

"Calm down," he said, stepping toward her, stupidly drawn by her distress. "I'm just telling you how it might have sounded."

"The whole thing sounds stupid," she declared. "It sounds like they're all paranoid."

"Judgmental of newcomers," Mac admitted. "They think if you're the new one, you should try to fit in and if you're obviously different from them, they assume you're doing it on purpose. And then they'll assume it's because you don't approve of how they are and you don't want to be one of them."

"I don't even know them!" she exclaimed. "How can I know if I want to be one of them? And how can they expect me to get to know them if they're snotty and suspicious with me?"

Mac shrugged. It was hard to explain. "They don't care if you get to know them, honestly. They have their family, their friends, their work, their way of life. And they love it. And they don't care if you fit in, like them, get to know them, stay here, or not."

"That isn't very nice," she mumbled.

"No, I guess it's not. It's like they have their club, and they're happy. They're not looking for new members and so anyone who wants to get in is going to have to try hard."

"I don't know if I want to be in their club," Sara pouted. "Why would I want to hang out with women who treat people like this?"

Mac grinned at the top of her head. It was cute to see Sara pout. She was never left out. She was never snubbed or judged. Everyone in Sara's world loved her and went out of their way to be sure she was happy and cared for and had what she needed.

He'd known Oscar would be like this for her. And he'd thought it would be good for her. Not just because it might convince her even faster that this wasn't the life she wanted, but because it might knock her down a peg or two. Being humbled once in a while wasn't a bad thing for anyone.

"I might have offended the grocer too," she said hesitantly.

Gus? It would be hard to offend Gus. "How?"

"I asked if there was a chance he could special order some things for me."

Mac fought a smile. "What kind of things?"

"Well, I really like nuts and he didn't have any other than the salted in the can. I wanted to see if he could get some fresh pistachios or almonds. And he only has iceberg lettuce. I was curious about some romaine and some fresh spinach."

Mac felt his mouth trying harder to curl. "What did he say?"

"No."

The smile slipped out. "That's it? Just 'no'?"

She nodded. "I said, would it be possible for you to special order some nuts and greens? He stared at me and then just said, 'no'."

Mac chuckled. "I'll get you some stuff from Omaha when I come home next time. But don't tell anyone."

She shrugged. "Okay. At least I did buy a few things from Gus. Maybe that's what I should do at the beauty shop—buy some shampoo or something. They probably don't carry my brand, but I could buy it anyway and just put it in the cupboard."

"Sara," Mac interrupted. He didn't think she was even aware of how Princess-y she sounded sometimes. "Is it possible that your hair could get clean with another brand?"

"Well, yes, clean," she said slowly. "But the shampoo I use makes my hair..."

"Don't buy anything you're not going to use," he broke in. "Then they'll expect you to need to buy more occasionally, right? Either you're going to end up offending them further when you never buy more, or we're going to have a cupboard full of unused shampoo."

Except she wouldn't be living here long enough to collect too many bottles, Mac reminded himself.

"Oh, I can take it to the center and let the girls take it," Sara said quickly. "They'll love anything."

Mac sighed. "Sara, don't take this the wrong way. You know I love those kids as much as you do." Mac spent three evenings a week, minimum, at the Youth Center where Sara had been the administrator. At first it had been to help keep an eye on her and spend more time with her. Now, even though she remained the largest draw for him, he found himself loving the interaction with the kids, the chance to learn about them and influence their decisions and be someone they could talk to and depend on. "If the women here found out you're buying their shampoo and giving it away to inner-city kids because you don't like it yourself...not sure that would go over very well."

She frowned. "That's ridiculous. Those kids are as deserving as anyone. They'd appreciate it more than most people who can afford it..."

Mac wrapped his hand around her upper arm and tugged her close, and covered her mouth with his. Her passion for the kids and her work had always drawn him. But with her obviously out of her element, feeling a little vulnerable and unsure for the first time in a very, very long time, he wanted her with an intensity he hadn't felt before.

Maybe it was because all of this, the life she was contemplating here in Oscar, was going to be fleeting. Maybe it was because he felt a little guilty for putting her in this position. Maybe it was simply because he *could*. Whatever the reason, he had to kiss her and he knew it was going to go far beyond that. And he wasn't going to stop it.

His lips pressed, then pulled, breaking contact for only milliseconds, lifting away, coming back to taste from another angle.

She didn't even hesitate in kissing him back, wrapping her arms around his neck, pressing close. He felt her soft belly press against his rock-hard fly and he cupped her butt with his big hands, lifting her up against an almost-painful erection.

She moaned, he groaned and the kiss grew hotter. She opened for him and he thrust into her, stroking her tongue, her bottom lip, then her tongue again.

Sara unabashedly pulled herself up and wrapped her legs around his waist. Mac walked forward two steps to set her on the countertop beside the uncut fruit. Not needing to hold her up any longer, he let one hand slide along the outside of her hip to her thigh and down to her ankle, then slid up the front of her leg, along the smooth skin to her knee. He paused, dipping his fingers into the softness behind her knee, then slid his hand up over the top of her thigh. His hand was so big that his thumb glided along the silky skin of her inner thigh. Until it came to the juncture where her leg met her pelvis. The pad of his thumb met the hot silk of her panties and he simply had to know the color of that silk.

He stroked his thumb back and forth along the lacy edge and reveled in the way her breath hitched. He trailed his lips along her jaw, to her ear. He sucked the lobe into his mouth, loving her moan, then licked along the side of her neck. "Sara," he said huskily.

"Yeah?" she breathed, tipping her head to give him better access.

"I need you naked."

"Okay." She reached up behind her and untied the string holding the bodice of her dress up.

Just *okay*. He marveled at his luck as he pulled back to watch. The dress dropped away from her breasts. No bra. He knew exactly how this was going to go.

"Lift up," he commanded.

Sara clamped her legs around him and lifted her butt from the Formica. He tugged the dress down over her hips, then when she released her hold on his waist, he whisked it down her legs and tossed it toward the refrigerator.

He stepped back. Turquoise blue. Her panties were the same color as her dress.

"Did you buy those to go with the dress?" he asked.

She nodded. "Perfect match."

"They need to go with the dress now too," he said, tipping his head toward the dress on the floor.

She hooked her thumbs in the top of the panties and wiggled on the counter, working them down one side at a time. They dropped to her ankles and she kicked them in the direction of the fridge.

Mac didn't look to see where they landed. Didn't matter.

"On the table," he said gruffly.

She looked over at the big wooden kitchen table. "What? The panties?"

"You."

Chapter Eight

Her eyes widened. "Me? On the table?"

"Now." He fisted his hands at his sides. He wanted her to follow his commands freely.

"Why not go upstairs? To the bed?"

He gave her a half smile. "Haven't you heard? I'm not into conventional sex."

She rolled her eyes. "I remember. The nipple clamps."

As usual, his body tightened in response to hearing her talk about things he'd never imagined her even knowing about.

"And you mentioned something about more than one woman," she added.

"Well, there's a spectrum of unconventional," he told her.

"Ah."

"Kitchen tables are not quite as far along the spectrum as ménages. Or, say, orgies."

She narrowed her eyes. "Good to know." Then she glanced around the kitchen. "It's the middle of the day."

"Yep."

"There are lots of windows down here."

"Yep."

"Someone might come by."

"They might."

"I..."

"Table. Now, Sara." He wouldn't repeat it too many more times. He could quite easily *put* her on the table. But he wanted to watch her get up there, lay back and offer herself up to him.

Finally, with a deep breath, she slid from the counter and padded across the linoleum to the table. He watched her breasts bounce slightly, the sway of her hips and the flush of excitement on her skin. She was breathing faster than usual.

He smiled. She'd started this.

"I brought your mail too," he said.

She turned to face him, the table right behind her. She braced her hands on the top of the table and pushed herself up to sit on the edge. "Thanks."

"There was a package."

"Oh?"

"Right there."

She looked in the direction he was pointing. The box from Scandalous Somethings sat at the other end of the table.

"Oh!" she exclaimed. "It came!" She hopped back down to the floor, seeming oblivious to her nakedness and the windows suddenly.

The box was, of course, already open and she gave him a grin when she noticed. Mac forced himself to stay where he was. For now.

She took everything out of the box, laying it on the table, like it was her birthday or Christmas morning.

"I've been wondering about this," she said, turning to face him and unscrewing the lid to one of the jars of body powder. She watched him as she lifted her index finger to her mouth and slid it past her lips. Withdrawing the wet digit, she dipped it into the jar, then pulled it out covered with yellow powder. She licked her tongue along the length of her finger. Slowly. Twice.

"You're not laying on the table," he said, crossing his arms and intentionally looking displeased.

She wasn't buying it. "No, I'm not. Yet." She crossed to where he stood. Her nipples were erect, her pulse beating rapidly at the hollow of her throat. Her eyes held mischief. She dipped her finger into the jar again and then held it up to him.

He circled her wrist with his hand, tugging her forward, until her breasts brushed the soft cotton of his T-shirt. She sucked in a quick breath and he smiled, feeling hungry suddenly. His closed his lips around her finger, his eyes locked on hers. He dragged his tongue from the base to the tip of her finger, swirled it around the pad, then sucked as he slowly pulled her finger free. She was holding her breath now. The powder tasted pretty good. He did love banana splits.

"I don't think this powder was made for fingers," he said huskily.

She licked her lips. "It's for...anything we want."

"I want, Sara," he said, his voice dropping to a near growl. "I want badly."

"Me too," she whispered.

"Get on the table."

He'd promised himself he wasn't going to have sex with her. He had not, however, promised not to touch her. Not touching her would have been smarter and easier in the long run. Hell, not touching her might have sped along the breakup he was trying for. But not touching her simply wasn't a possibility. He was a smart guy. He wasn't going to try to tell himself he could keep his hands to himself while living with Sara, even if it was for only a few days at a time.

And maybe all of the "unconventional" things he wanted to do would help convince her this wasn't what she wanted. But he was sure as hell going to enjoy them until she said stop.

Sara slid back up on the table.

Mac took the jar of banana split body powder from her. "Lay back." He hooked his arm under her knees and turned her as she lay back so that her legs were up on the table too. "And as long as this is here." He slid the pink fur-covered wedge down the table to her hips.

Wordlessly, she bent her knees and lifted her butt off the table. Mac slid the wedge under her so she lay on an incline, her hips up.

Perfect.

He took the powder puff that came with the jar and dipped it in the powder. Then he lightly skimmed it over her collarbones from one side to the other.

"Mmm." Sara closed her eyes and stretched her arms over her head.

Mac leaned over and licked the powder up.

She arched her back slightly, toward his mouth. He smiled and added more powder to the puff, then dragged it over her skin from collarbone to nipple. When the fluffy cotton touched the sensitive tip, Sara sucked in a breath.

He followed the trail of powder with his tongue, over her chest, to the nipple. She gasped and arched closer, and he couldn't resist. Foregoing the powder puff, he took a pinch of powder between thumb and forefinger and sprinkled it over her nipple and the areola. He licked it off, sucking on the tip before licking again, then sucking.

She was moaning, her head moving restlessly against the table.

"You know my favorite part of banana splits?" Mac asked, powdering the opposite breast.

"Um..." she murmured, clearly not focused on the question. Or forming words at all.

Mac bent and tasted her right nipple.

"Mac," she groaned.

"Hmm?" He licked and sucked another moment. "Sorry, I didn't answer, did I?"

He looked down at her, cheeks flushed with desire, nipples erect and wet from his tongue. She was everything he could ever imagine wanting.

Dammit.

It's just lust. It's just another beautiful woman, letting you do what you want, thinking you're the king right now... Been there, done that.

"What's your favorite part?" she asked, panting a bit as she tried to talk.

"The chocolate syrup." She was on his kitchen table, after all. Food was a natural combination in the kitchen.

He had to only take one step and lean a bit to grab the chocolate syrup from the door of the fridge.

"This is going to be cold."

Her eyes widened as he flipped the top open and turned the bottle upside down.

"Oh," she breathed as the first drizzle touched her skin.

He made a looping design starting between her breasts and dribbling down her stomach and stopping just below her belly button.

Before lowering his head, though, Mac moved to the end of the table, between her knees.

Without a word, her eyes on his, Sara let her knees fall apart.

He couldn't swallow. Or breathe. That seemed to be happening a lot around her.

"God, Sara, I've never seen anything more beautiful," he told her sincerely.

"Touch me, Mac," she said, her voice thick.

"Oh, I intend to, princess. Nothing could stop me." For the moment he was just going to look. She was all his. She would agree to anything, he knew. He could have her in any way—in every way—he could think of.

And it would still not be enough.

He was completely screwed.

He bit back a laugh at that. So true and yet, so ironic. He was screwed and yet that was the last thing he was going to be.

Hating the way his thoughts and emotions were jumbling on him, he concentrated on what he did know for sure.

Sara was naked, on his table, covered in chocolate.

What was he doing *thinking* anyway?

He lifted the bottle and squeezed. The thin line of chocolate fell, landing in the center of the triangle of soft hair between her legs, then drizzling lower, over the wet, pink folds begging for his attention.

Her eyes slid closed and she breathed in and out deeply, twice.

"Mac," she whispered.

"I know," he answered softly.

He started at her ribs, lapping up the chocolate, licking and kissing the sweeter skin beneath, even nipping gently at her hip bone and then dipping his tongue into her belly button. He spent a little extra time on her new crown tattoo from St. Croix. She was squirming and begging by the time he got to the final pool of chocolate. He followed that trail as well, his tongue picking up every drop, even if it took two, or three, or four licks to get it all.

"Open up, princess," he said, his hands on her knees. He nudged and she spread them even further. "That's it," he coached softly. "Just like that." He pulled the pad of his index finger through the chocolate on her mound, drawing it down into the sweetness of her body. She arched closer to his hand as his finger slid over her clitoris. He swirled just the tip of his finger around it, making her gasp, then dipped it in the powder and added that flavor as well.

Not that she needed it.

He knew he shouldn't do it. He knew it would only make him want more. He also knew there was nothing that could stop him. Mac leaned in and tasted Sara, long and deep and thoroughly. Anticipating her reaction, he'd clamped his hands on her thighs, keeping her from thrusting her hips too hard at the sensations.

His tongue stroked the outer tissue, flicked over her clit, then plunged deep.

"Mac!" she cried out. "Oh, please, please."

"Yes, Sara, that's it, honey." He licked again, then suckled her clitoris, making her sob.

"It's too much!"

"Let go, Sara."

She arched again and cried his name.

"Come for me, princess." He slipped two fingers into her tightness, hooking his index finger to find her G-spot and sucked again.

She shattered a moment later. His name left her lips in a loud cry as her hips came off the wedge, her hands grasping the edges of the table.

He kept his fingers in her, moving gently with the waves of her body, loving the feel of her muscles clenching and releasing as her climax slowly subsided. Her legs were trembling, when he finally slid his fingers free and lifted them to his mouth, tasting her as she watched him.

He licked his lips free of chocolate, powder and Sara. "Delicious."

"I don't think the table's going to hold both of us up here," she said, breathlessly.

"It won't."

"We're going upstairs?" she asked eagerly.

He just about threw her over his shoulder and headed for the staircase.

"I have to get back to work.

"Work?" She stared at him.

"Yeah, I'll see you Friday, princess. Around noon, probably." He almost couldn't walk he was so hard, but he had to go. To work. And away from his wife. The wife that he was going to have to somehow walk away from, for good, eventually.

Her eyes widened and she struggled to sit up. Difficult with the wedge under her. She finally rolled off of it and got upright. "What?

You're *leaving*?"

"My shift starts at seven."

"You knew you had to go back?"

"Of course. I always work Wednesdays."

"You'll be home tomorrow though?"

"No. Friday."

She didn't look angry. She looked disappointed, which flattered him. She also looked sad, which pulled at his heart. Dammit.

"You always work Fridays too," she said.

He shook his head. "No. Never Fridays. Unless we're covering someone."

"But...I never see you on Fridays."

"Does Sam work Fridays?" he asked.

She was still naked, flushed, tousled and sticky from the powder, syrup and sex and he was having a hard time not bolting for the door...or for her.

She frowned. "No. But you're never with us, you're never around."

"Sara, I don't work without the crew. We don't work Fridays. I can promise you."

"What do you..." She trailed off, suddenly looking sick.

Concerned he stepped forward. "What is it?"

"Nothing. I just figured it out." She wouldn't look at him as she slid to the floor and went to retrieve her dress.

He was distracted for a moment as she bent over to pick it up, but she straightened and held the dress up in front of her, allowing his brain synapses to work again.

"Figured what out?"

She sighed. "You see women on Fridays. That's why I never see you. I got it now. Never mind."

He should just let her think that. Instead he said, "I come to Oscar on Fridays."

"For a woman?" She looked appalled by the idea. "Oh, my God, Mac, do you have a girlfriend *here*?"

Absolutely not. "No, it's not that. I come home on Fridays. Because it's home. And I'm only here a few days a week when I don't work or...have something else in Omaha." Like her. The truth was, he spent more time in Omaha than he really needed to. Because of Sara. He convinced himself, and apparently his friends and her family, that he was there to help her, look out for her and enjoy his friends. The truth, that he was even just now fully understanding, was Sara was the draw. He loved the guys, would have spent a lot of time with them anyway, but without Sara in Omaha he would have been in Oscar a lot more.

"Oh." She clearly wasn't sure what to think. "So Friday afternoon?"

"I brought some of your books and movies and stuff," he said, as a consolation. He could, of course, come home tomorrow after his shift too. But he wouldn't. He wanted this to be tough on her. Just like he wouldn't go downtown and give the Style ladies a piece of his mind. If she was his wife, to keep, truly for as long as they both should live, he'd go down and tell Shelly and Angela and Karen to lay off. But if they gave Sara a hard time, it might make his job of convincing her to go back to Omaha, single, easier. "I'll bring the box and your clothes in."

"Great. Thanks." She finally met his eyes. "I do appreciate it."

He didn't know how to describe the expression on her face. "No problem."

When he came back in with the rest of her things, she was gone and he could hear the shower upstairs running.

He ran a hand over the top of his head. The scent of her drifted to his nose and he closed his eyes. None of this was turning out as he'd planned.

He didn't want her to go. Ever.

What a frickin' mess.

Sean picked her up Friday morning at ten, just as they'd arranged.

She walked toward Style With A Smile at ten nineteen. In the black and white workout pants and a loose white V-neck T-shirt that Mac had bought her.

Half of her felt her stomach flip at the thought of Mac. And his kitchen table. And chocolate syrup.

The other half of her felt her eyes narrow at the thought of Mac.

And the fact that he'd left her, on the kitchen table, after the most sensual experience of her life and the most amazing orgasm she could imagine, to go back to work.

He'd known all along he had to go back to work. Still he'd kissed her. Still told her to get on the table. Still used the powder and syrup. And the wedge.

She felt her body heat at the memory, even as she was annoyed beyond belief.

He'd made her come, laid out on his kitchen table and then walked out, as if they'd just had a sandwich together.

The jerk.

She hitched the pants up as she approached the door to the shop. Both the pants and shirt were a size too big. Fortunately the drawstring worked to keep the pants from falling to her ankles.

There certainly wasn't anything flashy or skimpy about them.

"'Morning ladies," Sara greeted. She took the huge box of muffins from the bakery to the counter where the stylists scheduled appointments.

The lady at the bakery had been pleasant enough. She'd also been too busy to spend much time asking Sara who she was or what she was doing here. Then again, Sara had her hair pulled into a simple ponytail, plain pearl studs in her ears as her only bling and just basic makeup applied. It had been absolutely no fun getting ready for this trip into town.

She loved to primp. Maybe that made her a snob. Or a princess. But she loved it.

Sure, she'd saved forty-one minutes getting ready today, but what was she going to do with forty-one extra minutes? She couldn't sleep past six thirty no matter how she tried. The Oscar paper didn't take long to read and it wasn't a daily paper anyway. The Today show could be watched even while straightening her hair, or waving her hair, or curling her hair. She didn't eat breakfast. So she now had forty-one minutes to think about all the wonderful makeup and hair accessories and body glitter she wouldn't be using. She had time to lament the invigorating face masks and hot-stone massages and vanilla-cinnamon—and other luscious varieties—body creams she was no longer going to be purchasing.

And what was she going to do with all the jewelry she had? What about the heels? What about all the nail polish? The girls at the center would think she'd gone crazy.

Her greeting still hadn't been returned.

"The muffins are fresh and my nails are in terrible shape," she announced to the, once again, full house.

"The nail polish and emery boards are in aisle six at the grocery store," one of the stylists said.

Of course they didn't wear nametags. In a town this small, everyone knew everyone else. Probably since kindergarten.

"So you don't do manicures on Thursdays either?" Sara asked.

"We don't do manicures at all," another stylist said, not even bothering to look over.

"How about haircuts?" Sara asked. "I could use a trim."

She'd just had her hair cut in St. Croix, but she'd sacrifice a quarter inch of hair to show these women she wouldn't be bullied.

The stylist closest to the door stopped clipping and turned to her. "We're full."

"I'll make an appointment for next week," Sara said.

"We'll be full."

"I'll make an appointment for next month," she said stubbornly.

"We all have full schedules. With regulars. We aren't open to new clients."

And what did Mac expect her to say and do now? Sara wondered. She couldn't drive to Omaha for fear of offending someone and she couldn't get in to the booked-up schedules of the only salon in town. Was she just supposed to let her hair grow indefinitely?

"Any chance there's a place in town that sells jeans?" she asked, giving up on the bonding over hairstyles and muffins.

Six pairs of eyes stared at her in the mirrors in front of the stylists' chairs. Looking around the waiting area, four more pairs of eyes regarded her with interest.

"No place that sells your kind of jeans," the stylist nearest the door, the one that seemed to dislike her most, said.

"My kind of jeans?" Sara repeated. "You mean the denim kind?"

Her sarcasm was not missed. Nor was it appreciated.

"I'm sure you're used to jeans that are a little better than what we have here."

"Better how? You only sell worn-out jeans here?" Her patience was pretty much gone. Sara had never been a sarcastic or nasty person in her life. She'd never had a need. But she was already regarded as a snob. She didn't want to be the snob that ran from the shop crying too and if she didn't parry their attacks that would be the only other thing she could do.

"I just don't think we have anything here of interest to you." If it was possible, the woman's tone had gotten cooler.

"Okay." Sara clapped her hands together and spun toward the door. "Thanks for your hospitality. I see why people are so drawn to charming small Nebraska towns."

She exited before she saw or heard a reaction.

She looked both ways up and down the sidewalk, trying to decide which way to go. She would hit the grocery store again before Sean picked her up, but she had a half hour until he would be ready to go home.

And she needed some blue jeans. Apparently.

She turned left, simply because she didn't have a better idea. Besides, the downtown area was situated in an old-fashioned town square design. The businesses literally lined four streets that made a complete square around the town park with a working fountain and a small bandstand in the middle. The square ensured she'd eventually make it to the shops that were now to her right. Either way, she'd see everything.

She was halfway across the square from Style when she passed a window with "Go Wildcats" in huge blue letters across the front and mannequins clothed in various T-shirts and sweatshirts in the school colors of royal blue and white. And blue jeans.

Relieved there was a place that sold clothes that weren't too-big sweatpants, she pushed the door open.

"Hello."

A man came toward her with a smile and Sara was relieved to see another person, besides Mac and Sean, who seemed friendly.

"Hi. Would you happen to sell blue jeans?" Might as well get right to the point.

The man nodded. "Sure. Back right corner of the store."

"Great." Relieved, Sara started in that direction.

She was amazed by the store as she walked. It was a lot bigger than it looked from the outside. It also contained an interesting assortment of items. She passed hunting supplies including tents, guns and camouflaged overalls and jackets. Next was the fishing section with several different poles and lures mounted on the wall, along with tall boots called hip waders. She wasn't sure what those were for, but was pretty sure she wasn't ever going to need them. Then there was the section that held basketballs, baseballs, footballs and other gear. Then, strangely, she found herself in the hardware section. Hammers, saws, nuts and bolts and even a few workbenches were on display. Next was apparently the automotive area. There were floor mats, motor oil, shammies, huge batteries and jacks. Nearing the back of the store she passed lawnmowers, hedge trimmers, barbecue grills and coolers of various sizes.

Finally she made it to the clothing section. Such as it was.

There were racks of blue jeans. There were also T-shirts, flannel shirts and a vast array of apparel with the school colors and logos on them. There were also some shirts and jackets with the Nebraska Huskers, the state's major university's team logo.

Okay. Well, it was clothing. And it was what the locals wore.

"You need some stuff for the big game?"

The store owner wore a name tag. "Steve" was watching her flip past hanger after hanger.

"The big game?" she asked.

"The scrimmage tomorrow night."

She really didn't care about the scrimmage. Nor did she imagine she would be there. But he seemed excited. "What stuff do you recommend?" Heave forbid she offend yet another business owner in Oscar.

"Well, it's still pretty warm during the day, but when the sun goes down it cools off quick. You might want to start in a T-shirt and bring a jacket along." Steve handed her a royal blue T-shirt with a huge white paw print on the front. *Wildcat Football* was scrawled beneath the print.

She smiled. "I don't suppose that Mac, I mean, Jason Gordon has an account here?"

"Um, no," Steve said. "I would certainly extend him any amount of credit, though." He smiled widely. "He's good for it."

"Of course he is," she said with her own big smile. "I'll be sure he stops by to pay you right away when he gets back to town."

Steve didn't seem surprised she would be charging things to an account for Mac. Which probably meant everyone in town knew Mac had a wife living at the farm. Not that she minded.

Besides, it was going to successfully clothe her in acceptable garments, so she would just be happy.

She left the store with three pairs of jeans, a pair of not-completely-ugly leather boots that went just up over her ankles, a pair of white tennis shoes and two T-shirts, a sweatshirt and pull-over jacket for the Wildcats.

The total bill was still less than she'd spent on one outfit at one of the "boutiques", as Mac put it, in Omaha.

She had just stepped out onto the sidewalk, pushing her sunglasses into place when she heard, "Sara!"

She turned to find Sean and two other boys coming toward her.

"Am I late?" she asked as he got close.

He grinned down at her from nearly five inches over six feet. "No. We were coming in to look at some new hunting gear Steve got in."

She smiled at the boys with him. "Hi, I'm Sara."

"I know," one of them said. Then when he got elbowed in the back by Sean, he said, "I'm Jared. Nice to meet you."

"I'm Zach," the other boy said. "Are you really married to Jason?"

She shrugged. "Really am."

"Wow."

"Yeah." She had to agree. It was pretty wow for her too. Even when he left her in a tingling pile of Jell-O on the kitchen table to go back to work after making her scream his name.

"Are you coming to the game?" Sean had spotted the royal blue.

"I think I am," Sara said. "You play?"

Sean chuckled and the other boys grinned. "Yeah. We play."

She looked from one to the other. "You're good, right?"

"We're okay." Sean's modesty didn't fool her.

"Well, now I'm coming for sure."

"Cool." Sean looked genuinely pleased.

"Yeah." She looked around the town square. She wished she had somewhere else to go, something else to do. Facing the empty farmhouse alone didn't sound appealing at all, but there wasn't much choice.

The next day when she went into town with Sean, she was decked out in one of her new T-shirts and blue jeans. She couldn't quite bring herself to wear the boots or tennis shoes, so she did slip into her flip-flops, hoping she could be forgiven for that one little thing. It was still summer as far as she was concerned.

She stopped at the bakery for cinnamon rolls this time before heading for Style With A Smile.

Conversation stopped the minute the door swung open. She gave everyone a bright smile. "Good morning, everyone."

She set the rolls on the counter, noting that the bakery box from yesterday was set next to the garbage can behind the counter. And it was empty.

Then she took a seat in the only unoccupied chair in the waiting area, swung her purse—which was Gucci, though she'd found it online for a steal—to her lap and dug out her new nail polish and emery board from the grocery store—aisle two, not six.

She started rounding off her tips, ignoring the fact that the shop was completely silent.

She hummed as she filed and buffed.

Finally, conversation, stilted as it was at first, started again.

By the time she had the first coat finished on one hand the women had decided to ignore her and were going about their business and conversations as usual.

It was quite enlightening. After thirty minutes she knew about kids, jobs, husbands and vacations. Probably more than she could have ever learned in even thirty minutes one on one. The women talked easily, asking questions about kids' illnesses, how the new grandbabies were doing, how the new paint in the kitchen looked and how the interview process for law school worked.

The women were quite obviously comfortable here and with one another. There was a camaraderie Sara envied. Though the questions were asked as a part of a semi-public conversation, it seemed clear that those asking the questions did care about the answers.

Sara wished she fit in here—or somewhere—like that. She was

supported. She had people who truly cared for her and loved her. But she didn't have...this. This acceptance from people who didn't have to like her, who spent time with her by choice.

There was something special about friendships like this. Her closest friends were also family, or those important to her family. Her brother, Mac, Dooley and Kevin, even Ben, had this kind of friendship. The kind that's chosen and tested and has survived over time.

She didn't.

She didn't have many friends. Dooley, Kevin and Mac had to like her because she was Sam's little sister. Ben and Danika had to like her because of Sam and Jessica. The kids at the center liked her, made her laugh, talked to her, looked up to her, but they weren't exactly friends.

She didn't have any girlfriends.

Sara kicked off a sandal and pulled her foot up onto the seat of her chair so she could reach her toes. She removed the decal and then wiped the polish clean with a portable polish-removing wipe. As she uncapped the polish and touched the brush to her big toenail she noticed the woman across from her watching intently. Sara continued with her pedicure. When all toes were polished she made eye contact and smiled.

"That looks nice," the woman offered.

"Thanks." Sara usually had other people do it for her because she enjoyed it and they were better at it, but she had watched enough times to know what she was doing. She glanced at the woman's foot, also in a sandal. "Here, give me your foot."

The woman looked startled. "Oh, no. I'm fine."

"I don't mind at all. I like doing it for others more than myself." She had no idea if that was true, but it seemed like potentially a good way to make friends.

The woman looked hesitant, so Sara leaned over, grabbed her foot and lifted it into her lap. The woman didn't protest, so Sara pushed her luck and unbuckled the sandal. She was acutely aware that the entire shop was watching them. She focused on the woman whose foot she was getting intimate with. "What's your name?" She slipped the sandal off and dropped it to the floor.

"Kathy." She looked uncomfortable, but didn't pull her foot back.

"Do you have kids?"

Sara had experienced more than her share of great pedicures. She began kneading Kathy's foot, pressing her thumb in and then rubbing along the arch. She massaged the ball of the foot, then stroked back to the heel, up over the ankle and then started over.

Kathy sighed. It was a small victory. It was hard to be snotty to someone who was rubbing your foot.

"I have three," Kathy said. "My youngest is fourteen."

"Wow, three," Sara said. "Are the other two still at home too?"

"One is."

"I work with teenagers every day," Sara shared. "But I don't have to live with them. I admire you."

"You work?" Kathy said. Then quickly added, "With teenagers, huh?"

Sara caught the small slip but ignored it. She smiled. "Yes. I was the administrator of a youth center. We helped give teens, especially those at risk for trouble, something to do, a positive place to go instead of the streets."

"And you were in charge of it?"

Sara also decided to ignore the surprise in the woman's voice and the interest the others seemed to have. "Yep. I got a master's degree in social work with the intention of running the center. My dad founded it and my siblings and I have run it ever since he died."

"Wow."

Sara smiled in response. That was nice. Maybe she was breaking some ice. She uncapped the polish and began applying it to Kathy's toenails.

"My sister is the director of nursing for the ER at St. Anthony's in Omaha. Her husband, Ben, is a trauma surgeon. My brother Sam is a paramedic, with Mac...Jason. And Sam's wife, Danika, is a social worker at the hospital."

Kathy smiled. "St. Anthony's is like a family reunion."

Sara laughed. "Yeah. Except we all see each other every day anyway."

They continued to chat as Sara did Kathy's other foot as well. By the time they were finished, the air in the shop seemed changed. Less tense. More comfortable.

She looked up, met the gaze of the stylist closest to the door and smiled. The woman didn't smile back, but she didn't glare, or look away either.

Small victories. One step at a time.

"You smell like cotton candy."

Sara turned to the woman next to her. "Thank you."

The woman seemed more puzzled than complimentary. "Do you have perfume that smells like candy?"

"No. It's body powder." She smiled. "Kind of."

"Kind of?"

Hey, the woman was conversing with her. She had to keep it up.

"It's body powder, but it smells and *tastes* like cotton candy."

"Really?" The woman leaned closer. "Where do you get that?"

"Scandalous Somethings."

She frowned. "Is that in Omaha?"

"No, it's a catalog and online. I just found it with Google."

"What kind of store is that?" A different woman asked the question now.

Sara debated for only a moment. "Sex toys."

Two words. Two small, simple words. And absolute silence descended on the shop. But it was different than before. It wasn't judgmental. It was interested.

"I guess body powder isn't technically a toy," Sara amended, looking around the room at the fascinated faces. "They specialize in things to use in the bedroom." She glanced around the shop again. No one said a word. "Or other rooms, I suppose. It doesn't have to be the bedroom." In her opinion, the kitchen had been just fine yesterday.

"Why are you wearing it now? Here?" Another salon patron joined in.

Sara turned to her. "I wanted to see if it would be sticky to wear it for a while. This book I'm reading says you should do fun little things that make you feel sexy and that will surprise your partner. I wanted to have it on when M—Jason…gets home tomorrow. I didn't know if it would be sticky to wear it all day or if I should put it on at the last minute."

The women all stared at her again. She looked at each of them. She'd told them she and Mac were married. If they were surprised she was talking about him and sex in the same sentence, that was their problem.

"Well?" someone asked. "Is it?"

"Sticky?" Sara asked.

The woman nodded.

Sara laughed. "No, it's not. And it smells good."

"Does it really taste like cotton candy?" someone else asked.

"Yep." Sara held her hand out, palm down. "Want to see?"

The woman's eyes widened. "You want me to taste it?" She sounded shocked.

Sara shrugged. "Only if you want to. Doesn't matter to me."

The woman didn't decline the invitation immediately. She just sat looking at Sara.

"What book said you should do that?" Kathy, with her freshly painted toenails, asked.

Sara reached down and dug out the book in her bag. "I have a bunch. This one is called *Sex All Day Long.*"

"Is it like an instruction manual or something?"

"No. It's more about relationships, honestly. I do have a couple books that are more instructional." Sara dug in her bag again and pulled out a smaller paperback. "And I have a few erotic romances. They're fiction, but they're steamy and have some good ideas."

No one said a word.

"There are a lot of electronic erotic romance books too," she went on, determined to not be intimidated by the long silences. "You can read them online."

None of the women would look at each other. A few seemed to be making a mental note.

Sara wasn't embarrassed by any of it. If these women believed she wasn't, or shouldn't be having sex, they were crazy. If they weren't having fun, steamy sex, they should be. And if it bothered them to think about Jason MacDonald Gordon having sex, they sure didn't know him as well as they thought.

The woman next to her was staring at the paperback in Sara's lap.

"I'll bring the powder in tomorrow and you can all try it."

No one declined the invitation, no one shouted *No!* and a few smiled.

"I'd better get going," she announced, standing and sliding her feet back into her flip-flops. "It was fun, girls."

"Bye, Sara."

"See ya, Sara."

"Thanks, Sara."

Sara was sure she was beaming. They weren't exactly friends yet, but at least she'd given them something to talk about again.

As she bent to tuck one book and the manicure-pedicure paraphernalia in her purse she surreptitiously slipped the romance novel to the woman who'd been sitting next to her.

Mac didn't make it home around noon, or even close to noon, the next day. He still wasn't home by the time Sara needed to leave for the football game, and she was ticked. She was sure he was avoiding coming home because he was avoiding her. She didn't completely understand everything behind that, but she did know he was still feeling bad about wanting Sam's little sister. She had to think Sam and Mac had talked about it over the past few days working together. She was also pretty sure nothing had been resolved. At least not her way. Otherwise, Mac would have come home as soon as his shift ended to be with her.

Sara called up the road to Sean's house. As a member of the team, Sean was already in town but his mother was happy to offer Sara a ride to the game, so Sara found herself tucked between Sean's mother and grandmother in the stands by the time everyone stood for the national anthem.

"Everybody's making a huge deal out of a simple scrimmage, aren't they?" Sara asked as they settled back in their seats.

Sean's mom, Pat, laughed. "There's nothing simple about it. Once boys in this town put their helmets on they play to win no matter who's on the other side of the line."

Sara could see that. It seemed like a real game to her. Everyone was dressed in school colors, the cheerleaders and band were there and the players were running and hitting hard.

It wasn't until the Riverside Wildcats' varsity team led by seven and a time-out was called by the visiting team that Sara noticed Mac.

He was standing down behind the team talking with the other

men who had gathered there. It seemed the women and other students used the bleachers, while the men—mostly dads, she was sure—congregated along the sidelines. They were separated from the team by a long rope and about thirty feet of dirt and grass, but they were there, watching and analyzing and discussing every play.

Mac also was dressed in the school colors, including a pullover and a cap, and he definitely seemed to be a part of the group.

Sara frowned at his back.

"Was there anything going on in town this afternoon before the game?" she asked Pat, not taking her eyes off of Mac.

"Oh, of course. They had a pep rally at school and then the big tailgate party in the parking lot."

"Why weren't you there?" Sara asked.

"I was, at the start. I helped serve for the first shift, then had to run home to get stuff for the after-party."

"There's an after-party too?"

"Football is what everyone lives for here," Pat said with a laugh. "We celebrate all season and then when it's over, we talk about it and anticipate the next season."

"Wow." Sara made a mental note to buy a copy of Football for Dummies or something the next time she was in Omaha.

"You didn't happen to see Jason down there at the tailgate?"

"Of course," Pat said. "I'm sure he was at the pep rally too."

"Uh-huh."

Sara excused herself and headed for the restroom. Fine. Her husband went to the school pep rally instead of coming home. Even though he'd been gone and hadn't seen her for forty-eight hours now. Even though the last time he'd seen her she'd been naked and willing with a box full of sex toys. Fine.

She emerged from the ladies' room and headed for the concession stand. If she wasn't going to see her husband and she was going to watch a game she barely understood, she was going to need chocolate.

As she stood in line behind a dad and a little girl who couldn't decide which flavor sucker she wanted, she heard a deep, very familiar voice say, "I wonder if they have cotton candy. I'm in the mood."

She whirled to find herself nose to chest with Mac and tipped her head back to look up at him. "How did you know I had that on?"

"I heard you were wearing it all day since you've discovered it doesn't get sticky and that you were interested in sex all day long."

She rolled her eyes. Even the title of her book had made it to his ears. "Who'd you hear that from?"

"Tim Stratton."

"Who's Tim Stratton?"

"Cindy Stratton's husband."

"Who's Cindy Stratton?"

"The woman you asked to lick you to see how your powder tastes."

She looked at the smile he gave her and raised an eyebrow. "That's not how I said it." At all. For one thing, the way Mac said it made it sound very sexual.

She turned back to the concession stand and ordered a Snickers bar and a bag of M&Ms. She didn't eat junk food very often but when she did it was chocolate. If she ever needed a sugar high, it was now.

"I want to lick you and see how your powder tastes," he said near her ear.

She headed for the bleachers, ripping the top off the bag of M&Ms. "I'm not sure I'm talking to you."

"Oh?" He fell into step beside her.

"You left things a little unfinished the other day."

"I heard you—very distinctly—finish, princess."

"I mean that *you* didn't finish things."

"You won't stay mad at me."

"Oh? And what if I don't forgive you? You going to threaten to never do any of that again?"

"I would never threaten that. Because that would be completely untrue. I fully intend to do all of that again. And again. And again. No matter if you think you're holding a grudge or not."

He caught her arm after a few steps and pulled her behind the concession building. He backed her up against the wall, pressed close, lifted her hair away from her neck with one big hand and leaned in to run his tongue from her collarbone to behind her ear.

She shivered in spite of herself. She tipped her head to the side too. "You shouldn't get to taste it now. You should have come home, instead of going to the pep rally, to taste it."

"Have to support my team," he said gruffly, tracing the wet path again.

"You didn't think I'd be here tonight, did you?"

"No. I'd hoped you wouldn't."

"Because..."

"Because just seeing you makes me want to lick you. All over. Right here and now."

Her blood heated with his words and the look in his eyes. "Why is that such a problem?"

"Because I shouldn't lick you. And I especially shouldn't lick you here in a public place where everyone thinks I'm a saint."

She sighed with pleasure. She loved having his hands and mouth on her. "They don't know you very well, do they?"

"They know me very well." His tongue traced around the outer shell of her ear.

"They don't know how cruel you are, withholding sex from your own wife," she said in a husky whisper.

"Not having sex with my best friend's little sister makes me a saint." He trailed his lips along her jaw.

"How so?"

"Do you have any idea how difficult that's been for me?" He kissed her, just once, softly.

"I hope it has been," she admitted. "It's been torture for me."

"Maybe I can help with that."

"Great, let's go." She didn't want to move, though. They were in a shadow here. The game went on, the crowd cheered, the band played, people came and went from the concession stand. They were hidden from it all. Someone could come around the corner at any moment and see them. The idea gave her a naughty thrill.

"Right here," he said against her lips. Then he kissed her with the heat and need that she felt herself.

"But..." She had to catch her breath. Her hands held the front of his nylon pullover in two tight fists. "This is a high school. With kids. And PTO moms. And..."

"Yep."

She kissed him this time, arching against him as best she could with their height differences. He helped her out with that when he cupped her butt and lifted her up against the wall and pressed in. She licked along his bottom lip, reveled in his groan, then stroked her tongue boldly against his. His fingers dug into her bottom and she wiggled against him, wanting to press skin to skin, to open to him, to pull him inside of her.

She'd had very plain and boring sex, but she knew there was more to it. If she hadn't, the Internet would have taught her quickly.

"Mac, I need you."

"I know you do, princess," he said gruffly. "I know exactly what you need. But I need just a little bit first. Just a taste."

With that he pulled her shirt up, the left cup of her bra down and sucked her cotton-candy-flavored nipple into his mouth.

He sucked and she gasped, then groaned. If he asked her to strip naked right here and now she'd do it and all she'd say would be thank you.

"That does taste as good as it smells," he reported. He took a bold swipe with his tongue across the skin on the upper curve of her breast. Then pulled back to look at her.

Chapter Nine

In the shadow of the building he couldn't see clearly. He looked his fill anyway. She was so damned beautiful.

He'd known she was there in the stands, but with Sean's mom and grandma she'd been safe, off-limits, untouchable. When he'd looked back to see her climbing down from the bleachers and heading off by herself, he'd sworn under his breath. He knew he had to go after her. He couldn't stay away. It was like an addiction.

"Mac," she whispered. "Do something."

"You want me just to take you up against the brick wall?" he teased.

When she nodded, he almost went to his knees. She'd let him. Like this. Where nearly anyone could find them. Unromantic, spontaneous, out of control. And she'd let him. From the look on her face, she'd like it too.

She was wearing jeans. He'd meant for that to be *less* appealing, to cover her up. Instead, she looked incredible. The blue denim showcased her small waist, her firm butt, and her slim legs. She wore it like she wore everything—with an easy style that made him want to howl with lust.

"Let's go home."

He wanted to. He really did. "It's only halftime. And I probably should warn you..."

"Princess Sara!" Dooley had her in a hug before Mac could finish his sentence.

"Dooley!" Sara squealed as her feet left the ground. "What are you doing here?"

"We came up to hang out with you. We miss you." Kevin moved in to hug her next.

Dooley stood back and watched. "You do smell like candy."

She turned a huge grin on him. "You sound like you expected it."

"Well, Steve told me you told his wife you're wearing some kind of special body powder."

She looked at Mac. "Steve is a friend of Tim's?"

"Yeah. I think Alan told Steve."

"Does everyone know?"

"That the hot girl married to the town's favorite son announced at the Style that she is wearing edible body powder from an online sex shop? Yeah. Everyone knows."

She rolled her eyes. "What else are they saying about me?"

"That you're loaning out books about relationships and sex," Mac said.

"That you're not pregnant," Dooley added.

"And that you give great pedicures," Kevin said.

"*You've* been talking to the locals?"

"Of course. We've been partying with them all afternoon."

"You've been here all day?"

"Yeah, we came up with Mac right after our shift."

She turned to Mac, eyebrows up. "Had to bring bodyguards?"

He grinned. Kind of. "They come up here with me most Fridays."

Sara frowned and turned back to Kevin. Kevin was the one that wouldn't lie to her, even to spare her feelings. "What? You come to Oscar a lot?"

Kevin shrugged. "Yeah. They have lots of games and parties and stuff."

"And nice Christian girls you can pray with?" Sara asked slyly.

Kevin blushed. "Well..."

She laughed. "Got it."

"Hey, Sara, tell me more about this body powder," Dooley said, stepping close to her.

"What about it? You put it on. Easy."

He took her hand and turned it palm up. Then he bent and licked the skin just above her wrist.

Sara giggled. Mac saw red.

He shoved Dooley back, pulling Sara behind him. "What the hell was that?" He glowered at his friend.

Dooley looked at him and licked his lips. "Yum."

Mac leaned toward him menacingly and Dooley had the nerve to smile. "Knock it off."

"Hey, a girl doesn't wear edible body powder if she doesn't want to be licked. Right, princess?"

"He's got a point Mac," Sara said from behind him.

"And you don't care who licks you?" he asked, still staring at Dooley.

He couldn't believe how seeing another man touching Sara like that had affected him.

"Oh, I care." She moved in closer to him. He felt her even though he couldn't see her. "I bought the powder with only one man in mind."

"Hear that?" Mac asked Dooley. "Stop licking my wife. Better yet, stop touching her altogether."

Dooley raised an eyebrow and smiled knowingly. "Right. Thanks for the reminder she's your wife."

Mac stared at him. He'd said that, hadn't he? He hadn't said "Sara". He'd said "my wife". She was, of course. Even though he was trying valiantly to not think of her that way. He also shouldn't sound so damned protective and possessive.

Shit.

"Okay, I won't lick her anymore," Dooley promised. "But I want the website address where you got that powder, princess."

"Stop calling her princess too," Mac said.

Dooley scoffed at that. "You're the one that started the name. She knows I mean it affectionately."

He was being irrational and knew it. Dooley and Kevin had called her princess as long as he had. The name had taken on a new meaning to him since this whole mess had started, though. He'd called her princess while he was making love to her. It was his name for her. Period.

"Of course I do," Sara said, giving Mac a strange look.

"You're still going to stop," Mac told Dooley.

Dooley shrugged. "Okay, the option is then 'sexy' or 'babe'. Which do you prefer?"

"Sara," Mac said flatly. "Or Mrs. Gordon."

Dooley, Kevin and Sara all snorted at that. Mac was no way a Mr., so his wife simply couldn't be Mrs.

"Second half is starting," Kevin interrupted, moving toward the field.

Dooley went with Kevin and Mac followed with Sara at his side. For the first time, Mac watched football and paid no attention to the game.

Sara smelled good, felt good against his side with his arm around her, and he could close his eyes and picture her—even hear her—coming for him.

Damn.

"Hey, Jason."

Mac turned to see Matt Thompson and Tyler Katz standing there. "Hey, guys." They were easily ten years younger than him—more Sara's age... He blocked that thought.

"We wanted to meet Sara," Matt said with a smile for her.

"Hi." She extended her hand and Matt shook it. Tyler repeated the action.

Mac frowned. They were more her age. She was gorgeous. And sweet. And wonderful.

But she was his wife. They knew that. And she was here with him. And Matt was married.

"What's up, guys?" Mac asked, his tone less friendly than usual.

"We were, um..." Tyler looked at Matt.

Matt was much less shy. He grinned and said, "We want some of the body powder everyone's talking about."

Mac arched an eyebrow. "What's that mean?"

"It was from a website, right?" Matt asked Sara.

"Scandalous Somethings dot com," she replied with a big friendly smile.

"Awesome. Thanks."

The guys moved off and Mac stared down at Sara in bewilderment.

He would have bet that something like announcing she wore

edible body powder would have labeled her as wild and a city girl and an outsider, if not worse—like slutty—in Oscar. Instead, she had become a legend.

Damn.

"Everyone knows your name, princess," he commented.

Sara smiled up at him and Mac felt it like a punch to the stomach. She was happy. Sincerely happy she'd made an impression.

"Not how I planned it," she said with a shrug. "I guess I'll take what I can get."

Mac felt a prick of conscience. She wanted to have friends. Sara was the type of person who had to have friends. And it was happening anyway. In spite of the fact he'd dumped her here, knowing no one, completely out of her element.

She was cute. That was the problem. If she was just gorgeous, just sexy, just someone he wanted with every ounce of lust his body was capable of, this would all be so much easier. But she was cute. Sweet. Fun. Someone he wanted for more than her body.

Which was why he was in love with her. Which was why he wouldn't mind staying married to her.

If things were different. If his life were different. If *he* was different.

He hugged her close to his side, taking a deep breath of the sweet smell of her hair. And as if in confirmation his eyes landed on someone over her head.

Heather Macintosh stared back at him. The first girl he'd messed with that he shouldn't have. She still hated him for talking her into her first sexual experience on the couch in Tim Conner's basement when he had no intention of even asking her to prom. And he deserved it.

"Yes!" Sara jerked under his arm and he looked down to find her jumping up and down. "Yes! Go Sean! Go!"

Mac pulled his attention to the field in time to watch Sean break free and run the thirty yards to the end zone.

"Did you see that, Mac?" she asked. "Wow, that was a great pass!"

Mac chuckled in spite of the dark thoughts from a moment ago. "You don't know football."

"I beg your pardon." Sara looked offended. "I watched Sam play and I've been forced to watch Husker games every Saturday for the past twelve years."

"Every Saturday?" he repeated. "They don't play year-round, princess."

"Well, it seems like it sometimes," she grumbled. "Anyway, being an intelligent person I was bound to pick a few things up after watching that much."

"I can only agree with you at this point," he said.

"Oh?"

"If I don't, it's kind of like saying you're not intelligent, right?"

She laughed and nudged him with her hip. "Right."

He liked making her laugh. He liked how easy it was to be with her. He liked pretty much everything about her. Except her insistence on being married to him.

The game ended three minutes later, the home team was victorious and the party on Main Street was in full swing within twenty minutes of the final play.

A local band provided the music—a mix of rock and country covers—the drinks were bring-your-own and the fun and laughter flowed easily.

"You gonna dance with me?" Sara asked, sliding onto Mac's lap after a dance with Dooley.

He shifted her so her butt wasn't against his groin, but didn't push her off his lap like he probably should have. "Doubt it."

"Why?" She wiggled.

He didn't trust that she'd wiggled without knowing what it did to him. He put his hands firmly on her hips to hold her still. "Don't want to."

"Why not?" She tried to wiggle, then gave a frustrated sigh. "Want to go home and have sex until Dooley and Kevin get there?"

"No," he lied.

She didn't look convinced.

"Want to make out in your car?"

"No."

"Want me to tell you all the places I put the body powder?"

"*No.*"

"Come on." She stood up and took his hand.

"What?" He let her pull him to his feet. Because if she *insisted* on taking him to the car and showing him where she'd put the powder, he wasn't going to make a scene by fighting her. "Where are we going?"

"If you're not going to let me rub against you on your lap or on the dance floor and you're not going to take me home or to the car to let me do more than rub against you, then I want a tour."

His body didn't believe one frickin' word that his brain thought when he agreed he didn't want to do any of those things.

"A tour? Of what?" he asked as they started down the sidewalk.

"The town."

He chuckled and gestured with his free hand. "Here it is."

"Not that kind of tour. The tour of your life here," she said.

He had to shorten his strides to stay beside her. "What do you mean?"

"I want to see the first place you had a job, the first place you got hurt and needed stitches, the first place you kissed a girl."

He looked down at her, a little amazed. "How do you know all of that happened here?"

"Because of how much you love it here."

Mac stopped, tugging her to a stop as well. "How do you know that?"

She smiled up at him. The streetlight shone on her hair. "I know you, Mac. I can tell when something matters to you."

It made sense. He knew what mattered to her, what made her laugh, what freaked her out. "I worked in the grocery store," he said. "Started when I was fifteen and worked every weekend and summer until I went to college."

"I've been to the grocery store," she said. "Okay, what else?"

He couldn't explain why, but he suddenly wanted to show her. Oscar did matter to him. It was home.

"Okay." They started walking again. The silence was comfortable and he loved how her hand seemed to fit perfectly in his even though his was so much bigger. Two blocks later he gestured to the tiny drive-in famous for their chocolate-dipped cones. "This was the first place I drove to when I got my license."

"Did you drive in from the farm?" she asked. She was studying the building instead of looking at him, almost as if she was imagining him there.

"The farm was my grandparents'. I lived here in town. Up by the Methodist church. It's about eight blocks from here."

She chuckled. "So not a long trip, but I'm guessing it was still monumental."

"Of course." He found himself smiling as well.

"Okay, so where were you when you first needed stitches?"

"I didn't need stitches until after college," he told her.

She lifted her hand and gently tugged the neckline of his T-shirt to one side. He knew what she was looking at. "How did this happen?"

"A bullet."

She grimaced. "On a call?"

Sara knew his work was sometimes dangerous. He and the crew worked the night shift as paramedics. They saw some nasty stuff at times. They were also at risk some of the time. They were called to fires, domestic disturbances, bar fights and more. They handled it well. None of them had ever needed more than an ice pack and a stitch or two.

"No. This was...a fight that got out of hand. I wasn't the target."

"You stepped in front of someone." She didn't ask it. She stated it. Like she was sure.

"Yes."

"Did you save them?" She traced her finger along the scar where the bullet had grazed his shoulder.

He took a deep breath before answering. "Not exactly."

She turned her gaze up to his face. "No?"

"After this shot missed, she fired again."

"She?" Sara repeated.

He didn't say anything. He was *not* going to tell her this story.

"A woman shot at you?"

"Not at me. I just got in the way."

"Who then? One of the guys?" Sara's eyes widened. "Was it my brother?"

Mac actually felt like smiling at that. He couldn't help it. It was kind of funny Sara would assume her brother was the target of a woman pissed enough to be shooting at someone.

"No. It wasn't any of the guys. It was before I met them."

"And it wasn't at a call?" she repeated. "Then what?"

"Sara, I don't want to talk about it."

She frowned at him. "Too bad. I think I should know."

"Why?"

"Because someone *scarred* you. I think, as your wife, I should know about all of the ways you've been hurt."

As she looked up at him, Mac realized she wasn't talking only about physical hurts either. She wanted to know about his wounds.

There was no way he was going to tell her.

"It doesn't matter. It was a long time ago."

"Fine. I'll just ask Sam. He'll know all about it, I'm guessing."

Shit. Mac squeezed his eyes shut. Of course Sam knew about it. And Sam would love more proof that Sara shouldn't be with him. It should have been a good answer—but Mac didn't want her to know that way.

"It was a woman, okay?"

"Who was shooting?"

"And who was being shot at." He opened his eyes and looked at Sara.

She looked thoughtful. "They were fighting over you?"

"Kind of."

Her eyebrows went up. "Kind of? I don't think people *shoot* other people over things that can be described as *kind of.*"

He sighed. "Want to see the place I first kissed a girl?" He was going to kiss *her.* As soon as possible. That was much preferable to all of this. It was much preferable to pretty much everything.

She crossed her arms. "*Now* you're going to initiate something physical?"

He stepped closer to her. "I'm pretty sure showing up in St. Croix would be defined as initiating things, princess."

"Uh-uh." She stepped back, shaking her head. "Forget it. I want to know why there was a gunfight over you."

"It wasn't over me," he said with resignation. He knew Sara. She wouldn't drop it. "But it was because of me. As in, I caused it."

"You pissed a woman off enough she wanted to shoot someone?"

He rolled his eyes. "Okay, here's what happened. I'm going to tell you this one time and then we're going to drop it."

She didn't agree, and he knew he'd be answering at least a dozen questions. Still, he felt the need to at least try to exert some control.

"I introduced a woman to...someone and she became obsessed. Then this person started to stalk the other person. She went a little crazy and..." He sounded like an idiot.

Sara's expression said she thought so too. "And?"

He hesitated. He'd been there and he had a hard time believing what had happened. This was going to sound ridiculous. But it had been real. Very real. "The crazy stalker one showed up one night with a gun and tried to kidnap the other one."

Sara watched him for several seconds. When he didn't continue she said, "And?" again.

"Right after she set my apartment on fire."

A couple more seconds passed. Then she said, "One of them set your apartment on fire and tried to kidnap someone at gunpoint."

"Right."

"Holy crap, Mac!" She smacked him on the upper arm. "You can't stop talking there!"

She was right. She would definitely ask Sam now if he did.

The worst part was she knew him well enough to know if he was lying. Or holding back.

Mac sighed, took Sara's hand and led her to one of the tables on the patio of the drive-in. She boosted herself up to sit on the top of the table, her feet on the bench. He stood in front of her, his hands in his pockets.

"I've never been with a woman that *I* didn't break things off with, Sara. I'm not bragging," he said as she started to speak. "I'm not proud of it at all. The truth is, I've never been satisfied completely."

She didn't say anything to that, just raised an eyebrow.

"Usually, when I tell a woman I want to break up, she cries and stops talking to me. Or gets mad and stops talking to me. Or says okay—and stops talking to me. But there were three who wanted to try harder. The first one was Heather. She was a virgin. We started out just dating, but I was a teenage boy, so of course I kept pushing things physically and she kept saying yes. Even then I knew she didn't want to have sex, but I also knew she wanted to be with me enough that she'd eventually give in. She did, to keep me from breaking things off, then hated me after."

"You were that guy, huh?" Sara asked.

"Yep." The guy who only cared about getting his. He'd definitely been that guy. He paced to the end of the patio, ran his hand over the top of his head and then turned back. The memories were more than a decade old, but he could still hear Bruce Springsteen on the stereo.

"And girl number two?" Sara asked.

He stayed where he was across the cement. "Danielle."

"Uh-huh." Sara leaned her elbows on to her knees, watching him intently.

"We were in college. Danielle was crazy about me. She was sweet, had only had a couple of boyfriends before me. She was fine with the sex." Very fine, as he remembered it.

"But there was a problem?"

"I always pushed. That's what I do. She said she'd do anything for me, so naturally I wanted to see what that meant."

"Sexually?" Sara guessed.

"Everything. But yeah, sexually too."

"And you said—"

"Great." He gave Sara a wry smile. "I got her to go skinny-dipping. And got her to go without panties. We went out and bought some toys. Which was good for a while. Then it was time to spice things up again. We did some role-playing, which was also fun for a while. Then it needed spicing up too."

"How do you keep topping yourself?"

"Exactly."

"What did you do?"

"Kept asking."

"Until you got to her limit."

"Right."

"Which was?"

"Blow jobs."

"Ah."

He crossed the patio to stand in front of Sara again. She didn't look shook up. Yet.

The big story was yet to come.

"It's a big jump from oral sex to guns and arson," Sara commented calmly.

"There were a few years in between. I stuck with girls who knew their limits and who weren't shy about letting me know. I didn't want any more sweet young things that I had to encourage and then feel guilty about. For a solid year, I dated only women older than me."

"But girl number three still came along."

"Yeah. Jenna. She fell in love with me at about the time I was wondering if maybe I was a little out of control."

"She was a virgin?"

"No. I had sworn off virgins in high school. She wasn't real experienced, but she kept up with me, no problem. She was willing to try anything and enjoyed it. And it was fun for me. Stuff was new to her, unlike most of the women I'd been dating. I also didn't have to talk her into anything. She was a novice, but willing."

Like Sara in so many ways. He stuck his hands in his back pockets and rocked back on his heels. That was a lot of his problem. Sara was more confident, more bossy about what she liked—and he was sure that would spill over into the bedroom—and more willing to initiate things. With Jenna he had *always* been the instigator. Still, Sara shared the innocence combined with curiosity.

"Eventually something happened to ruin the perfection, I'm guessing." Sara's tone held more than a hint of jealously.

Mac smiled. "You could say that."

"Go on." She motioned for him to continue.

"I got totally wrapped up in my fantasies. I took her to Omaha, to a couple of clubs where I used to hang out. We met some women and Jenna danced with them, even let one of them kiss her and touch her. Then they took her into a back room. She didn't come out running and screaming, but she was...flustered."

"Wow, she..."

"I'm not sure. She didn't tell me and shut me down when I tried to ask. She did ask me once if I'd ever been with two women."

"Which you had."

She didn't seem surprised or upset by it. Just matter-of-fact.

"Yes."

"And she was willing to be one of those women?"

"They'd apparently discussed it, but she never asked me to do it."

"Then what happened?" Sara also didn't look scandalized by the story.

"I didn't know it at the time, but Jenna went back to the club on her own to meet the women. Then, I guess she told them she just wanted one wild night. Which they had."

Sara's eyes got bigger but she stayed silent and still.

"After that, one started calling her. I didn't know about it. She just ignored it. Then, a couple of weeks later, the woman showed up at my apartment."

Mac still couldn't believe Jenna had done the things she'd done and that she'd hidden it all from him. But he remembered how embarrassed and scared she'd looked when the woman showed up at the door.

"Jenna tried to pretend she didn't know her, but I could tell right away she was lying. The girl, Lexie, showed up every day. She called. She'd send letters, packages. It got crazy. She claimed she was in love with Jenna."

"So she got a gun and some matches."

He nodded. His gut knotted as he talked but it wasn't the horrible nausea he usually experienced. "When Jenna told Lexie she was in love with me, Lexie turned jealous. Set the apartment on fire, then went after Jenna with the gun planning to take her away from me. Jenna wouldn't go, of course. I showed up in time to see Lexie pull the gun. I got in the way of the first bullet."

Sara was watching with wide, interested eyes. "The *first* bullet?"

The gut knot got a little tighter. He swallowed. "Yeah. The second one hit Jenna. It went through and damaged a kidney. She could have died. As it is, she has some permanent medical issues."

"Lexie went to jail?"

"Yeah." He sighed, feeling heavy and tired suddenly. "Two lives permanently changed all because I was...unsatisfied, or unwilling to be satisfied. Or something."

Sara looked at him, her head tipped to one side. "You feel guilty?"

He gave a short laugh. "Um, yeah. My grandma even thought it was my fault." Mac thought he should have been far past letting that bother him so much. He was a grown man. It had been years since everything happened. And he knew, deep down, his grandmother did love him. She'd been disappointed. Not to mention scandalized and embarrassed.

"She found out somehow and told me 'you better just leave nice girls alone'."

"Ouch."

That was it. Just a sympathetic acknowledgment.

Mac stood looking down at her. She was so amazing. She wasn't shocked or disgusted.

She stood up on the bench of the table so she could look at him more directly. "And you blame yourself for all of this?"

"Of course."

"Mac, you didn't mean for all of that to happen. You didn't mean for anyone to get hurt."

"I should have known better than to introduce her to that stuff."

"She didn't have to say yes."

"She thought she did."

Sara shrugged. "Well, that was her fault."

"What?"

"Come on, Mac. It was her choice to go along with it, to not tell you no."

"I would have broken up with her."

Sara shrugged. "Then she shouldn't have wanted to be with you."

He wasn't sure what to say to that. He'd known he and Jenna weren't going to have a happily ever after. He was pretty sure Jenna knew it too, all along.

"Besides, she didn't have to go back. Without you. To have a lesbian threesome."

He opened his mouth. Then shut it. Sara had a point.

"And you should know I'm not willing to try to be something I'm not just to be with you."

"Good."

"Because you love me just as I am. And that's how it should be."

He stared at her. The fact that she was right wasn't the problem. The fact that she knew she was right was the problem.

"So do you want me to go to that club with you?"

He stared at her. The club? Did he want to take Sara there? "You looking for a lesbian threesome?"

She laughed. "Not especially. And I'm not going to do anything I don't want to do. But I am willing to be adventurous in other ways. Not because of you... *with* you."

"*No.*"

Now she looked surprised. "Why not? You like adventurous women and, whether you've realized it or not, or admitted it or not, I want to be adventurous with you."

"No. Not...that." Not other people touching her and pleasuring her. No way.

"Why not?" She crossed her arms and looked at him expectantly.

"Because..." She didn't belong there. Not that Jenna had. And Sara was far more sexual than Jenna had ever been. Still he knew without a doubt he did not want to take Sara there. It was his job to protect her, more now than ever. Taking her to a club like that would be the opposite of protecting her. "That was a long time ago."

"So you don't find the idea of two women together exciting anymore?"

Well, he wouldn't go *that* far. He was like many—or most—men. Sure, two women together, with him, had always been a turn-on.

Just not Sara.

"No. I don't." It wasn't a total lie. Looking down at her, he had no desire for anyone, or anything else.

"You're still trying to protect me," she chided softly, laying a hand on his chest. "You don't need to."

Yeah, he did. That was exactly what he had to do. Even if it was from him.

For a few years after the incident with Jenna and Lexie, he'd purposefully chosen women who wanted that kind of thing, reveling in the pleasure and not having to worry about the woman—or women—or emotions, or expectations, or anything else.

Now here he was with Sara. The one woman whose emotions and expectations mattered more to him than anyone's. How had he let it go even this far?

But one look into that face and he had the answer.

All she had to do to get his heart pounding and him wanting her more than he wanted his next breath was touch him and look up at him with those eyes. It was the trust. He knew it. He was no psychologist, but it wasn't hard to figure out he was responding to her unconditional faith in him—faith that he would take care of her, that he loved her and that he would do the right thing. He hadn't felt that trust in a long, long time. And he craved it.

Sure, his crew trusted him, his patients trusted him, the hospital staff and the cops and the firefighters he worked with trusted his judgment, his skills and his intelligence. But no one, in longer than he could remember, trusted him like Sara did. Completely, in all ways, with everything she had.

Women had either been disillusioned and hurt by him emotionally or they'd withheld their emotions. He preferred the latter. The women he dated now were in it for the sex and the good time. No one had even come close to falling in love with him in a very long time.

So he was not going to let Sara down. He was not going to let her regret trusting him. Which was exactly why he should be concentrating on what else he could do to drive her away before he made her sorry she'd ever met him.

Sara put her hand against his cheek, making him look into her eyes. "I'm not going to do anything I don't want to do just because you want me to, Mac. I mean, anything I *really* don't want to do or can't live with, okay?"

He really wanted to believe that. "You've already bought a boxful of toys you didn't want."

She frowned. "Who says I didn't want them?"

"You wouldn't have even looked at that catalog if you didn't think I liked that stuff."

"And I would have been missing out. I *love* this body powder."

He must have looked as disbelieving as he felt, because she shook her head.

"Mac, because of you I watched *Lost* for the first time. I got hooked on it, because I loved it. I tried it because of you, but I kept doing it because I wanted to. And if not for you I would have missed out." She smiled mischievously. "Nipple clamps could be the same way."

Heat surged through him even as his mind vehemently rejected the idea. He really wanted to see Sara in nipple clamps. Which meant that there was no way in hell he was ever going to.

In fact, that seemed like a great plan: he was going to do the opposite of whatever he *really* wanted to do.

She slid her arms around his neck. "You realize, don't you, inviting Kevin and Dooley up here is going to backfire on you?"

"How's that?" He loved when she rubbed her breasts against him.

"Well, you brought them here because you thought it would keep us from having sex on the kitchen table." She rubbed again.

"It will. One thing I'm not into is exhibitionism."

"Sure. It also means we'll be in the same bed tonight."

"Well, I..."

She just watched him process it. Kevin and Dooley would take the two extra bedrooms.

"There's the couch." *He* didn't even believe he was sleeping on the couch. He could, certainly. He'd done it the first night when he hadn't trusted himself to even be on the same floor with her, but he barely fit on it and hadn't slept well. Besides, he didn't want to be on the couch. He wanted to be in the bed with Sara. Dooley and Kevin were the perfect excuse. Just like his subconscious had known as soon as they'd put their butts in his car seats.

"You're not sleeping on the couch," Sara said unnecessarily.

"I know."

He gave in just like that. He'd known all along it would come to this. Sara had known. All of Mac's friends, including Sam, had known. So what was the point in resisting? He would make love to Sara. The way she deserved to be loved. At least once. Maybe because he needed her to know how it should be. Maybe to prove to himself that he could do that. Just that. Whatever the reason, he couldn't stay out of her bed one more night.

Mac didn't know or care where Kevin and Dooley were. They knew their way to his house and would have no trouble sweet-talking someone—someone female, no doubt—into giving them a ride.

Once he'd let his mind and heart accept that he was going to make love to Sara, he couldn't wait to get her home.

There would be time for scaring her off tomorrow. Or the next day.

"Take your clothes off, princess," he said the minute he put the car in gear.

"Right now?" He didn't miss the breathlessness in her voice.

"Yep."

"There are people around." She pulled the sweatshirt she wore over her head as she spoke.

"So start at the bottom," he said, feeling a bit breathless himself.

She kicked off her shoes, then slowly peeled one sock off at a time. They were already at the outskirts of Oscar—the beauty of living in a small town—so when Sara lifted her hips and started to wiggle out of her jeans, Mac was the only one to appreciate it. Which was exactly as it should have been, in his opinion.

"Keep going," he said gruffly as her jeans hit the floor.

"You haven't even looked." She pulled her shirt off.

"I have to drive without wrecking."

"Good thought," she laughed. She tossed her bra into his lap.

Mac tightened his grip on the steering wheel and wondered why he'd started this. They still had a few miles to go. He just didn't want to waste time once they got to the house. He needed to be inside her. Had needed it for weeks. Years. He felt like a dam about to burst.

Her panties landed on his thigh. Had he said dam? More like *damn.*

She was totally naked.

"Sara," he said, teeth gritted.

"Yeah."

"Get yourself ready. We're about three miles from home."

"I'm ready, Mac."

"I mean *ready.*" How he was keeping his mind, not to mention his eyes, on the road he had no freakin' idea.

"I'm *ready,*" Sara promised.

He quirked a smile. She sounded sincere. But he had to be sure.

"Princess, I'm not going to be able to go slow and gentle."

He felt her slide closer. He smelled that damned cotton candy and her arousal and nearly pulled the car over.

"Don't touch me," he growled, pressing harder on the accelerator. "Touch yourself."

She sucked in a quick breath.

"I want to touch you."

He saw her hand move toward him. "You're gonna kill me," he muttered. He grabbed her hand. "Put those pretty fingers between your legs, honey."

"I want *your* fingers there."

"They will be," he said with a small smile. It wasn't like he was actually seeing anything outside of the windshield. His thoughts were quite firmly on Sara and all the things he wanted to do to her. At least his brain was recognizing the white and yellow lines that meant the car was still on the road. "Come on, princess," he coaxed—damned near begged. "Do it for me."

In his peripheral vision he saw her hand move away from him. "Tell me what you want me to do."

"Touch your nipple," he rasped.

She moaned in response. "Mac."

"Pull on it. Imagine it's my mouth. Sucking on you."

"*Mac*," she gasped.

He risked a glance. Her head was back against the car seat, her hand doing as he'd said, tugging on one nipple.

"Son of a bitch." He swerved back to his side of the road. There were no other cars but there were ditches.

"Now between your legs, princess." His voice sounded like he was strangling. "Tell me you're ready for me." He saw the knee closest to him shift, widening the space between her legs.

"I want you, Mac," she panted.

"I know, honey, I know."

His erection felt swollen beyond anything he could remember.

"Are you wet?"

"Very."

"I want you to come, Sara."

"I'm sure I will."

He smiled in spite of the incredible tightness below his belt. "I appreciate your confidence in me. I mean right now."

"How are you going to do that?"

"*You're* going to do it."

"Mac..."

"It will make it easier on you when I get you home and do everything I've been imagining doing to you. Over and over again."

"Oh," she breathed. Then her breath hitched and she moaned.

He couldn't keep his eyes from her then. She was flushed, her head against the headrest, her hand between her thighs. She met his eyes and her fingers moved, sliding in and out.

He glanced back at the road. Damn. He was sweating. He was driving home on a somewhat-chilly fall evening, and he was sweating. His pulse was racing and his throat felt tight. Just riding home with Sara was a workout.

"Mac," she whispered as she came.

He took the corner into his driveway fast enough that it threw Sara up against him. His arm snaked around her waist and the moment the car was in park he hauled her in for a scorching kiss.

She straddled his lap and his hands were all over her—breasts, back, hair and between her legs where she was hot and ready for him.

Her hand stroked over his erection and he groaned into her mouth. "God, yes."

"Hood of the car or backseat?" she asked. "Or right here?"

Mac wasn't sure he'd be able to walk to the house, but his mind rejected every scenario except taking her for the first time in his bed.

"Inside. Now."

"Yeah." Her hands smoothed over his head. "That's where I want you too."

He groaned and laughed at the same time. "Inside the house."

She kissed him, licking along his lower lip, nipping gently, then sliding her tongue boldly in against his. She pulled back, breathing hard.

"I don't mind being out here." She wiggled in his lap. "It feels naughty."

Mac grinned. He couldn't help it. Sara was on his lap, bare-ass naked, wanting him to take her in the great outdoors. He could picture taking her from behind with her leaning over the hood of his car, or having her ride him sitting on the porch swing, or standing up with her against the side of the barn. All were temping, but...

"What I want is you spread out on my big old bed, legs wrapped around me and my hands under your ass, lifting you up so every single stroke goes nice and deep," he said against her neck.

She let out a deep breath. "That's exactly what I want."

That was all he needed to hear.

Chapter Ten

Sara preceded Mac into the house, walking gingerly over the rocks and grass of the front yard. She'd only taken three steps though before Mac suddenly grabbed her upper arm and swung her around. He lifted her so they were belly to belly. She wrapped her legs around his waist and arms around his neck.

"Oh, this is—" She lost her breath as the denim-encased erection slid against her bare cleft. As he carried her across the yard, up the porch steps and into the house, the friction on the aroused flesh was enough to have her breathing hard again by the time he set her back on her feet at the base of the stairs leading to the bedrooms.

"Upstairs. Now." He started undressing as she ran up the steps.

He was right behind her and naked as he cleared the threshold and stalked toward the bed, never taking his eyes off of her.

"Spread out on my bed," he reminded her.

Sara sat on the edge of the bed. She'd been aroused before. She'd been aroused with Mac before. But she'd never felt this jittery, pounding, aching *need* before. Even on the brink of orgasm with him prior to this, she hadn't felt this level of want. It was like a deep thirst or terrible hunger, but combined with the strange deep fear that if she was satisfied now, it still would never be enough, she would always feel this craving.

He came toward her and she scrambled back up the bed toward the headboard, watching Mac wrap his fingers around his erection as he walked.

She tingled all over, heat and awareness teasing every nerve. She was half-afraid he'd continue to torment her with his mouth and hands, not giving her the part of him she really wanted. She had to push him to the edge with her so that he wouldn't hesitate to jump over.

Sara went up onto all fours and crawled forward as Mac knelt with one knee on the mattress.

"Now there's a pretty picture," he said gruffly. "But not what I was imagining."

She smiled. "Hold on."

He did pause and she got to him before he realized her intention. She wrapped her hand around his on his shaft. As she bent her head forward Mac groaned. "You are gonna kill me."

"Want me to stop?" she asked, her nose nearly touching the head of his penis.

"No. Yes. No." His hand went to the back of her head and urged her forward. "Mostly no."

She licked his tip and the pleasure of his moan danced down her spine. Turning Mac on was as good as being turned on by him. To know this strong, stubborn, experienced man could want and need her touch so much gave her a thrill she'd never grow tired of.

His hand dropped lower on his cock and she took him farther into her mouth. She'd seen enough on the Internet that soon his hand dropped away entirely as she stroked down his length while she sucked and slid him in and out of her mouth.

"Sara," he rasped. "Get on your back..."

The need in his voice was enough to make her do as she was told. The ache in her had also increased to the point of near pain.

Mac climbed up her body, kissed her greedily, then hooked her knees over his elbows, braced his palms on the mattress, spread her wide and eased into her.

In spite of how wet she was, it was tight and she felt every centimeter of him stretching and filling her.

"Oh, Mac," she gasped.

"Princess," he panted. "God, you feel good."

He pressed against the spot already throbbing for him. She arched closer.

"Easy, honey," he said. "Easy. I want all the way in, but we have to go easy."

Sara dug her heels into his butt. "More, Mac."

He withdrew slightly instead, then pushed forward again. "Easy," he repeated in a whisper.

Sara looked down to where they were joined. He wasn't even halfway in yet. "You're so big," she whispered back.

He chuckled. "Thanks."

When she glanced up though the strain was evident in his face.

"Should have used the pink dildo," he said. "To get you ready for me."

"You're bigger than that even."

He grinned. "Yeah, but you're smaller. It would have helped you stretch."

He withdrew an inch, then pressed forward.

"Harder," she begged. "More. Something."

She was sure this wasn't a usual problem for him. The women he was used to could take all he had to give and dammit, she would too.

Sara uncrossed her ankles, put her heels against the mattress and pushed up.

"I don't want to hurt you," Mac groaned. "Stop, Sara."

She felt stretched, needy, wanton and hot, but not in pain. "*Please.*" She moved her legs farther apart. That helped. Then a thought came to her. A tight fit needed more lubrication.

She reached between them and found her clit, circling it as Mac moaned. "I'm not gonna last watching that."

Sara smiled up at him. She did love driving him crazy. "Harder," she whispered.

With a curse, Mac thrust his hips forward and slid home.

"*Yes,*" Sara hissed. He moved, dragging out against her inner walls with delicious friction. Then thrust forward again. And again. "Faster," she urged, sensing that was what she wanted more than knowing.

At that word Mac must have realized she was fine, because he took her suggestion, thrusting harder, deeper and faster until she felt the sudden release of the tight coil of desire. It was like the other orgasms with her fingers, his fingers, his tongue...and yet so much *more.*

As her muscles contracted they had something to squeeze against, something to draw on and Sara cried Mac's name as her body's pull on his completed her release.

A moment later Mac groaned, “Sara,” and she felt the pulsations of his climax.

He slumped to one side so he wasn’t directly on top of her, but stayed sheathed inside of her, chest to chest.

When she finally caught her breath, she smacked him on the butt. “I can’t believe you made me wait this long for that. We could have been doing that every night for the past—what?—ten years?”

He shuddered and rolled more to the side. “You were sixteen ten years ago.”

She laughed. “Okay, eight years.”

He shook his head, his nose and hot breath against the side of her neck. “Let’s say five.”

“Okay. Five years is still a lot of deprivation on my part.”

“I guess I have some making up to do.” His big hand stroked from the outer edge of her breast to her hip.

“Guess so,” she said already feeling the shimmer of desire starting again. “Think you can keep up, old man?”

“We always have the dildo if I can’t.” His hand stroked across her belly.

“A stand-in, huh?” She rolled toward him.

He took a nipple into his mouth immediately, his hand now cupping her butt and pressing a growing erection against her belly. She groaned, ready for him too.

“Well, I don’t think you’ll have to worry about running the batteries down on your vibrator any time soon, princess.”

For the first time in almost ten years Mac didn’t want to go to work. He loved his job, loved his crew, had nothing to keep him from wanting to be there.

Until Sara.

He’d made love to her again in the night and once that morning. Still, leaving her naked and wrapped in his sheets was the hardest thing he’d ever done. He couldn’t get enough of her. The feel of her, the way she sounded, tasted.

Maybe stranger still, he’d chosen the missionary position in bed all three times. Well, there had been the few minutes when she'd ridden him, but he'd definitely finished with her on the bottom.

He couldn't remember the last time he'd chosen the missionary position at all.

But with Sara it seemed right, and he couldn't wait to get home and do it all again.

Dooley was asleep in the passenger seat, Kevin was reading in the backseat, leaving Mac alone with his thoughts. He was surprised. They hadn't given him any trouble at all. The only even slight hint at any ribbing was finding his clothes folded neatly on the bottom step of the staircase after he'd left them in a pile by the front door.

He risked a glance at Dooley, then in the rearview mirror. Neither seemed interested at all.

Strange. But he'd enjoy it.

They drove past the community center, then the drive-in, then the city park and swimming pool before leaving the Oscar city limits. Mac was usually fine seeing Oscar fade away behind him on his way back to Omaha.

Now Sara was there and even though he'd see her again in less than twenty-four hours—having decided he would drive back and forth each day now—it still seemed a long way between Omaha and Oscar.

When he'd offered to take her to Omaha with him and the guys today she'd insisted she had things to do. He'd asked what, but then the sheet had slipped low—accidentally or on purpose he didn't know, or care—exposing her right breast, and he'd been a goner.

Now he couldn't wait to get back to Oscar after his shift.

It wasn't completely a foreign concept to him.

Oscar had been his home. He'd loved it growing up. He'd planned to raise his family and grow old there. Then as the women and years went by without anyone feeling right, he'd started to think of his work, Omaha and his little adopted family as his whole life.

But he loved this town.

Dooley woke up fifteen minutes from the hospital and Kevin closed his book. Mac braced himself for questions, jokes, a lecture...something. But they only talked about the game last night, some girl named Tara that Dooley had spent a lot of time with and how they had to stop staying out late and drinking—in Dooley's case anyway—on nights when they had a shift the next day.

Mac breathed a sigh of relief. Apparently his taking Sara to bed last night had been monumental only to him and Sara.

His peace lasted until four minutes after they stepped into the locker room at the hospital to change into their uniforms.

Which just happened to be when Sam came in.

"Oh, hey, Mac, I found this on the steps and forgot to give it back to Sara. You better take it home tonight." Dooley tossed Mac a hot pink thong.

She'd probably dropped it on the way into the house last night.

It wasn't a big deal. Except that the tossed thong nearly hit Sam in the face.

Mac caught the scrap of lace and put it in his pocket, bending to tie his shoes without a word. He was going to kill Dooley. He was pretty sure Dooley knew it so it didn't need to be said out loud.

"Oh, and I think this is yours too, right?" Kevin tossed him one of the finger vibrators from Sara's toy box. Which no way had just fallen out on the table or floor. They'd gone looking through the box.

Mac caught the vibrator and put it in his other pocket. Without a word, he crossed to the coffeepot. It would be harder to kill a good guy like Kevin. Hell, Kev didn't even swear. But God would understand.

Especially when Kevin said, "I had to clear the kitchen table for breakfast this morning, so I put that pink fur wedge in the pantry. Don't know what it was doing on the kitchen table, but it was taking up all the space."

Mac tried valiantly to not remember exactly what it had been doing on the table. It was damned tough.

"Thanks." Was there any chance, any chance at all, that they were done? He poured a cup of coffee he didn't want.

"Hey, since I didn't see Sara this morning, I was hoping you could give her a message for me," Dooley said.

Of course they weren't done.

"Tell her I've been thinking about what positions she should try and she'd look great in any of them, but The Couch Canoodle would be fantastic for her."

Mac turned slowly to face one of his best friends. Sam and Kevin were staring at Dooley with the complete disbelief that Mac was sure was apparent on his face.

"What the *hell* are you talking about?" Mac finally asked.

"The Couch Canoodle?" Kevin said at the same time.

"You sure you want to hear this?" Dooley asked Kevin.

"I think I *have* to hear this," Kevin said.

Dooley chuckled. "Okay, she's on your lap on the couch—or a chair would work, I'm sure. I mean you just have to be upright..."

Kevin motioned with his hand for Dooley to get to it.

"Then she leans back. All the way back. Until she's horizontal. Not only does it feel great, but the view..."

"Stop. Oh my God please stop," Mac said, plunking his coffee cup down on the counter and stepping toward Dooley, ready to do physical damage if needed. "I don't know what you want but you can have whatever it is. Just fucking stop talking."

Dooley gave him a this-is-going-according-to-plan grin. "It's Cosmo. I left her the website."

"Stop imagining my wife in *any* position—even doing dishes—stop giving her sex advice, stop leaving her websites. Just, for God's sake, stop."

"I'll stop all of that if you look Sam in the eye and tell him you're in love with his sister and to get over it."

Mac stared at Dooley. Dooley simply crossed his arms and stared back. Then Mac looked at Sam. He thought about how Sara had looked that morning. Satiated, certainly. Sexy, sweet...and happy. Dammit. She'd been happy. Because of him. And she knew everything. There was no pedestal for him to precariously balance on. She knew him, knew about his past and was still happy with him.

He huffed out a big breath. "Okay, what the hell? Sam, I'm in love with your sister and she's happy." He spread his arms wide. "I don't know what else to say. I can't promise to never piss her off. But she's happy. With me."

Sam met his gaze steadily, his arms crossed over his chest, legs wide, defensive.

"I know."

Mac rolled his eyes. "It's not like you're perfect either, but Dani puts up with your sorry ass because she loves you. Is it so hard to believe Sara loves me?"

"No. It's not."

"And I didn't expect this. Okay? I was ready to just stay her friend. I told you that. But this is what she wants and, dammit, I can make her happy. I honestly believe I can."

"I think you can too."

"And you need to leave her alone. You don't need to take care of her all the time. Jessica doesn't need to give her opinions on every damned thing. You take care of Danika and Jessica can nag Ben. I know it's a habit and Sara lets you get away with it, but *I'm* taking care of her now."

"Okay."

"Sam, you're a stubborn ass—"

Kevin shoved him hard from behind. "Shut up, Mac."

Mac glared over his shoulder. "What the hell, Kev?"

"Shut up and listen. Sam's trying to tell you something."

Mac looked back at Sam. "Fine, say it. Get it over with. Then duck, because I'm done with this bullshit and I'm probably going to hit you."

Sam took a big step forward, his arms still crossed. "What I've been trying to say, jackass, is that I know Sara's happy. And she's safe with you. And you'll take care of her and probably give in to anything she wants. Whether that's good or bad for you is another question. For me, it's great. So we're good. It's all good."

Mac stared at Sam waiting for the *but*, or whatever else was coming. "And?" he finally demanded.

"And it's about time you stood up and threatened to hit me if I said no. That's how I know you're serious about her."

Mac narrowed his eyes. "You're just fine with all of this? Suddenly it's all peachy?"

Sam narrowed his eyes in return. "Yeah. Peachy."

"I'm sleeping with your sister, Sam."

"I know. Sara called Dani this morning. It's about time for that too."

"Oh, really," Mac said sarcastically. "Like you've been begging me to do her since day one."

"It's what Sara wanted. So she told Dani all the time. Of course I don't want her spending her life with some guy who isn't going to be a real husband to her."

"I'm using a pink fur wedge with her." Well, that one time he had.

"So I heard," Sam said dryly.

"She's wearing edible body powder for me."

Sam relaxed his stance, dropping his arms to his sides. "As long as it's what she wants."

"It is," Mac said. "I am." The confidence he felt with those words was liberating. His relationship with Sara was different than any other he'd ever had. Which was as it should be. He couldn't be as sexually uninhibited as he'd been with other women—he simply couldn't go there with Sara. She was special, different. But it was fine. He'd had his time to play, his wild days. He was a married man and it was time for him to settle down.

"Okay then."

Sam pivoted away and headed for his locker.

"So that's it? After all your crap, now it's all just fine?"

"You're gonna make me say it?"

Mac thought about it, for about three seconds. "Yep."

"Fine. I was wrong. I overreacted."

He felt a huge weight lift from his shoulders. "Okay."

"It takes a big man to say he was wrong."

"Okay."

"I mean, not every guy can suck it up and say they're sorry."

"Okay."

"I'm not going to get any credit for this?"

"Nope."

"Fine." Sam turned back to his locker. "But I am a hell of a guy," he muttered.

Sara wished, for maybe the first time ever, that she knew how to make banana bread. Or any kind of bread. Or anything that could be called a baked good.

It would have been nice to walk into Style with something *she* made for a change, but the bakery did a great job and the women at the shop were in the habit of having the coffeepot full and the napkins out by nine thirty when Sara made her appearance.

The banana bread was a hit no matter who made it. Sara sat in the chair between Cindy and Kathy, pretending to study the book of hairstyles. She was sort of, kind of contemplating a change in color. More she was wondering how long it would take for her to get her own chair in the salon waiting room. She was the only one who seemed to have to move each day. There were four regulars, present every morning, but the other three chairs changed occupants depending on the day of the week and who had to work or run errands. One woman worked at the library twice a week, another took her toddler to daycare twice a week so she could be at the Style on Mondays and Thursdays, the third went to see her mom once a week for lunch so surrendered her chair.

Yes, they all got their hair done and tanned in the tanning beds at the back of the shop, but really they all showed up for the socialization, laughter and gossip. And now the treats that Sara brought in.

"My son says she's a city girl and he can't wait to show her that we grow our own Christmas trees," Sonya said. "I'd love to see her tromping through the snow with an axe."

They all chuckled.

"You grow your own Christmas trees?" Sara asked. She couldn't help it. She was a city girl too.

"We grow the whole town's Christmas trees," Sonya told her.

"And trees for lots of other people," Monica piped up. "They own the Christmas tree farm out north of town."

Sara thought about that. She supposed Christmas trees, like all other trees, had to grow somewhere. She'd just honestly never thought about it. Or the people who had to chop them down.

"Have you ever chopped one down, Sonya?" Sara asked.

She knew she should feel self-conscious about being the new girl, the not-quite-welcomed girl, who kept asking questions that were probably dumb. She'd decided not to care. She wasn't going to let the women ignore her. She was a nice person who just wanted to make some friends.

"Well, yeah, honey. I chop trees down all the time."

"That's why not everyone around here gets manicures," Angela said from where she was rolling a woman's hair in curlers.

Angela rarely spoke directly to Sara and when she did, it was usually to point out something silly Sara had said or to mockingly answer a question. Everyone else seemed to be warming up somewhat. But not Angela. Sara had yet to be brave enough to ask why.

Sonya held out her hands for Sara to see. Her hands were dry, the nails short, calluses evident. Sara looked down at her own hands. "I'm pretty sure I've never even picked up an axe."

Angela snorted. "I'm pretty sure you haven't either."

The other women laughed and Sara even found herself smiling. "Pretty obvious, huh?"

"Um..." Sonya gave her a smile that could have been described as friendly. "Yeah, Sara, it is."

Sara thought about it. "I used a screwdriver one time."

"What for?" Monica asked.

"To take the back off of my portable CD player to replace the batteries."

There was a long moment of silence. Then an outburst of laughter. Finally someone said, "One time?"

Sara was smiling with them as she shrugged. "I've got a sister, her husband, a brother and three of his best friends looking out for me all the time. I never change batteries, light bulbs...anything."

"Wow, you're like a princess," Sonya said.

Sara had to smile at the inadvertent use of her nickname.

"Yeah, tell us some more fairy tales," Monica said. "About a land where a woman doesn't have to do anything and has others to take care of her all the time."

Sara looked at her, but found Monica's expression to be friendly.

"You all work really hard, don't you?"

"Monica helps her husband milk cows every morning," Nancy said.

Sara knew her eyes were wide. "You milk cows? With your hands?"

Monica shook her head. "Not anymore. We have milking machines now, but we still have to get the cows in and hooked up, then unhooked. And we milk three times a day."

"Seriously?" Sara looked around. "What about the rest of you?"

They must have read the sincerity on her face because they started talking about one another. Nancy was a nurse, who worked the night shift at the nursing home. Sonya and her husband had the tree farm—not just Christmas trees, it turned out—along with a large greenhouse. Kathy cleaned the school with her daughter after school hours, as well as the two churches in town. Cindy helped with the books for her husband's construction business.

"So now tell us about you," Monica said to Sara.

She shrugged. "I don't do anything. I mean, I work with the teenagers at the youth center. A lot of that is talking, listening, just being there. I think it's important, but it's not...what you all do." She turned to look over at Angela and the other girls. "I mean, I could never be on my feet all day long."

"Makes it tough to wear heels," Angela said.

Sara looked down at her feet. "I do love my heels." She wasn't going to apologize. Maybe that's what Angela and the others wanted, but she did love her heels.

"So tell us about having five men at your beck and call," Cindy said. "Sounds like heaven to me." She rubbed the side of her neck and rolled her head.

"You okay?" Sara asked.

"A headache. Nothing unusual."

"Here, let me try something." Sara stood and moved to stand behind Cindy's chair.

"Oh, you don't have to..."

"I get a massage every week." She shot a glance at Angela who, predictably, rolled her eyes. "I've picked a few things up."

"You get headaches?" Angela asked. "How is that even possible?"

"I don't get headaches too much," Sara admitted. She started rubbing Cindy's shoulders. "And my blood pressure is extraordinarily low." She was going to be herself with these women and they were going to see she was an okay person anyway. "I think it's because of the massages and yoga." She could feel knots along Cindy's right shoulder in particular. She pushed her thumb in on the tender points, holding the pressure until she felt Cindy's shoulder relax and then moving to the next.

"You do yoga?" Kathy asked.

"Of course she does." Angela shook her head. "Just like we all would if we didn't have a million other things to do."

Sara shrugged. "I also like aromatherapy—I have lots of relaxation scents. And I try to get plenty of sleep."

"Just like we all would..."

"Yeah, yeah," Sonya interrupted Angela. "Go on, Sara."

Sara didn't dare glance at Angela. She moved her hands up to the back of Cindy's head, pressing and rubbing in small, gentle circles. Cindy's head dropped forward and she sighed. "I have another secret for relaxation," she said.

"Hot kinky sex?"

Surprisingly this did not come from Angela. There wasn't a sound for several seconds. Sara turned to face Sonya.

"I was going to say cartoons. I love them. Especially the old ones, Looney Tunes and stuff."

"Oh." Sonya looked around at the other women. "What? You were all thinking it."

Kathy and Monica looked embarrassed. "Sorry, Sara," Kathy said.

"Um, no harm done."

"It's just...well, most of the women in town are a little intimidated by a woman who can keep up with Jason MacDonald. And maybe a little jealous."

Sara had to admit she liked having someone who was willing to be honest with her, even if—maybe *especially* if—it wasn't complimentary. And as the words sunk in she felt a smile building. Maybe it *was* a compliment, come to think of it.

"I thought I was just annoying you all with my unwillingness to clean my own house and my high heels and my need for weekly facials."

"Oh, honey, all of that is really annoying too," Angela said.

The rest laughed and Sara just smiled bigger. She couldn't completely explain it but she felt good. These women gave each other a hard time, like Mac and the guys did, like friends did. She was growing on them. She could feel it. Besides, Angela had just called her honey.

"Oh, my *Gawd*," Cindy sighed just then. "My headache is gone. This is the best I've felt in days."

Sara felt warmth spread through her. "That's great," she said sincerely.

Cindy smiled. "You have a gift."

"Well, I don't know about that, but I'm glad you feel better."

"Seriously, Sara," Kathy said. "The other day when you massaged my feet...wow. That was heavenly."

Sara smiled and reclaimed her seat, listening to the women talk about how they deserved a good massage and how bad their husbands were at it.

The shop closed from eleven to three in the afternoon, opening in time for the kids after school and people after work. As the women left the shop, Sara hung back until it was only her and Angela.

"Um, hey, Angela?" Everyone else called her Angie or Ange, but Sara wasn't feeling that brave.

"Hm?"

"Do you have Internet on the computer here?"

She knew they did their scheduling and accounting on the computer, but wasn't sure what the Internet access was like in Oscar.

"What kind of net?" Angela asked from where she was scrubbing out her wash basin.

"The Internet. On the computer. You know..." Sara couldn't think of anything to compare it to.

"Oh, we don't have a lot of that fancy city stuff here." Angie turned on her sprayer and rinsed soap bubbles down the drain.

"Do you know if somewhere else in town has Internet access?" Sara wished she'd just kept her mouth shut. She didn't think that Angela would loan her a cup of sugar not to mention a pleasant conversational exchange.

Finally, Angela turned to face her. "Of course we have the Internet on the computer here. This isn't Mars, for God's sake."

Sara felt her cheeks heat. "Oh. Would you mind if I looked at a couple of things while you clean up?"

Angela tipped her head to one side. "Tell you what, you use my computer, *you* clean up."

Sara looked around the shop and shrugged. "If you trust me. Considering I have very little cleaning experience."

"Honey, we put harsh chemicals and dyes in these sinks and on this floor. I doubt you could hurt anything." She took her apron off, tossed it over the back of her chair, grabbed the broom and dustpan as she walked past and handed them to Sara. "Don't forget the corners."

She crossed to the counter, took a piece of banana bread, poured a cup of coffee and settled into the chair Sara had occupied earlier. "I think you're going to need an emery board when you're done here, though."

Sara said nothing. She didn't know if Angela was picking a fight, trying to make conversation or was just pointing out a fact. So she just started sweeping.

She hadn't checked her e-mail or Facebook in days. She hadn't thought about it until now, though. She had some high school and college friends she should let know about her wedding and new address, but it was nothing that couldn't wait. She needed to talk to Mac—or an even higher power like her sister, Jessica—about getting a computer and access out at the farm.

What had prompted her question to Angela though, was the idea of massage therapy. She knew there was a school—or maybe even more than one—in Omaha. She had no idea how long it took or what was involved, but she felt a little flutter in her stomach when she thought about it.

She could do that. She liked people, making them feel better, making them happy. She was good at social work for all of those reasons, however Oscar didn't seem in desperate need of its own social worker. Besides, social work had seemed a natural degree to get for the work her sister and brother had already decided she would do at their dad's youth center. They both wanted to keep it going but they'd been called into medicine—Jessica with her nursing degree and Sam as a paramedic—because of their experience with their father's death. Social work was not, however, Sara's dream job.

She didn't know if she had a dream job. The idea of having her own business... She felt like she'd just gone over the biggest hill on the roller coaster. Something she did entirely on her own, exactly how she wanted, even with a few mistakes. Something she could do with her own hands, create or influence. Something she could point to and say *that's mine*. No help from anyone. She needed that.

"How long have you owned this business?" she asked Angela.

The woman was looking at a *People* magazine, sipping coffee.

"Eight years," she answered without looking up.

"You started it all on your own?" Sara swept the pile of freshly trimmed hair to the wastebasket by the desk.

"I have the loan payment every month to prove it." Angela flipped a page.

"So you got a loan from the bank?"

"Well, my money tree got uprooted by the tornado I call *life* so yeah, I went to the bank." She took a drink of coffee.

"I'm impressed."

Angela glanced up. "What?"

"I said I'm impressed. I wouldn't know the first place to start with something like that."

Angela looked wary but she said, "You just open the door, walk in and announce I need some money. People come running with bags of it."

Sara smiled. "Sure. That sounds about right." She dumped the dustpan of hair into the garbage. "It must have been fun designing the place. I love the color blue you used."

Angela looked at the wall to her left. "Um, thanks."

"I mean, it must have been exciting picking out what colors you wanted to use and the name of the shop...everything from scratch. All your own ideas. All yours."

Sara went to the middle wash sink. She took a towel from the shelf just below and began wiping the sink out. She wasn't sure if she should use soap on it or not. Seemed that there had been a lot of soap on it already with all the shampoo and it didn't *look* dirty.

"You have to *scrub* the sinks," Angela said. She stood and crossed to the sink she used, grabbed the purple sponge sitting on the edge and tossed it to Sara. "That's when you use the muscles in your arms."

"You mean the ones I use to pick up my lattes and carry my designer bags?" Sara asked.

For just a moment Angela seemed startled by the banter. Then she said, "Those are them."

Sara hid her smile as she ducked her head and began scrubbing the sink. She did, after all, like lattes and had a lot of bags. If that's what it took, her muscles were in great shape. Not to mention that she did scrub her own kitchen and bathroom sinks in her apartment. Which Angela probably wouldn't believe anyway.

She finished scrubbing, rinsing and drying the third sink. Then she spotted the cleaning supplies under the front desk. She sprayed the mirrors with glass cleaner and wiped them, dusted the front counter and the shelves that held hair-care products by the front door and straightened the magazines on the table in the waiting room, stepping around Angela's feet to do it.

Sara started to climb onto a chair to dust the light fixtures over the stylists' chairs when Angela got to her feet.

"Okay, the computer's all yours. Lock up when you're done." She went to the front door and opened it.

"You're leaving?" Sara asked, climbing down from the chair.

"Yep. I'm starving." Angela took one step out the door and turned back. "And yeah, doing everything to get the shop open was fun." The door shut behind her before Sara could think of something to say.

She was humming, though, as she typed "massage therapy schools, Omaha, NE" into the Google search box.

"And that space right next to Angela's shop would be perfect. It's too small for anything else and it would be pretty much the same people who go to Style that would want to come to my place."

Mac couldn't believe he was naked in bed with Sara and her mouth was so busy with things *other* than what he'd had in mind. She was so excited about her idea to open a massage business. She'd apparently researched it extensively and had gone to Mary Stotten's real-estate business the same day to ask about available spaces.

For some reason Mary hadn't told Sara he owned the building.

"Princess, if you want a shop, let's find one in Omaha." He ran his hand over her bare hip.

She frowned. "I don't want a shop in Omaha. I want to do it here."

"Why? People in Omaha are a lot more likely to get massages."

"There are a hundred massage businesses in Omaha. I'd be the only one here. I'd be able to offer a service no one else can."

He pulled back and looked at her. She was serious.

"That's important to you."

"Yes."

"Why?"

"Everyone here contributes something." She sighed and propped herself up on her elbows on his chest. "There aren't any businesses here that don't matter, that aren't needed. There's no nail salon, no froufrou coffee shop, no purse stores. Those are all extravagances. Here everything makes life better somehow. I want to do that, contribute, be someone that they...need."

She ducked her head, not meeting his eyes. Mac lifted a hand and tilted her chin. "Why is that so important? Why here? Why them?"

"Because I've never done that before."

"Done what?"

"Contributed."

He swallowed hard. It should have sounded pathetic, but it didn't. It sounded matter-of-fact. Still, it made him feel bad. Because she was kind of right. Not really, of course. She contributed in...intangible ways. For instance, she made him laugh. She made him look forward to every day. She made him...happy.

"Princess, you contribute."

She gave him a sexy smile. "I can't contribute like *that* to the whole town."

"No, you definitely can't." In spite of her teasing, he couldn't help the little rush of possessiveness he felt. "So contributing to me isn't enough?" Yeah, that didn't sound Neanderthal at all.

"No, it's not enough," she said, without blinking. "For one thing, you're easily satisfied."

"By you, I am," he said honestly, moving closer and kissing her shoulder.

She sighed happily. "I need something I have to...work for, try at. For another, I can't spend all my time in this house, in this bed."

"Well..."

She giggled. "Stop."

He sighed. "I know, princess. I just don't see why Oscar is so important to you."

"Because it's important to you."

Mac felt his throat and chest tighten.

"And it's a challenge for me. If I can make it here, I can make it anywhere."

"You sound like Frank Sinatra."

She smiled. "These people work hard, Mac. They don't take the easy way out or do anything silly."

"And you want to massage them."

She smiled slightly. "I do."

"I don't know, Sara."

"Uh-oh."

"What?"

"When you call me Sara instead of princess it's serious."

She was right. "It's just that I know this town. I know you're determined to win them over, but it isn't that easy. You're not from here, never will be. You just don't get the same treatment."

"Then I'll have to work hard, won't I?"

He shook his head, giving up. "It does bother you that your sister just gave you the job at the center, doesn't it?"

Sara snorted. "She didn't just give it to me. She made the whole thing up."

"She was taking care of you."

"I know. And now I want to take care of others."

"You've done that with the kids," Mac said, believing it and wanting her to know it.

"I have," she agreed. "So have the rest of you."

"You need something that's all yours, huh?"

"Yep."

"You want a shop here in Oscar."

"Yep."

God, he loved her. It was so ironic that the woman he most wanted to care for and make happy most wanted to do something completely without his help.

But there were some things he now knew she loved and wanted that he *could* give her. Things she *needed* him to give her.

"Come a little closer and maybe you can talk me into it."

Sara grinned and wiggled closer. "Well, you're not really the one I need to talk into this."

"Oh?" He was only half listening anyway. Her skin was so silky and warm and he wanted his hands and lips on every inch of it. Again.

"The bank has to agree to let me use that space. I pulled up some sample business plans on the Internet too. I'm thinking Angela might help me with it. I don't know. I'm probably reading too much into the fact that we kind of talked..."

"You don't need a business plan, princess."

"Mr. Carlson said I did."

"Mr. Carlson? You mean, Scott? You talked to Scott?" Scott was a high school buddy of Mac's. And was the vice president of the bank.

"Yes, of course. Right after I talked to Mary I went to the bank to see where to start."

"Princess." Mac attempted to pull her close—and under him. She came as far as his chest. She even let him kiss her. When she pulled back he said, "Scott was messing with you."

"Why? That doesn't make sense."

Mac pulled back slightly and smiled. "I own that building, princess. If you want to put a massage business in there, that's not a problem. If you want to store old chairs in there, that's fine. Whatever."

"You *own* that building?" she repeated, frowning.

"I own that whole side of the square."

She gaped at him. "What?"

He shrugged. "Those buildings were falling apart and the city was considering tearing them down. At the same time the town wanted to keep the square intact and wanted businesses in there. I found out there were some businesses, like Style, that wanted space but couldn't afford to restore the buildings themselves. My parents' life insurance policies were significant and I decided that was a good use for some of it."

"So...I don't have to... I still need money for inventory and furniture and..."

"No, you don't. I can cover all of that."

"I don't want you to." She put her hands on his chest, pushing instead of stroking.

"What do you mean?" He tried to pull her close. "Sara, I can take care of whatever you want or need."

"But..." She gave up struggling against his hold and flopped onto her back. "I thought... Shit."

"Shit?" He chuckled. "I've had women have opinions about my money, but never that one."

"I wanted to do this myself. I thought you... You don't act, or live, like you have money."

"Sorry?" He wasn't sure why he was apologizing exactly.

"I'm spoiled, Mac."

He had *no* idea how to respond to that. Agreeing seemed less than intelligent. Disagreeing wasn't likely to get him points either for some reason.

"I am. I've always had whatever I wanted. Now I want to work for something."

"You want to work for something?" he repeated. "What does that mean?"

"You don't have to sound so skeptical. I can work."

"Define work."

"Try. Sweat. Put effort into. Take a risk."

Mac propped up on one elbow to better look at his wife. "What's this about, Sara?"

"This is a working town. They do hair, they milk cows, they grow trees... I have manicures and high heels."

Mac blinked a few times, then said slowly, "And you feel like..." He hoped she would just fill in the blank.

"They all think I'm too spoiled to get my hands dirty, too lazy to climb a ladder, too dumb to do accounting."

"Who cares what they think?"

"No, it's not that I care what they think." She took a deep breath and sat up, crossing her legs in a very distracting way. She noticed his preoccupation and pulled the sheet up to cover her lap. "It's that...I'm afraid they might be right."

Mac's brows slammed together. "You are *not* dumb or lazy or..."

"I have to prove it. To myself."

He was still frowning. Hard. "How?"

"I want to take classes in something completely new. And I want to paint and stain wood. I want to learn to balance books and I want to *use* my hands somehow to *do* something."

Mac considered that. She looked determined...and excited. What the hell? He was a sucker for her anyway. If Sara wanted something, he was going to move heaven and earth to help her get it. Even if that meant letting *her* do the heavy lifting.

"I have a few ideas about how you can use your hands to *do* something," he growled, finally succeeding in pulling her body under his.

And he kept her there for a very long time.

Chapter Eleven

Sara cleaned Style With A Smile every day after the morning rush, while Angie sat and ate whatever treat Sara had brought in and looked through magazines or did book work. Then Sara spent a couple of hours on the Internet. Interestingly, Angie always left her alone during her computer time. So clearly she didn't think Sara was going to steal anything or ransack the place. Sara wondered why Angie stayed during the cleaning. She probably just enjoyed watching Sara do manual labor.

They did talk, though. It wasn't exactly conversation, since that would require a back-and-forth exchange. But there was verbalization. Angie liked to give yes or no answers to her questions, but Sara had no trouble filling the silence. She talked about her siblings, her friends, the Bradford Youth Center, movies she wanted to see, books she'd read, places she wanted to vacation. She also told jokes. Thanks to Dooley and her brother she knew some pretty raunchy ones too. Angie had yet to laugh out loud, but Sara had seen a smile more than once.

Sara figured if the shop owner was annoyed by Sara's noise she could contribute herself, leave or tell Sara to leave. She did none of the above.

Two weeks into the arrangement, Sara finally asked, "So why don't you like me?"

Angie sat in one of the stylist chairs as Sara cleaned the front window.

There was a long silence, during which she continued scrubbing.

Finally, she heard Angie sigh. "I find a few things about you annoying. But mostly I don't mind you."

"Then why do you act like you don't like me?" Sara took the glass cleaner and rag to the front door, thinking that perhaps she didn't want to see Angie's face during this conversation. Like confession.

"Because it's easier to be bitchy to you than nice."

"That just a personality thing or something specific to me?" Sara asked.

She heard Angie chuckle and almost turned for that rare occurrence. "A little of both, I suppose."

"Because I'm new?"

Angie didn't answer right away. When she did finally reply, it was soft. And honest. "Because you walked in here in high heels I would kill to wear but can't because my back and legs hurt, looking great and confident, energetic, perky—which I haven't been in longer than I can remember—talking about needing a manicure when I could barely make it through the clients I had scheduled. It just happened to be the worst day I've had in quite a while."

Sara did turn then. "I'm sorry. Are you... Is everything okay?" Something about Angie's tone made her think the answer was more than just being overworked or overstressed.

Angie met her gaze. "I have fibromyalgia. My doctor had just called that morning to confirm it."

Sara wasn't sure what to say. "I've heard of it. I don't know a lot about it."

"It's a chronic condition—no cure. It's all about feeling tired and sore all the time. Lots of fun."

"There's no medication for it?"

She shrugged. "They're working on some things. There is a new one out now that's working okay for me. But you can't get rid of it. They say it's like arthritis in the muscles."

Sara frowned. "I'm sorry, Angie. That must make it tough to be on your feet all day."

"It does." She pushed herself up from the chair. "Anyway, you're not the only person who comes in here who I wish I could trade bodies with, but you are the one I can take it out on since I haven't known you for twenty years."

Somehow, that made Sara feel better. She smiled. "I can take it."

Angie lifted an eyebrow. "Yeah, I was really worried about running you off." Her sarcasm was blatant.

Sara just grinned.

"You really going to open a massage therapy business?" Angie asked her then.

Sara smiled and nodded. "Yep, right next door. Lucky you."

Angie rolled her eyes. "You can't talk through the massages. You're supposed to get people relaxed."

Sara laughed. "I'm glad you find my conversation so stimulating."

"Your *conversation* is incessant chatter," Angie muttered. "You have to learn to just be quiet, Sara. Let people just be."

Sara thought about that as she stored the cleaning supplies. "I'm not sure I know how to do that," she finally answered.

Angie sighed. It had been quiet in the shop for about three minutes straight. Sara knew that was a record since she'd been there.

"You just keep your lips together," Angie said. "It's not hard."

"It is. I'm used to noise and interruptions and advice." Sara leaned an elbow on the front counter, thinking about her words as she explained them. "I constantly have people asking me how I am, what I'm doing, what I'm planning, if they can help. Nobody's ever just let me be."

Angie looked up from her magazine. "Is that a good thing?"

"Um, yeah. Mostly." Sara was trying very hard to remember the last time she'd been in the same room with someone and *not* talked. She couldn't come up with one single occasion. Her life was filled with a bunch of rambunctious teenagers and a nosy, bossy bunch of friends and family. The new ones, Ben and Danika, were no exception.

"I'm always the center of attention."

"I'm shocked."

Sara smiled at that. "Don't think I didn't like it when I was younger. But eventually, believe it or not, I grew up a little and tried to do some stuff on my own without their advice or help."

"Whose advice and help?"

Sara tried to hide her surprise and pleasure over Angie's interest. "My sister and brother. And all of my brother's friends. Like Ma—Jason."

"You can call him Mac, I think I can keep up." Angie closed the magazine. "What happened when you tried this stuff on your own?"

"It freaked them out," she said honestly. "It made Jessica sad, because I didn't need her anymore. It made the guys even more overprotective because they weren't right there taking care of me."

"What happened?"

"I didn't do it again."

Angie's eyes widened. "Didn't do what?"

Sara shrugged. "Anything without them being involved."

"Anything?"

"I let them be involved in everything I do."

Angie just sat looking at her, running her thumb up and down over the edges of the pages of the magazine. Finally she said, "Why?"

"They insist."

Angie shook her head. "I don't buy it. You're smart and sassy enough to not let them get away with that. Unless you like it."

Sara felt strangely complimented. "It's not about me liking it." She waved her hand dismissively. "You're not interested in this. I should just shut up."

"You dragged me this far into this conversation and now I don't get to hear the rest?" She crossed her arms and sat back. "No way. No computer time until you spill."

Sara smiled. "Okay. It's not because *I* like it. I involve them in everything because they need that."

"What... You mean you let them have an opinion about everything for *their* sake?"

Sara grinned. "Yeah. It's so important to them. At first they needed to take care of me just as much as I needed them to. It gave us all an anchor after my dad died. My mom walked out when I was just a baby, so it was always just dad. When he was gone, taking care of me was what kept Jess and Sam grounded, gave them something to *do*, to focus on."

"How old were you when your dad died?"

"Ten." Sara took a deep breath and let it out. "He was shot. Interrupting a burglary at Jessica's apartment."

Angie frowned. "My God."

"It was rough." Sara truly had been protected from so much. There had to have been financial worries and legal issues for Jessica, and even Sam, to deal with. But Jessica had been there through it all for Sara, acting as a buffer, keeping things as normal as she could.

"But after I was pretty much grown up, they still needed to be sure everything was perfect for me, smooth, worry free. It's what they do."

"What about now that you're living here?"

"It's driving them a little crazy," Sara said. "But it's good. It's...liberating."

"For you?"

"Yes. And for them. I'm too far away for them to do much for me, they *can't* see me every day so now they have a chance to pay attention to something else." She laughed again. "I just realized that's why I haven't been more upset about not having a car. Without a car there's no question of my driving back to see them. There's no guilt, because there's no choice. This is just how it is."

Angie shook her head. "You know what this means, right?"

"What?"

"You don't need manicures or someone to clean your house. You've been a princess for them, not because you really are one."

"I have to clean my own house now?" She pretended to pout. Angie knew good and well that Sara had already been doing that.

"Yep, sorry." Angie pushed herself up from the chair. "And no more princess treatment around here."

Sara laughed. "The Queen would be appalled if what you've been giving me is the royal treatment."

Angie pushed the front door open and stepped through. "Ah, the Queen can bite me."

Sara was still grinning when the door swung shut and Angie disappeared around the corner.

Then she spent the next two hours on the computer researching fibromyalgia.

Sara knew painting the walls in the unfinished building she'd chosen for her massage studio before she'd even started classes—that would take her eighteen months to finish—probably counted as jumping the gun. Still, she saw the rooms, including the colors, she wanted vividly in her mind and once the bank agreed to give her the loan she'd applied for, she'd needed to *buy* something to make it feel real. And paint was the easiest thing. Because it was the only thing she knew she needed for sure and could pick out by herself.

Obviously she needed furniture, flooring, new windows, new doors, a computer, some plants, pens, paper... She didn't know what she was doing. So she bought paint. A perfect sage green that would look amazing with white wooden trim around the windows and doors and a pale yellow for accent. Cool, peaceful, relaxing.

She hummed as she spread out the plastic sheets she'd bought at the hardware store. There wasn't anything specific to cover, but she hadn't ever painted before and with her luck there was some trick to the whole thing that involved plastic sheets.

She squatted next to the can of paint and started to pry the lid off with the little silver tool the guy had insisted she needed. She also had a stirring stick—which she could figure out—and three brushes in various widths. As she dipped one of the new brushes into the can she felt a little zing of happiness. She was doing this, by herself, without advice or help.

"There you are!"

She whipped around quickly to see her sister coming through the door.

"Jess!" The brush and paint forgotten for the moment, she ran across the floor and grabbed her sister in a big hug.

"Watch the paint!" Jessica said laughing as she pulled back.

And like someone had flipped a switch, suddenly her quiet little someday-shop was filled with her friends and family, noise, laughter and teasing.

Ben, Danika, Sam, Kevin, Dooley and Mac all crowded through the door. Kevin and Dooley were each carrying a cooler, Mac and Sam each had a big cardboard box and Danika had a tote bag over each shoulder.

"What are you all doing here?" she asked, her eyes wet and her throat tight for some reason.

"Mac said we should come see what you were up to," Danika said, catching Sara in a hug. "Basically he finally gave us permission to come," she whispered in Sara's ear.

Sara laughed and found her husband's eyes. He'd been at work and she'd had plans for his return home, but the look he gave her over Dani's head was full of promise for when they were finally alone. He knew how much she'd missed her friends and family. That he'd told them to come meant a lot.

“What happened to your hair?” Sam asked, in that annoying-brother tone of voice he’d long ago perfected.

Sara touched the bandana she’d tied around her head. “Nothing.”

“Why are you covering it up?”

“To keep from getting paint in it.”

“Paint?” Sam asked, standing near her can of paint.

She knew she was beaming when she answered, “Yeah, I’m painting.”

Sam turned in a full circle, then asked, “Painting what?”

“The shop.” Sara gestured with her arms wide. “My place.”

Sam looked at the can of paint and then at the walls and then at her. “Oh.”

“So this is great timing. We’ll help.” Kevin put his load down and started toward her. “With all of us, this will go fast.”

“No!” She said it more forcefully and louder than she’d intended, but it did result in him stopping halfway across the floor. “I mean, thanks, but I want to do this myself. All by myself.”

“You’ve never painted anything, Sara,” Sam pointed out.

“So?”

He must have seen something on her face that made him realize an argument would be pointless. “Okay.” He shrugged. “Go for it.”

Dani grabbed his arm. “Um...”

“She’s going to do it by herself,” Sam said to Dani. “Leave her alone.”

Danika looked around the shop a little helplessly. “Ooookay.”

Sara didn’t care what they were talking about. She didn’t know what she was doing. So what? She didn’t care if she made some mistakes. That never happened. Which to most would sound like a good thing, to her it was...boring. And a little pathetic. And high maintenance.

“Oh my gosh!” Jessica took one of Sara’s hands. “You cut your fingernails!”

Everyone stopped talking.

“Let me see that.” Dooley took her other hand. “Holy crap, Sara. I’ve never seen you without those long sparkly nails.”

"They'll break off while I'm working," she said. Truthfully, it had been a bit traumatic to take the polish off and cut the beautiful French tips from her nails. Her hands looked like they should belong to someone else. But it had to be done. She was a working woman now.

"And what's with your shoes?" Ben asked, frowning at her feet.

Sara looked down at her white tennis shoes. "What?"

"Those don't have a heel on them."

"And they're *bright*," Dooley added.

She shrugged. "I needed shoes to work in. You can't climb ladders with heels on."

"So you bought brand-new tennis shoes to wear as your work shoes?" Ben asked. "Why not just wear an old pair?"

She felt like an idiot as she admitted, "I don't have an old pair."

"Well, a not-brand-new pair."

"These are the only tennis shoes I have," she said, wiggling one foot.

"You don't own tennis shoes?" Ben asked.

"What would I have tennis shoes for?" she returned.

"Walking, working out...painting."

Sara just watched him and waited a few seconds. Then he realized what he'd said. "Right. You don't work out or...paint."

"You walk," Dooley pointed out.

"Well I don't *walk*," she said. "I don't go any distance that can't be comfortably covered in heels."

"What about yoga?" Ben asked.

She shrugged. "You go barefoot during yoga."

"What about on your way *to* yoga?"

"Why would I buy shoes just to wear on my way to yoga? I wear my work clothes—and shoes—since I go straight from the center."

Sara grinned at Ben's and Dooley's amused and disbelieving expressions. Her brother and sister—and Mac—didn't seem one bit surprised though.

"But now I'm going to paint. And do other manual labor."

Danika grinned. "Can you define manual labor, sweetie?"

Sara knew these people loved her, which was the only reason her feelings weren't hurt. "I'm going to stain wood, nail things, hang things...” It sounded a little stupid even to her.

“Stain wood?” Danika repeated. She looked around. “What wood?”

There was no trim around the windows or doors, or baseboards, or...anything.

“The floor. I want to put hardwood floors in.”

“Um, honey, those come already stained. And the guys who put it in for you...” Dani stopped at the look on Sara’s face. “You’re not seriously telling me that you think you’re going to put the floor in by yourself?”

“I’m sure I can learn.” She wasn’t sure at all, but her pride insisted she say it.

“I’m sure you can too, but why?” Dani asked. “I wouldn’t even do a wood floor by myself...even though I *could*.” Danika was a self-taught miss fix-it. She knew how to do *everything*. More than Sam did. Which was a constant source of amusement for all of them.

“I just...” Sara puffed out a frustrated breath. “I just want to do something by myself for a change. So—” she squared her shoulders, “—I’m going to paint. You’re all excused.”

She figured they were staying for dinner and maybe beyond. But she had her painting clothes on, her can open, her paint stirred and her brush dipped so she was going to paint. Dammit.

“You have one can of paint?” Kevin asked.

Sam nudged him. “Leave her alone.”

“You’re using a *brush*?” Dooley added as she dipped her brush again.

“Shut up,” Sam muttered. “Just let her do it.”

“The windows aren’t even done yet...”

“Dani,” Sam said warningly.

“So we’re not going to tell her she should put the windows in before she paints?”

“Nope.”

Danika sighed. “And we’ll just come back and put the windows in and then help re-paint.”

“Right.”

“Okay, but this is—” Danika stopped talking mid-sentence but Sara didn’t turn to see how Sam had shut her up.

It was nice Sam was the one listening to her and keeping the others from giving her a hard time. Of course she knew she didn't know what she was doing in turning this empty, somewhat-run-down building into a cute, comfortable massage business. But they didn't have to be pointing it out so readily.

Sara crossed to the closest wall and painted one wide sage green stripe down the center of the brown, non-dry-walled wall. The moment she did it, she realized a few things. One, she really did like the color. Two, the green would be a lot prettier on a finished wall. Three, this was going to take *forever* with one brush. Four, she didn't want to do this by herself anyway.

She sighed and turned. The conversation behind her hadn't stopped, it had simply switched focus. They were all sitting around on the floor or on the coolers, passing around food and drinks and talking about the Oscar Wildcats' chance of making it to a state playoff in football.

They were eating pizza from Zio's. Her favorite pizza. The best in the world.

They were also eating cheesecake from Maria's. Her favorite dessert. The best in the world.

It was not a coincidence.

"Okay, fine. You can help."

They stopped chewing and talking, and one by one they started to grin. "I thought you'd never ask," Danika said from her place on the floor leaning against Sam's left arm. "This place is going to look amazing."

They started jabbering about the supplies they'd need and everyone's schedule and when they could get back to Oscar to start.

And just like that Sara was crying.

Mac was, of course, the first to notice. He was on his feet, across the room and had his arms wrapped around her within ten seconds.

"It's fine. We're all proud of you. This doesn't mean you're lazy or superficial or dumb," he said into the top of her head.

Sara tried to giggle in the midst of crying and it turned into hiccups. She hiccupped in his arms for a while, just loving the feel and smell of him. Eventually she held her breath, quieted the hiccups and then pulled back.

"I'm crying because I just realized I'm damned lucky to not know the first thing about painting or milking cows or cutting hair. Because I'm lucky to have all of you who have been taking care of me for so long."

Mac's big hand rubbed up and down her back. "I'll always take care of you, princess. Swear to God."

Her heart melted a little. "I know. But I want to learn stuff and do stuff. Stuff I'm interested in, stuff I'd be good at. I admire the other women here in Oscar. They work hard, but it's at things that really matter to them, because it's their business or their family or it's taking care of their friends and town. I want to do something I choose that really matters to me."

"I thought the center mattered to you," Jessica said from where she shared a cooler with Ben.

Sara turned to her sister, who was so much more than just a sister. "It does. Very much. But I want to volunteer there like you all do because I love it. I don't want to *work* there because my sister made up a job for me."

Jessica didn't nod her agreement, however she seemed to be thinking about it, and Sara knew she'd understand.

"You sure massage therapy and having your own business here in Oscar are what you want to do?" Mac asked.

"I think so." As she said it, she felt like a bright light had been turned on inside of her. She felt happy. "I want to do something from scratch, the hard way, like everyone else. I want to be here in Oscar where everyone will know me and they'll come in for the conversation as much as for the massage."

She turned to look at the group who she considered her family, blood siblings or not. "You're all the best. I love you all so much. But I want to be accepted into a group because of who I am, not because I've just always been there or I'm someone's little sister."

"Hey, we all love you too," Sam protested.

She grinned at him. "I know. And this group is my rock. But I want to start a group of friends from scratch too. Where I do stuff for them as much as they do for me."

"You do stuff for us," Mac inserted.

"Well, you do more stuff for *some* of us than others." Dooley waggled his eyebrows suggestively.

Sara felt Mac tighten his arm around her. "Damn right," he

growled. "You won't be starting from scratch with that."

She wrapped her arms around him too and smiled. "Damn right."

"Oh, shit, Mac, you're killing me," Sam groaned.

He and Mac were watching Dooley and Ben measure the windows.

Mac faced him. "What?"

"I see how you watch her. Damn, what am I supposed to do when you look at her like that?"

Mac frowned. "Like what?"

"Like Sam watches Danika," Ben said, coming up beside his brother-in-law.

Mac and Sam looked at each other. Mac had seen exactly the expression Ben was referring to on Sam's face a number of times.

"I look at her like that?"

"Yeah," Sam said softly. "You really do love her."

Mac frowned at him. "You thought I was just saying that?"

Sam shrugged. "I guess it didn't hit me what it meant until now. If you feel for Sara the way I feel about Danika... Well, damn, buddy, there's nothing I—or you—can do about it anyway."

Mac rolled his eyes. "Well, no shit."

Ben laughed and shoved Sam. "You both should just wallow in it like I do. Just be sickeningly in love. Who cares what anyone else thinks?"

Mac and Sam both readily agreed Ben and Jessica were sickening. Inside Mac was pretty sure he was looking forward to being exactly the same way with Sara.

"You mean like this?" Sam asked, catching his wife's arm as she walked past. He swung her around, backed her up against the closest wall and kissed her like they were completely alone in their bedroom.

Danika's cheeks were pink when he finally let her go. "What was *that* for?"

"Medical advice," Sam said simply, looking very smug.

Her eyes flickered to Ben and she simply said, "Oh." Then moved off to re-join the other girls, still looking a little dazed.

"Sickening enough for you?" Sam asked.

"Kind of hot," Ben admitted glancing around the room. "Where's Jess?"

Mac knew exactly where Sara was. But he wanted a little privacy for *his* display of affection. Sam might be okay with them being together, but watching Mac undress his little sister might be pushing it.

"I think it's time you all head back to Omaha."

Sam started to say something. Then he met Mac's gaze. Slowly he nodded. "Probably is. We'll be making a bunch of trips up here anyway to finish the shop."

"Right." Mac started walking him toward the door. "Dani, you're ride's leaving!" he called over his shoulder.

Ben was already packing up the coolers and Mac heard him tell Dooley to "shut the hell up" about something.

Mac really liked Ben.

Within fifteen minutes they were all packed up, loaded in their cars and heading out on Main Street.

Mac turned to his wife. "Let's go home."

She gave him a playful grin. "We just started painting."

"We're not going to be painting until we dry-wall."

"Maybe we should start on that." She started backing away as he advanced.

"Don't have any materials."

"We should go and get some." She giggled as she had to skirt the can of paint.

"No, we shouldn't."

She reversed until her back met the wall. Mac stopped directly in front of her, cupped the back of her head and bent to put his nose behind her ear where he breathed deep.

"Are we going to do this here?" she asked breathlessly. She looked more than interested.

He touched the skin behind her ear with his lips, then his tongue. "If I took you up against this wall, you would think of it every time you were in here."

She pulled in a shaky breath, her hands gathering the front of his shirt in two fists. "Yeah."

Mac felt a surge of heat and desire jolt through him. "But," he said, lifting his head to look her directly in the eye, "I've developed a definite affinity for my bed." That was where Sara belonged. In a bed. With a husband who cherished her. Not some guy who could have sex anywhere, any time. He could wait until they got home. He would make a point of waiting. Sara deserved that.

"Okay," she said with a sexy smile. "Take me home. To bed. But hurry up."

He proved he could wait. But he did break the speed limit.

Sara didn't see her breakfast guest right away. But she felt him.

Her big toe came into contact with something in the middle of the kitchen. Something weird. The something wasn't heavy or immoveable, it didn't hurt her toe, it didn't make a noise. It felt a little like she'd kicked a jump rope.

She really didn't want to open her eyes then.

She did, of course, because she didn't want to run into anything that was actually heavy, immovable or painful to kick. Then she wished she hadn't.

The jump rope was about the right size and shape. But it was black and orange. And had a head.

She felt faint as the snake slithered away from her. She was glad he was moving in the opposite direction, but was not very happy he was moving at all. Or even that he was *there*.

What the hell was a snake doing in the kitchen anyway?

She closed her eyes but her head spun, so she opened them again. The snake was still there.

She wasn't sure which was worse—closed and spinning, or open and not alone.

The snake slithered in the direction of the living room. That was really one of the big problems with snakes, she decided then. It was the slithering. Made them all the more creepy.

As it neared the arched doorway, she shook herself. "Uh, no way." It was *not* going into the living room. She looked around frantically. She had no idea what to do with a snake but she was not letting it into the rest of the house where there were lots of things to get under and hide and wait to freak her out. As it was she was never going to walk into a room without looking for black and orange objects again.

She noticed the big plastic bowl she'd used for popcorn the night before. Tossing the unpopped kernels in the trash can, she tiptoed toward the snake.

A shudder went through her. Snake. Even the word was creepy.

Not to mention his coloring. Black and orange was just naturally sinister. Nothing friendly, warm and cuddly was ever black and orange. Okay, maybe the occasional kitten. But black widows were black and orange too.

And poisonous. Sara froze. Were there poisonous snakes in Nebraska? Hell if she knew. She'd never been this close to a snake—that she knew of anyway—of any color.

She eyed him critically. She didn't want to get much closer, but she also didn't want a potentially poisonous and definitely creepy snake loose in the house.

Dammit. She had to do this. She moved closer, leaned over and reached as far as she could, holding the edge of the counter with her opposite hand to keep from falling as she half placed, half tossed the bowl over the snake, trapping him underneath. She managed it on the first try.

Breathing deeply for the first time in several minutes, she eyed the bowl. It was just plastic. Not all that heavy. She ran to the living room, grabbed one of the books from the ancient set of encyclopedias and balanced it on top, weighing the bowl down and preventing any escape from thrashing angry snakes.

She breathed again, shivered once and headed to find her cell phone.

Maybe Sean would come over and get rid of the thing. Even covered with a bowl and the thickest book in the house, she did *not* want a snake within one hundred feet of her. Two hundred would be even better.

The call went straight to Sean's voice mail and she realized with a glance at the clock that he was in school. The snake could *not* stay in the house until four o'clock or whenever Sean got home. Mac would be home in the next two hours, but for some reason she knew she had to do this before he got home. He was a part of the gang who didn't think she could paint a wall by herself. Facing a snake by herself would shock them.

She heard the snake bump against the side of the bowl and her eyes widened. He was getting mad. How strong was a snake like that? Especially ticked off? He was a wild animal. His survival instincts had to be colossal.

Then she frowned.

There were no air holes, of course. How long could he stay under there and not have air? Probably not long. His lungs... Did snakes have lungs? They had to. Right? Anyway, if he had them, his lungs were tiny.

She sighed. She didn't want him to move in and wasn't thrilled he'd stopped by, but she didn't want him to die. Especially because she really didn't want to deal with a dead snake.

Crap.

Yeah. He had to go.

Now.

She glared at her phone. She had no one to call. No advice. No one to come do it for her. This was awesome. Yeah, right.

She sighed again. Fine. Okay. She could do this. As long as he didn't bite her—or jump, or get away.

Surely she could tip the bowl over, scoop him into it, cover it and then run like hell outside to dump him out. Far, far, far away from the house.

How far was far enough? Would he come back? Would he bring friends.

If only she had Google.

Muttering expletives, she surveyed the kitchen. There was a lid that went with the bowl. All she needed was something to scoop him with. Something with a *long* handle that would enable her to stay as far away as possible. And she needed something to cover every single centimeter of bare skin he could even possibly bite.

She took the stairs two at a time, quickly donned two pairs of socks and her tennis shoes, jeans and a long-sleeved shirt of Mac's. Back in the kitchen, she pulled on oven mitts, grabbed the longest-handled utensil she could find—the barbecue tongs for the grill.

Wishing for some kind of face mask, she approached the bowl.

Just get it over with. Just do it. You can breathe later.

She took the book off, swallowed hard and flipped, scooped,

covered and ran.

She didn't stop until she was out of breath.

She ran back to the house too. She didn't really think the snake would follow her. But she wasn't taking any chances.

It took her almost an hour to search the entire house, under and in everything a snake could use to hide from her. She shuddered the whole time, hoping she wouldn't find anything.

When the house came up clean, she drank a glass of wine and slid into the tub, relaxing her tense muscles into the strawberry-scented bubbles. Only after she'd soaked for thirty minutes and the wine had slipped into her veins did she finally smile.

She'd gotten rid of a snake, all by herself.

Ha!

"Princess?"

Her smile grew. Mac was home.

"In here." She swirled her toes in the water, anticipation tightening the muscles she'd just loosened.

"What are you…" He trailed off as he saw her lying in the tub.

"Want to join me?" She swirled her hands, causing the bubbles to shift and float away from her breasts.

"Yeah." He started undressing, pulling his T-shirt off and tossing it to the side. "But the tub isn't very big."

His belt came off as he pushed his shoe from his left foot with his right.

"We'll have to stay really close together, then." She sat up partially, letting the water and bubbles slide from her breasts to just below her belly button.

His eyes firmly on her already-erect nipples, Mac stripped out of his pants and underwear.

"Come here."

"You come here."

He shook his head even as he stepped up next to the tub. "I want plenty of room to move."

"I want you right here, right now."

"On the bed."

The sex was amazing. She couldn't get enough of him. But it was always on the bed. She wanted something...naughtier. He was always in control, everything perfectly orchestrated. She wasn't complaining about the results. But she wanted him crazy. So hot for her that he couldn't wait to take her wherever they were. Even the first night when he'd had her naked in the car, he'd still managed to wait until they were in the bed. She wanted something...wilder.

She stood, water sluicing off of her body, bubbles trailing down her hips and thighs. "You sure?" She reached out for his hand, bringing it to her breast. "I'm wet and warm and smell like strawberries."

"My favorite." He cupped her breast, then plucked the nipple. "But I can keep you wet and warm no matter where we are."

He reached for her waist with both hands, lifting her from the tub and up against him. She wrapped her legs around his waist and he slid home that easily.

They both groaned. But Mac started for the bedroom anyway, not stopping until he laid her on the bed, where he had plenty of room to move and took full advantage of the fact.

She stopped minding about ten seconds in.

It wasn't until later that she realized Mac still hadn't lost his mind over her.

Chapter Twelve

"Did I tell you Sean is teaching Sara to drive the old pickup in the barn?"

"That thing runs?" Dooley asked, fishing his car keys from his pocket on his way to the parking lot from the hospital.

"Now it does." Mac shrugged. "Sean overhauled the engine."

"Why?"

"He wanted to. To help Sara."

"Ah, she's charmed him too."

Mac nodded. Not that it was a surprise, of course. There were very few males on the planet who would be immune to Sara.

"But if it runs, what does Sean have to teach her?"

"It's a stick shift," Mac said with a grin, stopping beside his car. "With an ignition that needs wiggling just right, terrible shocks and a driver's side door that has to be opened from inside."

Dooley shook his head. "And she hasn't complained once?"

Mac was amazed too. He'd been expecting the whining to start the first day she realized she was stranded without a car. Instead, she'd made friends with the neighbor and bummed rides from him until she was fed up. Then, instead of insisting someone bring her own car to Oscar, she'd asked Sean for lessons in driving the beat-up pickup that Mac's grandfather had parked in the barn years ago.

She hadn't told him, of course. Sean had. When he'd called to ask Mac if he could work on the engine. She was resourceful and showed no signs of leaving Oscar. Not that the truck would make it far, likely.

"They named it Sully," Mac said.

"Sully?" Dooley asked.

"Like the big blue monster in that Disney movie, *Monsters, Inc.*"

Dooley laughed and Mac grinned wider.

"I like that. Sara's so cute," Dooley said.

Cute. He supposed Sara was cute. He used to think the same thing. But it was really such an inadequate word for everything she was.

"Apparently she can make it from the barn to the end of the driveway only killing it once."

"It's amazing she's stuck with it." Dooley smiled affectionately. "She's never been very good about doing stuff that isn't easy for her."

Mac looked at his friend in surprise. "You noticed that?" Dooley was right, of course.

"Yeah, I noticed." Dooley slugged Mac lightly on the arm. "You're not the only one who's loved her a long time you know."

"I know..." Mac trailed off, uncertain suddenly. "At least..."

Dooley rolled his eyes. "Not like that."

"You sure?" Mac wasn't sure why he asked. Of course Dooley wasn't *in love* with her. But he still wanted to hear it. Out loud. In English. Maybe twice.

"Yes, I'm sure." But Dooley clearly hesitated.

"*What*?" Mac fought not to grit his teeth.

"I just, well, I've always seen Sara as amazing, of course. And she's turned into a beautiful woman. But that's a fact, not just an opinion. Like the sky is blue and the Yankees are the best team in baseball."

Mac snorted.

"I just don't see her like you do," Dooley said. "I think she looks gorgeous in those heels she always wears, stuff like that. At the same time, I'm not *attracted.* I can't imagine kissing her. It would be—awkward."

Mac shifted. "I wouldn't say..."

"Not for you," Dooley said quickly. "I didn't mean that. But..." He stopped and shook his head. "Forget it."

Mac scowled at him. "But what?"

"Nah, I shouldn't ask you this."

"Why?"

"It's inappropriate."

Well, so much for normal conversation and being fine. "When has that ever stopped you?" Mac asked. "Most of the time that's *why* you say things."

Dooley shrugged. "Yeah, good point."

"What do you have to say about this?"

"Was it weird? The first time you kissed Sara?"

The word "weird" reverberated in his head. Dammit. Mac flashed back to Sara climbing onto his lap at the wedding reception. Surprising, yes, Sexy as hell, yes. But weird?

"Maybe a little."

"I just..." Dooley paused and looked at Mac cautiously. Then clearly made up his mind to continue. "Seeing her naked, all of that, when did it stop being weird?"

Mac supposed that this was inappropriate. Still, he and Dooley had talked about nearly every inappropriate thing under the sun. "Seeing her naked was..."

Lots of words. Amazing, breathtaking, the most erotic thing in his life. Unexpected. Definitely unexpected. Guilt-inducing. Oh, yeah definitely that last one.

Dooley, never one for deep ponderings, seemed unconcerned with Mac's inability to describe it. "I'm glad it's not weird for you anymore, man. Seriously. That would suck."

Mac shifted his weight again, definitely uncomfortable.

"I should have known it was fine between you two when she seemed pretty damned comfortable with the body powder," Dooley commented.

"Yeah." Over the past month or so, she'd tried getting comfortable with all of the stuff in the box she'd ordered. Fortunately, he'd been able to distract her from the toys fairly easily. So far.

Not that using toys with Sara would be weird. No, *weird* was too harsh. He'd liked the body powder just fine and the pink wedge had been fun. But that had been spontaneous, spur of the moment, fueled by basic biology and chemistry. And lack of real thought. It was when he got to *thinking* that things seemed not quite...uncomplicated.

"She keeps up with you then?" Dooley asked.

Mac knew exactly what he meant. Mac had shared lots of stories with the guys—some of them were even true. Knowing Sara as they did it was no wonder Dooley had a hard time reconciling Mac's style with how they thought of Sara.

They had no idea what a seductress she could be. How hot, how curious, how enthusiastic she was.

He suspected all of it was a surprise to her as well.

"I can't talk about my wife like this," Mac said, shoving Dooley back a step. Rather than admit that Sara could very likely keep pace with him and enjoy every minute, or that for Mac it was...a little weird, Mac decided instead to keep a few secrets from his friends. For the first time since meeting them.

He thought about the conversation all the way to Oscar.

He was content. That was absolutely the best word to describe how he'd felt in the past month. He drove home, to a real home rather than an empty apartment, every day after work. He now had throw pillows on the couch, a wife who made a habit of having breakfast ready for him when he got home—though the cinnamon rolls were from downtown Oscar and she stuck with French toast after the one incident with the pancakes—and an answering machine that said *Mac and Sara*.

He loved it.

It was the last thing he'd expected, but he liked hanging out at home, grilling on the back patio, going downtown for ice cream, talking about some landscaping ideas for next summer, sitting with Sara at the football games.

It was stuff he'd always wanted but hadn't thought he would have. He'd always assumed he would choose the drinking-dancing-clubs-I-only-need-your-first-name-tonight lifestyle over the dinner-at-home-mow-the-grass-watch-TV-with-one-woman-every-night lifestyle everyone else seemed to find satisfactory.

Turned out he'd just been waiting for Sara.

Sara definitely made him want to be home with her every night.

It was undeniable he loved his new life and didn't want it to change. Seriously. He'd turned into Ward freakin' Cleaver and he loved it.

He had no idea what had happened other than to attribute it to being in love, for real, finally.

Mac breathed deep as he came through the front door of the

house. It had become something of a habit. Strange, sure. But he loved the way his house smelled since Sara had moved in.

She liked scented candles, she wore lots of lotions and body sprays, she used furniture polish and carpet freshener and all kinds of other things that made the house smell good. Like home. Like Sara.

He tossed his duffle to the side and started for the stairs, taking them two at a time and strode through the bedroom door, ready to smell her up close and personal.

Sara wasn't there.

But the room smelled like her. Stronger than anywhere else in the house. It was arousing and comforting at the same time. He inhaled deeply. "Princess?"

"Hi." She came into the bedroom from the master bath, rubbing lotion on her arms and hands. Her smile was sweet and seductive.

"Hi."

He started around the edge of the bed, but stopped as his eyes dropped below her chin.

"Oh, my..."

"You like?" She twirled, showing off the sheer floor-length robe she wore. It was white—kind of. It was really mostly see-through. Except for the red satin hearts right over her nipples and the bright red bow tied between her breasts.

"You've..." He cleared his throat. "You've been shopping on Angie's computer?"

"Yep." She smiled.

She might as well have been naked. She was underneath. Which he could see clearly.

Mac couldn't move. He was used to Sara greeting him dressed for the day. Not that she always stayed that way, of course, and she wore pajamas to bed, but they consisted of soft cotton short shorts and a matching tank top. Which were quite sexy enough.

He hadn't seen her in lingerie.

"Do you like it?"

"Princess, there's nothing there not to like." Except his tenuous hold on his control.

"So how come you're standing way over there?" She came toward him, fingering the bow between her breasts.

"I'm so stiff I can't move."

She grinned at him and he felt his desire grow.

"Then I'll have to do the work." Her hands began tugging at his T-shirt and he let her slip it off over his head. Then her fingers went to work on the snap of his jeans and the zipper.

As the metal tab dragged down his length, his breath hissed out between his teeth.

He kicked the jeans off, but before he could remove his boxers, she put her hands on his chest and pushed. "Sit."

He sat on the edge of the bed and she climbed into his lap, straddling his thighs and facing him. His hands went to her hips, drawing her against him, rubbing her sweet cleft against his barely covered erection.

She kissed him long and deep, making his fingers curl into the softness of her butt. When she let him up for air, she ran her hands over his head.

"I have a surprise for you." She wiggled her hips, eliciting a groan from him.

"I love it already." He lifted his hands and untied the bow between her breasts, then skimmed the robe off of her shoulders. He cupped her breasts, thumbing the tips and making her moan.

"It gets better," she breathed.

"Never." He kissed her again, plucking at her nipples.

She pressed down against his straining erection. Mac reached to remove the final barrier between them, but Sara said, "Suck on me, Mac."

He paused, wanting to be bare against her, but not able to ignore a plea like that.

Palm flat against her back between her shoulder blades, he pushed her forward as she lifted herself. He took her nipple into his mouth, swirling the tip with his tongue, then sucking slightly. She cupped the back of his head, urging him to give more. He sucked harder.

When her right nipple was hard and wet, Sara pulled away and reached past his left hip.

"Look what I got."

Before Mac registered what was happening, she leaned back and applied a little silver clamp to her right nipple.

Mac felt like he'd been punched in the gut.

The sight was shocking and erotic and amazing and horrible.

He throbbed with lust and his chest felt tight. Sara's nipple was clenched in the teeth of a tweezer clamp. All he could focus on was the sweet pink flesh being squeezed and how wrong it looked on her. Too dark, too slutty, too...like his old life.

"*No*," he said firmly. He released the clamp and promptly pulled the nipple into his mouth. Rather than foreplay, the suction provided some relief from the pain that occurred after releasing a nipple from a clamp. The clamp cut off blood flow and the sudden return could hurt. She'd only had it on for a few seconds, but he still reacted to prevent any pain at all.

Sara squirmed on his lap, pushing his head away. "Stop. Mac, stop."

He let go but was breathing hard, working on controlling the emotions coursing through his body.

God, he'd never seen anything like that. Other nipples, other clamps, other women, yes. But on Sara it was...weird. Part of him wanted it. He couldn't deny it. He wanted Sara's body pushed to the limits of pleasure. For her sake. For what she could feel and experience. But he couldn't—obviously—handle what that would mean. He couldn't do it for *his* pleasure.

A bruise from taking her on a table, a scrape from being thrust into against a rough wall, a mark of any kind caused by him, for him, would make him crazy.

He knew it was an irrational reaction, that Sara had bought and applied the clamp herself. But he'd given her the idea. She was doing it for him, because he'd said it was what he wanted.

In the past four weeks, he'd carried her to the bed to make love each time, in spite of her starting things in the living room, the shower, the kitchen. He had barely managed it, but he had worshipped her body in the way she deserved. The way a woman who was loved and honored and cherished should be treated.

The other women, the one-night stands, the flings, the crazy wild stuff had been about lust, gratification, pleasure. Not love. Not forever. Not commitment and marriage and promises.

Not Sara.

Dammit, sonofabitch, hell, fuck, shit. Okay, crazy sex was *weird* with Sara. He hated that word, but it was pretty accurate at the moment. Not because of her—she was amazing—but because his head, his conscience, his memories wouldn't leave him alone.

She deserved to be made love to. Not the stuff he was used to feeling for and doing with women. What the hell did he know about making love? He'd never done it before Sara.

And she could get the crazy wild stuff with any pervert on the street—hell, any man she knew pretty much—while *he* was the only man who was going to truly make love to her. Ever. Whether she liked it or not.

So, yeah, all of this was strange.

And the world was *not* a normal or good place if Dooley was right about something.

Breathing deep through his nose he slowly lifted his head to look at her.

She looked—understandably—confused. "What's going on?"

"I was joking about the nipple clamps." He tried to call her princess. He really did. It just wouldn't come out.

She gave him a look that said there was no way she was believing this. "Why? You've tried it before and didn't like it?"

He couldn't quite bring himself to lie. "That's not it."

"You don't like it on me?"

She hadn't covered up and his eyes dropped to her breasts. His traitorous body hardened in spite of his best intentions. "I'm not that into it," he said, unable to look her in the eye.

She leaned in and reached past him again. "How about these?" She held up four pink silk ties.

He swallowed hard. "What do you mean?"

"Tie me up, Mac." She dragged one of the cool silky strips across the back of his neck.

"Then what?" he asked. Stupidly.

"Whatever you want."

His gut clenched and his cock throbbed beneath her, like it was seeking her heat. With absolutely no input whatsoever from his brain.

"This is what I want." He rolled her beneath him, tossing the nipple clamps out of reach.

Her robe fell away as they rolled, her naked body completely exposed and accessible. He pressed against her and she caught her breath, even as she started shaking her head.

"No, wait."

"What for? I know you're hot and ready." He slid his hands between them, then a finger into her.

She was definitely hot and ready.

She clutched at his shoulders, always responsive to him. Still she said, "Mac, no, wait."

He could slip his boxers off and slide home. Hell, he could simply spread the front panel open and slide home. She would be gasping his name in no time. But the "Mac, no" stopped him.

Panting, he put his forehead against hers. "What, princess?"

She wiggled under him and he let up his pressure on her hips. She stretched and then held up the pink vibrator.

"Tie me up, use this. Please."

The image she put in his mind, the begging, the heat of her under him made him insane. He wanted to do all of it—his body did, anyway. He could imagine her like that. The ties holding her open for him, the tugs on the chain between the clamps making her pant and moan, the vibrator bringing her to orgasm just before he thrust into her, taking her to the height again right on top of the first.

But he wasn't going to do any of it.

She was his *wife*, his friend, the woman he'd promised to protect and treasure.

He didn't know a damned thing about honoring and cherishing someone, but he was going to give it his all and the tie-me-up-dildo-thing just didn't seem like the way to go.

Sweet, not weird. Sweet, not weird. That was going to be his new mantra.

He moved his finger in her, circling her clit with his thumb. She wiggled against him. He bent his head to her breast and again teased the nipple, sucking softly, then hard. She wiggled, more aggressively. He lifted his head and moved to kiss her.

She turned her head.

"Mac. *Stop.*"

Dammit.

He rolled off of her and threw his arm over his eyes.

He felt Sara shift on the mattress, then leave the bed. Her footsteps faded away, the closet door opened and shut and then he heard her return to the side of the bed.

"We have to talk."

Yeah. They probably did. There were some things that Sara needed to understand.

He pushed up to a sitting position, rubbed a hand over the top of his head and looked up at her.

She was now wearing a fuzzy pink bathrobe, tied securely around her waist.

He wanted her like that too. More. It was crazy. He knew that. But *this* was different. This was comfortable and nice and...normal.

He'd seen more than his share of lingerie and toys. He'd never done the bathrobe, watch-the-*Late-Show*-together thing. Neither had Sara. He wanted stuff that was new to both of them. Was that so bad?

"What's going on?" she demanded, hands on her hips.

"I just tried to make love to my wife and she told me no." He sounded put-out. And he was. Though he felt nauseated too.

"*I* tried to make love to my husband and he told *me* no."

"You tried to have *sex* with me."

"Well, excuse the hell out of me!"

"I don't want that stuff, Sara."

"Bullshit," she returned bluntly.

"I don't."

"You have in the past. With other women."

And he was now going to pay for his past, as he'd always known he'd eventually have to.

"Yes," he said honestly.

She looked surprised he'd admitted it. "What am I supposed to do with that?"

He shoved to his feet. "I don't know. It doesn't matter what I've done before. I am *not* going to tie you up or put nipple clamps on you. Ever."

Sara felt her stomach dip sickeningly. Mac stood in nothing more than his boxers looking frustrated and nearly angry.

Her body still hummed with unfulfilled need for him and reacted to him even as she felt anger and—worse—trepidation building.

Something was wrong. And this wasn't the first time she'd suspected it.

They made love every day but she'd been trying to entice him over the past month into something, *anything,* outside of the bedroom. She'd almost had him in the shower and once in the living room, but every time he would pull back at the last minute, seem to remember something important and take her right upstairs to the bed. The sex was amazing. But it was always in the missionary position, no toys, no dirty talk.

This time she'd pulled out all the stops. The nipple clamps were supposed to be the final straw, the thing that would push him over the edge no matter what. In fact, she'd even stuck to the bedroom in case there was some strange reason he had to be in that bed.

Still he'd pulled back.

She hugged her arms to her body and fought the fear. This was not the Mac she'd been hearing stories about for twelve years. "Why not?" she finally managed to choke out. "What's wrong with this?"

"It's just...not you."

She stared at him. "Not me? How do you even know that? We've never done this. This is all new to me."

"So why don't you just trust me? I know all of this and I know you."

"I do trust you," she insisted. "I would never let anyone else do these things. Only you."

"I just..." He looked pained. "I can't. I don't want to do these things with you."

"But *I* do. I won't do anything I don't want to do, Mac. I promise. But I want this."

"I can't explain it, Sara. It just doesn't feel right."

Her stomach dropped. This was bad. "When you hold back like this, I wonder what other ways you're holding back from me, Mac."

He said nothing. And he wouldn't look at her.

Her heart started to race. In panic. "I want your all. Everything you have. In every way."

"I can only give you what I can, Sara. Going in to this..."

"It was all my idea." She tried to swallow, and failed, against the huge lump of dread and regret.

Dammit. It had all been going so well. They were happy, they were very compatible, they were in love.

But was it enough?

Suddenly she wasn't so sure.

Yes, she had more than many women. But every woman should want, should demand, it all. Everything they wanted and needed. A man who would help her fulfill every fantasy, every desire.

Every woman should have a man who gave everything he had in loving her.

If nothing else, Sara had long lived with the idea that she could have it all—anything she wanted. Especially from Mac.

She wasn't ready to break that habit.

"You're a lot of big talk," she finally said.

"Yeah, I know."

"Why?"

"Why what?"

"If you didn't want to do this stuff with me then why all the talk about nipple clamps and toys and wild and crazy sex?"

He took a deep breath.

She didn't want to hear this. Even before he opened his mouth, she knew it. He'd been calling her Sara for the past several minutes. That was never a good sign.

"I was trying to run you off."

"Off?"

"Convince you that you didn't want all of this."

"This."

"Me. Us. My life. Life with me. I wanted to scare you off."

"And now *you're* the one who's scared." She felt as bitchy as she sounded.

He winced. "I just don't see you that way."

"Are you actually going to give me the *let's just be friends* speech?" She preferred the fury that was slowly building to the feeling of desperation and anxiety that had been filling her before. "Because we are way past that, Mac."

"No. I want things to be the way they have been. It's been good, right?"

She couldn't deny that it had been good. But it could be more, she knew it. "Good isn't good enough."

"Dammit!" He finally exploded. "You've been pushing since day one. Can't you let up on anything? Can't you just be satisfied for a change?"

Sara wondered why she didn't feel hurt, or even angry at his words. But she knew this had to be bothering him. Mac had always given her whatever she wanted. It had to be just as strange, and difficult, for him to say no to her as it was for her to hear it.

"Satisfied? With you giving me and this marriage a half-assed effort?" she shot back. "No, sorry. I can't be okay with that."

"Half-assed?" He looked truly offended. "I have lived up to every single vow I said to you, Sara! I'm here. I'm with you. Only you. Forever."

"But you're holding back. There's something..." A thought occurred to her that made her chest literally hurt. "You don't think I'll be enough for you," she said quietly. "You're afraid I won't be as good as the other women and you'll be disappointed, but won't be able to get out of it. But if we just stick with the basics, then you can always blame that for being less than satisfied, rather than blaming me."

He looked like she'd just kicked him in the groin, shock and pain obvious.

"No," he said firmly. "Not that."

"Then you think you're protecting me. Sweet little Sara shouldn't be exposed to this naughty stuff." *That* idea pissed her off. "For some reason you need to cling to the idea of me being conservative and straight-laced."

"Maybe a little," he said cautiously. "But not really."

"Then you're afraid I'll think less of you if you *really* tell me what goes on in your brain?" she pressed.

"Yes! No! All of that and none of that!" he exclaimed. "I *hate* when you try to psychoanalyze me. You got a B in Human Psychology!"

She gasped. That B had devastated her. And she'd ended up graduating with honors anyway! "I got an A-plus in *Abnormal*

Psychology though!"

"I was just trying to get rid of you!" he finally bellowed. "I can't have nipple-clamp sex with you Sara. I don't totally get it either, but it's just too...*weird.*"

Her anger dissolved like salt in boiling water. It was just gone. It didn't matter why he felt the way he did. It just was.

A deep, heavy depression pressed in on her heart.

"That was why we came to Oscar, isn't it?" she asked, the truth clear. "And the frozen burritos and no car and the sweatpants? You pulled out all the stops to get me to leave."

He nodded, looking as exhausted as she felt.

The plan made sense. It should have worked. If she was the woman Mac thought she was. The woman she'd even believed she was until recently.

But what she knew now and he didn't realize was that she was a princess by choice. Not out of necessity, not because she couldn't help it. But because it had worked for everyone, including her, for a long time.

The problem was Mac saw himself as the servant boy or the black knight, not completely worthy of the princess.

And she honest to God didn't know what to do about it.

Maybe they had rushed into all of this after all. She'd believed just being together would be enough, but it was obvious Mac had some misconceptions about who she was.

In spite of the past twelve years, he didn't really know her. So he couldn't see he was the best man for her.

She really hated it when everyone else was right.

"You've always been the one to help me solve my problems," she said. "Now that you are my problem, what do you suggest?"

"You've been okay with the missionary position," he pointed out.

She felt the tears building. "That's not the point."

"What is the point?"

"You're only seeing me as you want to see me. Pretty much how you've always seen me. Me being the damsel in distress, needing you to save and protect me, was something you needed as much as I did." She took a deep shaky breath. "You and my brother and the guys, are heroes. You take care of people. Thinking of me as someone you needed to worry about was easy, it's what you do. Thinking about me differently will take some effort, might make you uncomfortable, might be a little confusing for a while. Guys like you like to be in charge. You don't like to be uncomfortable and confused."

"You're doing it again..." he said in warning.

"I'm a grown woman. I have needs and ideas that are bigger than any of you can imagine. I need a partner, a lover, a friend...not a guardian."

"Maybe I've had too many years of seeing you only one way."

She nodded as her throat tightened. Maybe. Maybe some ideas just couldn't be undone.

"I want you to love who I really am, Mac."

"I do love you."

"Part of me," she agreed. Which wasn't enough. That she was sure of.

There was a long silence between them.

Then quietly he asked, "Now what?"

She took a deep breath. Her stomach hurt. Her heart hurt. But her thoughts were very clear. "I think it's time for me to do what you've been wanting me to do since St. Croix. I'm going home to Omaha."

He stared at her, as if letting the idea sink in. For a moment she thought he was going to protest. Then he nodded. "I'll take you."

"*No*!" God, he'd agreed with her. Her head had expected it. Her heart rejected it. She shook her head vehemently. "Absolutely not. I'm not going to be cooped up in a car with you for the next hour."

He raised an eyebrow. "Fine. You can take the car."

Apparently he wasn't going to try to talk her into staying.

Sara shook her head again. "You need it for work tomorrow. I'll take Sully."

"He won't make it all the way to Omaha."

She shrugged. "If not, I'll call Jess or Sam."

He accepted that, because he couldn't argue they would come in a heartbeat. She'd be fine. It was the middle of the day.

She had to get away from him and headed for the closet, praying her tears would hold off. She thought of other things instead. At home she could go to the Cheesecake Factory and get four pieces to go, swing through Starbucks, then get into her Jacuzzi bathtub, turn on the Home and Garden network and then crawl into bed under her down comforter...and stay there for the next week or so.

Of course, as soon as Kevin heard her footsteps on the floor above his head, he'd be at her door with a pizza and the rest of the gang on their way.

Which also sounded really great.

She emerged in the stupid baggy sweatpants Mac had bought her because they were the first things she grabbed. Not caring a bit how she looked, she also put on the first shirt and shoes she grabbed.

Mac was not in the bedroom—thank God—when she came out. She didn't see him again at all as she headed for the barn with only her purse and car keys.

The sob that had been building since she realized her marriage was falling apart finally broke free. She angrily wiped the tears away as she climbed into Sully's passenger seat and slid over behind the wheel. He started right up, bless his heart, but he died before she cleared the barn doors. She gave him the love words he needed, then clutched, shifted and started forward again.

Things were good until the end of the driveway.

It was going to be a long trip to Omaha.

By the time she pulled into the Gas and Gulp to fill up, she was over the worst of the crying and was feeling pretty proud of keeping Sully running without incident at the stop sign on the outside of town.

She started the pump and decided to list all of the reasons Mac was an idiot to let her go instead of crying.

She made it to *great dancer* when she heard, "Sara? Are you okay?"

Sara turned to find Angie heading for the car parked on the other side of the gas island.

"Sure, why would you ask?" she said in as cheerful a voice as she could muster.

"Um, because of that," Angie said, indicating Sara's clothes. "I've never seen you look like...that."

Sara glanced down. The too-big sweatpants were gray, the flip-flops on her feet were bright green and the fitted tank she wore was purple. With sequins. She also knew her hair was coming down from the twist she'd put it in, she had no makeup on, her eyes were probably red from crying and her toenails desperately needed the polish touched up.

And she didn't care.

A true sign things were definitely not okay.

"I'm on my way to Omaha."

"Oh."

Of course, that didn't answer Angie's question about if she was all right and didn't address the unspoken question of why she looked like she was wearing bad hand-me-downs.

"Somebody sick?" Angie asked.

"No." Unless she counted the horrible nausea she couldn't get rid of. And the death of her marriage, of course.

"Just going to visit?"

"Kind of." She got busy unhooking the gas nozzle and recapping the tank.

"Mac going with you?" Angie leaned a shoulder against the post between the gas tanks, obviously not planning for this to be simple small talk.

Sara choked, then tried to cover it up. "Um, no."

"So what's going on?"

"Nothing."

"You sure this truck can make it that far?"

Sara glanced at Sully. "No."

"You need anything?"

Sara leaned in through the truck window and grabbed her purse. "No, I'm fi..." Her wallet wasn't there. Of course. She rested her forehead against Sully for a moment. Then she sighed.

A few weeks ago, Sara would have never believed she would ask Angie for anything. She would have never believed Angie would ask to give her anything for that matter. Sara felt like an idiot but she was a distressed idiot. Now that her mind and heart had settled on going home to Omaha, she was feeling a little desperate to get there. "Can I borrow twenty bucks?"

"Yes," Angie said without hesitation. She reached for her wallet.

"Thanks."

"But after you pay for the gas, I'll take you to Omaha."

"What do you mean?"

"I'll take you to Omaha. You shouldn't drive when you're upset."

"I'm not upset."

Angie pushed away from the post. "Sara, I've been married long enough to recognize the signs of a big fight."

Sara started to protest, then decided there was no point. "Okay. Thanks." Driving away from Oscar, away from Mac, seemed like a monumental task she wasn't sure she was up to.

All she needed was to get to Omaha where she could fall into her bed, spray her cinnamon *Good Night* pillow mist and sleep for the next sixteen hours.

"Don't you have to be at the shop today?" Sara asked after she'd paid for the gas, parked Sully around the side of the Gas and Gulp and climbed into Angie's car.

"Yeah, but we'll just reschedule. No one dies without a haircut."

"No one will be mad?"

"They'll understand when they find out a friend was in need."

Sara felt her surprise melt into a smile. "We're friends?"

"You've massaged my hands and wrists, neck and feet. You brought me an aromatherapy candle. You gave me that article about how to boost my serotonin. If I had money, power or fame I'd think you were just kissing up, but since I don't, I'm thinking maybe you did it because you're a nice person who found out I have fibromyalgia and is trying to help. I'm smart enough to be friends with someone like that."

Sara didn't care that Angie was not an overly warm and fuzzy person. She leaned in and awkwardly hugged the other woman. "I made a friend, all on my own."

Angie didn't answer and Sara could almost feel the eye roll. She smiled anyway.

They drove for nearly fifteen minutes in a relatively comfortable silence.

But Sara slowly felt the desire to talk build until she said, "I got a snake out of the house the other day."

Angie looked genuinely surprised. "Good for you."

"And I had to clean out the fridge the other day."

"Good."

"There was some nasty stuff in there."

"You've never done that before?"

Sara shuddered. "No way. I rarely eat at home and I hate leftovers so nothing stays in my fridge more than a day or two."

"But you survived."

"Yeah." Sara got quiet again for a while. Then she said, "I didn't tell Mac about either of those things."

"Why not?"

"I suppose for the same reason Mac can't see me in nipple clamps. Force of habit."

Angie coughed in surprise. "Well, that's fixable," she announced as she recovered.

Sara wiped away the one tear she'd let fall. "I don't know. I think once you decide that cheesecake is best with raspberries and you really, really like it that way, then there's not much motivation to change the perception."

Angie didn't say anything at first. Then she asked, "Are you the cheesecake or the raspberries?"

Sara snorted.

Angie grinned. "I assume that you're worried that Mac really, really likes his perception of you and doesn't really want to change it? But I'm not clear if he really, really likes your cheesecake...or your berries."

Sara couldn't believe it but she laughed. "I guess I'm the cheesecake. Our relationship is the raspberries. He likes the raspberries, has liked them for years, so doesn't want to try anything else."

"Raspberries are really good on cheesecake," Angie offered.

"Sure they are. But the Cheesecake Factory has made a fortune on the fact that there are lots of things just as good or better."

"Good point."

Sara sighed. "Do you think you can change someone's perception of something even if they don't want to change it?"

Angie looked at her in disbelief. "Seriously?"

"Yes, seriously."

Angie laughed out loud. "Sara, you *forced* me to change my perception of you. You refused to let me see you only as the girl who wore killer heels, body glitter and was only interested in manicures.

You brought us cinnamon rolls, talked my ear off, cleaned the shop."

"I won you over?" Sara asked, somewhat teasing.

"You did." Angie sighed heavily. "In spite of myself. And *I* wasn't madly in love with you. I'm sure you can change how he sees you."

"How?"

"Tell him about the snake, for instance."

"Um..."

"Come on, Sara. Show him who you are. Don't let him get away with just seeing the heels and body glitter. Show him that you can scrub sinks and rub someone's shoulders and paint someone else's toenails. Show him what you're made of."

"More than raspberries?" Sara asked with a smile. Regardless of what Mac thought, Angie liked her. That had to count for something.

"You're obviously more than raspberries," Angie said.

"Obviously?" Sara repeated. Then laughed. "Yeah, obviously," she said with sarcasm.

"You've been out of your element for almost two months and you're doing great," Angie said. "You've figured out how to get around not having Internet access, not having a car, not having any friends. You've even figured out how not to starve."

Sara thought about that. "I did make spaghetti the other night."

"Sauce in a jar?"

"Yeah. It was great."

Angie laughed and shook her head. "There are all kinds of amazing things that come in jars and boxes and mixes."

Sara smiled and settled back into her seat. Was Angie right? Was this fixable?

She wasn't sure if things were fixable with Mac. He might not ever see her as anything other than the little girl he'd always taken care of. But *she* could see her as more than that. And maybe that was the most important thing.

Chapter Thirteen

Mac had never been in as bad a mood as he was in the weeks after Sara left.

Oh, he knew exactly where she was and he wanted to go to her. Badly.

But he also knew he shouldn't. He shouldn't have gone after her in St. Croix. This was his second chance to *not* follow her and mess up both their lives. So he was going to do it right this time.

"Of all my friends, I thought you were the bright one." Sam crossed to the coffeepot without even looking at Mac.

"Nope. That would be Ben." Mac kept his eyes resolutely on the TV screen in front of him. He'd seen the movie at least twice before but there was lots of shooting and swearing and things blowing up, which fit his mood perfectly. As it had for the past ten weeks.

"Well, sure. Ben can save my life if I'm impaled with a sharp object. But you're the one who knows stuff about *stuff.*"

"That's stupid," Mac told him.

He wasn't in the mood for whatever this was. Why couldn't his friends just leave him the fuck alone? Every one of them had tried to talk to him about Sara in the days right after their breakup. Since being told, explicitly, where they could each put their opinions they'd backed off a little. Not completely of course. That wasn't their style. But it had been only one of them spouting off every two to three days versus all of them hitting him every day.

Another explosion, taking out three cars and a warehouse. *That* was what he wanted to pay attention to. Shit being destroyed.

"You helped me realize how I felt about Danika."

"That was completely obvious though. You were just being a jerk."

"Yeah, well, you're being a jerk now, so I guess we'll be even."

Mac kept his eyes forward. Sam was treading on thin ice, to be sure, but hitting him wouldn't get Mac anything.

He tipped back his can of soda and decided ignoring Sam was the best course of action.

Probably the most impossible too.

"You made a promise to me, Mac," Sam said quietly.

It was the serious tone that finally pulled Mac's eyes away from the car chase and machine guns. "What?"

"You promised me she would be happy."

Mac stared at his friend. He and Sam had been through a lot. Sam knew him. Mac's mouth felt dry, his throat scratchy with regret as he said simply, "Yeah."

Sam's expression was somber. "So tell me what the hell this is."

Mac had beat himself up in every way possible. He'd been drunk every night he hadn't worked and had gladly suffered the hangovers the next morning.

He'd suffered through seeing Sara twice and not being able to touch her, hold her, *really* talk to her. It was all superficial—much more than it had been when they were just friends—and it felt wrong.

It was punishment he deserved.

He hadn't been sleeping or eating worth a damn. When he did sleep he tossed and turned with dreams and nightmares of Sara being hurt, never seeing her again, and having her hate him.

And there wasn't a minute in the day when he didn't think of her. Most of the calls they'd had at work had been routine, not requiring much mental power beyond the tasks he could literally do in his sleep.

Simply put, he was tortured. He was mentally and physically hurting and exhausted. With no end in sight.

Now, on top of all of that, his best friend was pissed at him.

"She wants things I can't give her," Mac finally said. "I thought I could show her that life with me wasn't what she wanted. Turns out, life with her isn't what I want."

"Bullshit." Sam came to stand right in front of him, blocking the TV. "There's never been a thing that Sara's wanted you couldn't or wouldn't do."

"Now there is."

"The one thing you've always done is kept her from being hurt."

"Right. That's what I'm doing."

"She's hurt *now*, Mac. By you. She's miserable. It's been almost three fucking months."

Mac didn't want to be happy about that. He shouldn't want her to miss him. That was ridiculous when he was the one that told her to leave. "She said she's miserable?"

"No. I've barely seen her," Sam said. He paced a few steps away, then back. "It's driving us all nuts."

"All?"

"No one has seen her much. She's not home most evenings. She doesn't always answer her cell. She comes to about half the dinners and stuff we invite her to. What's going on?"

Mac frowned. It wasn't his problem. It couldn't be his problem. That was the mistake he'd made in the first place—getting too involved with Sara, jumping in when she did something a little out of character.

"How should I know? I haven't seen or talked to her."

"She'd take your call."

Mac shook his head, positive that wasn't true. "I'm the last one she would talk to."

"What happened?"

Instead of angry, Sam suddenly sounded worried and that was a hell of a lot harder to resist. "I can't talk to you about it."

"Why the hell not? She's my sister—"

"Exactly. I'm not talking about my marriage to your sister with you."

Sam stared at him. "It's about sex?"

Mac sighed. "Kind of." But not really. That was just how the whole thing had manifested.

"You want to talk to Kevin about it?" Sam asked.

"No." He couldn't talk to his reformed Christian friend about the deeper meaning of nipple clamps.

"Ben's in surgery," Sam said. "What about Jess or Danika?"

"Well, Jessica is also Sara's sibling so she's out," Mac said dryly.

"Right. Dani?"

Mac thought about that. "Where's Dooley?"

"Dooley? You want to talk about a *relationship* with Dooley?"

"He might get it."

Sam was clearly confused by that. "Dooley? Doug Miller? The guy who panics if a woman expects him to spend more than fifty bucks on a date? *He* might get this?"

Mac shrugged. He agreed it seemed strange. "One time he said some things that got me thinking."

"Oh, my God, hell is freezing over as we speak," Sam muttered, starting for the door into the kitchen area. "Fine. I'll go get him. Whatever it takes to pull your head out of your ass."

Two minutes later, Dooley strode in. "It's a sad day when you're looking for my advice."

Mac agreed, but didn't say so out loud. "Do you have any?"

"Advice?" Dooley took the chair to Mac's right and propped his feet on the coffee table. "About Sara? Hell yeah."

Mac waited. Dooley watched a building blow up in the movie. "You want to share it?" Mac asked, sounding more patient than he felt.

"I did."

"When?"

"That first day I saw you after you guys broke up."

Mac thought back, scowling. Everyone had shared advice and opinions from a simple, *You're an idiot* to *Leave her alone* to *Take her back to St. Croix.*

"What did you say?"

Dooley pinned him with an intent look. "I said to just do whatever it is she wants you to do."

"Yeah, that sounds easy, but..."

"And now I have more to add to that advice," Dooley interrupted.

"Okay," Mac said slowly. "Lay it on me."

"You sure?"

"Yes."

"Listen to her."

Mac thought there might be more, but when Dooley turned back to the movie, he had to ask, "What does that mean?"

Dooley kept his eyes on the TV. "Just listen to her. None of us really do that."

"How do you... What do you mean?"

Dooley swung his feet back to the floor and leaned his forearms on his thighs, looking at Mac again. "I've been spending more time with Miss Sara since you haven't been around. Old habits die hard and Sam and Ben wanted Kevin and I to still hang out with her when she's at the center."

"She went back to work?" Mac couldn't explain why that disappointed him a little. Sara had realized she wasn't rewarded working there in a made-up job.

"She's volunteering like the rest of us," Dooley corrected. "Anyway, I've been spending more time with her. As long as you've been around the rest of us didn't spend more than an hour or so with her at a time. Now I've been spending like half a day. And I realized a couple of things."

"Things I missed?" Mac was angered by the insinuation. More by the fact that it might be true.

"Yeah," Dooley said, never one to worry much about someone else's feelings. "She's not who you, we, think she is."

"She said something like that too."

"I'll give you an example. The other day she unstopped a toilet at the center."

Mac could admit Dooley had surprised him with that. "A toilet?"

Dooley nodded. "Yep. And it wasn't the first time. She was pretty comfortable with the plunger."

That was hard to believe.

"And one of the boys got a bloody nose playing basketball and she took care of it."

"Blood?" Mac asked. That didn't seem like Sara at all.

"Yeah. No problem. The kids said she's done it several times. But you wouldn't know that because if you'd been there you would have taken care of it."

"And she would have happily let me."

"Maybe," Dooley agreed. "But it doesn't mean she *can't* handle something just because she chooses not to."

Mac had to give him that point.

"Did you know she got a snake out of the farmhouse by herself?"

Mac's eyes widened. "A snake?"

"A completely harmless garter snake," Dooley said. "But she didn't know it was completely harmless. Which makes all the difference."

Mac tried to picture it. Sara and a snake. Sara not freaking out about a snake. Sara handling a snake.

He couldn't quite do it. But he was impressed anyway.

"What are you really saying, Dooley?"

"That she isn't the little girl who needed someone to help her with math or drive her to piano lessons or nurse her through chicken pox."

"I'm just supposed to snap my fingers, change my mind, take twelve years of habits and change them overnight? I've tried. Believe me, I want to. I can't."

Dooley pushed to his feet. "No. You can't just change your mind like that."

"Then what?"

"Date her."

"What?"

"Date your wife. Listen to her. Get to know her."

"I know her. I know her better than anyone."

"You know her as your friend's little sister who's always been around as part of our group, who's there for pizza night, who can kick your butt at most video games, who taught you how to do the Macarena. You don't know her as a woman, someone you could have a one-on-one relationship with, someone who will love you even when you screw up."

Mac wasn't sure what shocked him more—that Dooley was making a big speech about relationships and emotions or that he was right.

"The one-on-one thing is probably the hard part," Dooley concluded. "You've always had the rest of us to buffer your not-great moments."

"My not-great moments?"

"We all have them. But when we're all together, they don't seem so bad. When you're one on one there's a lot better chance she'll realize that you make mistakes, say stupid things and don't always have the answers."

Mac missed the next explosion in the movie. He didn't care about the car chase. He didn't even care about the heroine with the ripped tank top showing a bunch of skin.

He just sat and stared at Dooley, processing his words.

Finally he said, “Holy crap.”

“What?” Dooley had been watching the girl with the ripped-up tank top.

“*You're* not supposed to be the smartest one of us.”

Dooley smirked and pushed to his feet. “Just because I don't share my insights, doesn't mean I don't have them.” Dooley grabbed a soda from the fridge, popped the top and left the room whistling.

An annulment was surprisingly easy to get when both parties were agreeable, when they hadn't been married long enough to have any shared assets and when Mac had helped save the life of a very grateful judge.

The day it was final, Mac had gotten blisteringly drunk.

He knew an annulment was the right decision. He wanted to be married to her, but she had to want it too. They needed to start from scratch in several ways.

In addition, their friends had been very clear about the fact that they were not going to choose between Mac and Sara and everything had to be just as it was before. So for the past three months everyone had been acting like they always had, like the kiss at Sam's wedding, the trip to St. Croix and the marriage had never happened. And they were all stubborn enough to pull it off. Mostly.

“I have something I need to tell all of you,” Sara said as she passed the bowl of salad to Kevin.

All conversation around Jessica's dining room table ceased immediately. It had always been that way, the spotlight on her whenever she wanted it, but lately there was a general feel that no one knew what to expect from Sara. Announcements got major attention.

This one was likely even more monumental because the near-weekly dinner their group had enjoyed for years had only occurred three times since Sara had moved back to Omaha.

“What's up?” Sam asked.

Mac could see he was trying hard for a nonchalant expression.

“I'm taking a vacation.”

Jessica stared at her. "You just took one."

That was as close as anyone had come to bringing up St. Croix, or anything remotely related, with Sara and Mac both in the room. It was as if everyone was holding their breath.

"I know. I have to go again."

"I thought you had this class now."

Mac frowned. He didn't know she was taking a class. Were the massage therapy classes starting already? He'd thought she had to wait until the new session started in January.

"It will be done by the time I leave. I'm going in a few weeks."

"Where?" Kevin asked.

"Italy."

"With who?"

"Alone."

"No, you're not." Sam plunked a piece of bread onto his plate. "You're not running off again. And certainly not alone."

"I am." She said it calmly, looking directly at her brother. "There is absolutely no reason for me not to."

"You're a young woman who would be traveling alone in a strange country. You don't speak Italian, you don't know the money exchange..."

"*Mi imparare l'italiano. Mi fa molto bene.*"

Sam just blinked at her.

"I'm learning Italian. I'm very good at it," Sara repeated in English. "That's the class I'm taking. And I do know the money exchange. I talked to the bank about how to prepare and..."

"You're taking *Italian* in this class?" Sam asked.

"Yeah. Turns out I have an affinity for foreign language. Who knew?" Sara picked up her wineglass and lifted it toward her brother. "And I'm learning about wines and some Italian art and history. There's a house for rent that I can..."

"No!" Sam said firmly. "For God's sake, Sara. You know this isn't a good idea."

"Really, Sara," Jessica agreed. "Another country? What about a trip to New York or something?"

Mac watched the exchange with a growing mix of emotions. He

had been taking Dooley's advice and had been simply listening to Sara more. What he was witnessing was a variation on a scene that had repeated itself hundreds of times over the years. Sara was talking, proving she had put thought and preparation into the idea, but all Sam and Jessica heard—and all he would have heard prior to Dooley's insight—was that she wanted to do something that worried them.

"I think it's a great idea."

Everyone at the table turned to look at him. Surprise was the predominate emotion.

"You think she should go to Italy?" Sam finally asked.

"I do," he said. He did. He wanted Sara to be the type of woman who could—and would—travel to a foreign country alone. Because then he could start getting used to that woman.

"You plan to go along?" Sam asked.

"No." She had to do this alone.

"What if she gets lost? Gets her purse stolen? Some guy makes a move?"

"She'll have to ask for directions. Or talk to the police and call to have her credit cards suspended. Or use the self-defense skills we insisted she learn a few years ago."

Sam stared at him. Mac understood why. In the past, Mac would have protested something like this even more adamantly than Sam.

"Sara's smart and resourceful, Sam." She had made life in Oscar work, even when there had been intentional curve balls thrown her way. "If she wants to go to Italy, she should go."

He finally glanced at Sara. She was staring at him with more surprise than her brother.

"Are you okay?" she asked.

"Completely fine, thanks."

"Hit your head on anything lately? Running a fever? Finished a bottle of wine all by yourself?"

He lifted his beer in toast. "Just paying attention."

Her eyes narrowed, but she didn't say anything more to him.

The group dropped the subject, somewhat reluctantly, and they moved from salad to chicken. Just as everyone was served, the doorbell rang. Ben got up to let Chad Pearson in. *Dr.* Chad Pearson.

Mac shifted in his chair, his almost-good mood dead instantly.

Dammit.

Chad was Ben's new intern and had been invited to the other two group dinners as well.

He annoyed the shit out of Mac.

Chad came into the dining room, laughing with Ben. He greeted everyone with his big smile, then leaned in and kissed Sara on the cheek.

Mac breathed in through his nose, consciously relaxing his hold on the sharp utensil he held.

He hadn't seen Chad kiss Sara before but he'd suspected interest on the young doctor's part from the start. Now it was quite obvious.

"Sorry I'm late," Chad said as he pulled out the empty chair next to Sara. "Emergency hip fracture. I agreed to stay."

Mac wondered why he hadn't noticed the empty chair. He'd sat opposite of Sara on purpose. It was easier to watch her from across the table. But he'd thought nothing of the chair next to her, because everyone else had already been accounted for. Or so he'd thought.

Ben passed Chad a full plate. "We all know how that goes."

Mac glanced at Sara. She was refilling her wine glass.

Mac watched Sara nod at something Chad whispered in her ear and chewed his chicken harder than necessary. He washed it down with a long swig of beer. Something about Chad drove him nuts. Not his perfect hair, his genius IQ or that everyone at the table thought he was incredibly funny. Mac's friends, being who they were, made sure he knew all about Chad's family's money, his dedication to charity work and his recent support of the Bradford Youth Center, as well as the fact that he had completed three triathlons. It wasn't even that he was interested in Sara. It was more...ambiguous than that. He didn't quite fit with Sara and he didn't seem to be trying very hard.

Mac accepted another beer from Ben, finished his dinner and managed enough uh- huhs and grunts to keep anyone from asking him what was wrong. The whole time he watched Chad.

He wanted to punch him. Not surprisingly. But it was odd because he didn't want to punch him because Chad touched Sara too much, or because he was making her laugh, or because he hung on every word she said. In fact, he didn't do any of those things throughout the dinner.

The damned idiot.

She was sitting right there, in a light peach-colored clingy dress—the type she'd given up for blue jeans in Oscar—and looked amazing. Which Chad had commented on. But he was keeping his hands to himself. He seemed to think what Dooley was saying was more important than looking at Sara.

Idiot.

Maybe it was because they weren't alone. Maybe he didn't think her family and friends would appreciate public displays of affection. He didn't know them very well, but maybe deserved points for respect.

"Chad, you want another beer?" Mac asked. He had no idea who had been talking or what topic he'd just interrupted.

Chad looked at him. "Uh, sure."

"Could you grab me one too?" Mac tipped his bottle back and finished off the one in his hand. He knew it was rude. He didn't care.

"Mac, I'll just—"

Jessica started to get up as Chad predictably broke in with, "No. Please, Jessica, let me." He pushed back from the table. "Anyone else need anything?"

Everyone, predictably, declined.

As soon as Chad disappeared around the corner Mac got several *are you kidding me?* looks and a "What was that?" from Ben.

He ignored them. His eyes were only on Sara.

She didn't seem upset that her ex-husband had been rude to her new potential boyfriend. She just picked up her wine glass again.

"Sara, you should go get some more bread," he said.

She frowned at him. "If you want bread..."

"Just go." Something in his face or tone or body language kept her from arguing.

She stared at him for a moment then narrowed her eyes, stood stiffly and muttered, "Fine," through gritted teeth.

Mac sat back in his chair and glanced at his watch. It was quiet around the table for twelve seconds.

Then Danika asked, "Do I want to know what's going on?"

"He's been sitting next to her for almost forty minutes. She looks and smells amazing. He should have a chance to show her how interested he is without the rest of us watching."

Mac knew Sam, Dooley, Kevin and Ben thought he was insane—or perpetually drunk—since his breakup with Sara. They would just chalk this up as further proof.

"Wait, you want him to make a move on Sara?" Danika asked.

The idea made Mac want to howl. And drink. And punch something. Then again, Sara was a very sexual person—as he well knew—and deserved to be with a guy who couldn't keep his hands off of her.

"She at least deserves to have the option. To have the option, she has to know he's interested. To show he's interested he needs some privacy."

"You want her to have options?" Danika asked softly.

"She needs to find the perfect guy for her. To make a choice, you have to have options."

He grabbed the beer in front of Sam and downed what was left in three swallows.

Sara was back in less than two minutes. She set the French bread loaf on the platter in front of Mac that still had half a loaf on it.

He gaped at her.

"What?" she snapped, whipping the napkin off of her chair so she could sit.

"That was fast."

"It's already baked," she said. "How long did you think it would take?"

If she'd come into a room alone when he was in there? Nothing less than thirty minutes. Longer if the door had a lock.

"Fucking idiot," Mac muttered, getting to his feet.

"Mac, wha—"

He stomped down the hall to the kitchen, ignoring the partial question from his hostess.

"What the hell are you doing?" he asked Chad, who was clearly looking for a bottle opener for the two beers in his hand.

"Um, I can't—"

"Sara was just in here with you."

"Yeah. She got the other loaf of bread."

"What did you get?"

Chad looked confused. He held up the bottles. "Beer."

"Did you cop a feel, run your hand up under that skirt, *kiss* her?" Mac demanded, coming farther into the room.

"Uh." Chad looked more confused and a little concerned. "Of course not."

"Of course not? What's that mean?"

"I, um, well we're—"

"Sara's amazing. And you're an idiot."

"Excuse me?"

"The front of that dress dips low and with those straps she isn't wearing a bra. You could have easily slid a hand in. Let her know what you're thinking."

Chad looked completely shocked.

"At least mess her up a little, a good long wet kiss, something—"

"Mac!"

He turned to find Sara and Jessica in the kitchen doorway behind him. Sara's cheeks were red which he guessed was more due to anger than embarrassment.

"Have you even heard of a Super Wedge?" he asked Chad. "At least seen a picture?"

"A—a wedge?" Chad asked, stuttering in surprise.

"How about experience with clitoral gels?"

Chad couldn't even stutter that time.

"Okay, how about basic things about *her*. Do you know that she loves to play chess but she sucks at it?" Mac asked. "Do you know that she likes to take baths and prefers strawberry-scented bubbles? Do you know that she's read all of the Harry Potter books twice? Do you know that—"

"*Okay,*" Sara interrupted. Her voice was a little hoarse. "That's enough, Mac."

"Come here." He motioned Sara to him.

She raised an eyebrow and crossed her arms. He could almost hear the *Yeah, right.*

He grinned. He liked that. She wasn't quite as enamored with him as she used to be. That was good.

"Fine." He grabbed Chad by the front of his shirt. "Then *you* come here." He pulled him forward until Chad stood in front of Sara. She straightened in surprise. Mac grabbed Chad's hand and put it on Sara's butt. "Every time you get a chance your hand should be there," Mac told him. "Now kiss her."

"Mac!" Sara protested, her cheeks pink.

Chad's hand didn't move. He even pulled her forward. Which was good Mac told himself firmly.

"Kiss her," Mac said again, pretty sure his voice didn't sound menacing. Much.

When Chad leaned in, Sara glared at Mac, then wrapped her arms around Chad's neck and lifted her lips. Chad kissed her. Even with a little tongue. Mac's molars took additional punishment but he didn't tear them apart—or dismember Chad—which he counted as personal growth.

When they parted, Chad was breathing harder.

Sara wasn't. She wasn't even a little flushed. She looked almost disappointed. And she should have been. That was not a kiss.

"No," Mac said, impatiently. "Like this." He grabbed Sara's arm and spun her up against him. He put his hand right where Chad's had been on her butt, then tunneled the other in her hair. He pulled the strands just enough to tip her head back, then sealed his mouth over hers.

It took three seconds for her to melt against him, to raise on tiptoe and to wrap her arms around his neck. She groaned, and he slid his hand from her butt to her thigh and then pulled her leg up to his hip. Fitted against her where he craved her most, he backed her up to the wall and pressed close.

"Mac," she gasped, tipping her head so he could taste her neck as he slipped one of the straps of her dress from her shoulder. The bodice started to slip and Mac's lips followed.

Suddenly cold water splashed against the side of his face. Sara gasped and he jerked his head up. He turned to find Jessica holding an empty glass. She raised an eyebrow.

Mac looked down at Sara. "Something like that," he murmured.

Now she was breathing heavy, flushed and ready. For him. He let her leg go, feeling it slide along the length of his thigh. He pulled her strap back into place. Jessica tossed her a towel for the water that had splashed on her as well.

"So, Chad," Mac said, turning. "Do you think you could come up with a couple positions on a Super Wedge?"

"Mac!" Sara exclaimed.

"Because Sara has pictures of at least five," he went on. "And if you're going to deserve her, you'd better get a book or something."

"Mac..." Jessica said, warning in her tone.

He focused on Chad, ignoring the women. "Do you know how to pleasure a woman like Sara? Because it can't be over the top. No leather or anything. But you'd better be creative with chocolate syrup and not be shy about some public stuff."

"Oh, my God!" Suddenly Sara was in front of him, her hands flat on his chest, pushing him back. "Shut up, Mac! You're *not* telling other men what I like sexually! What is wrong with you?"

He wrapped his fingers around her wrists and held her, truly looking into her eyes for the first time in weeks. "You deserve the best. You deserve someone who makes you laugh, who takes care of you but knows when to let you struggle a little on your own, someone who will think you're sexy in high heels or tennis shoes, who will take five hours to show you how to cut, stain and put up wood trim even though he knows you'll never do it yourself. And then be happy to do it for you."

She pressed her lips together and nodded. He heard Jessica sniff behind him.

"You also need someone who can be what you need and whose needs you can completely fill sexually. Don't settle for someone who can't love you the way you deserve and worship that amazing body, heart and soul."

"You told me to come home," she said softly.

Grudgingly, he said, "This is supposed to be better for you than what I can offer."

Sara felt her heart swell with love and hope. "You don't think it is?"

He didn't look happy about it. "I thought we always gave you everything you wanted. Turns out, we give you what we think you need, do what we think you need us to do and don't listen or pay that much attention to you really. That's how I missed that you'd grown up. I think we all did."

"Hey," Jessica protested.

Sara shot her sister a look. "I've got this, Jess."

"Come on, Chad," Jessica said with a sigh. "Apparently no one in here needs either of us."

Chad looked more than happy to leave.

"By the way," Sara said to Mac. "Chad's engaged."

Mac looked at the other man's retreating back. "Oh."

"To someone else," she clarified as the door swung shut behind them.

"He kissed you when he first got here tonight."

"On the cheek. And he kissed Jessica and Dani too."

"He did?" He'd totally missed that. Completely focused on Sara as he'd been, it wasn't really surprising.

"So no worries there," she said softly.

Mac focused on her again. "I've done it too, princess."

"What?"

"Assumed I knew best what you need and want. I haven't spent a lot of time listening to you."

"Well," she said slowly, knowing she had to share with him what she'd learned in the past month without him, since Oscar. "The thing is, you all had to assume, because I didn't know all of what I needed or wanted. And I didn't realize how much of what I wanted I could get for myself."

"And now you've figured it out?"

"Some of it," she answered honestly. "I'm working on the rest."

Jessica and Sam were expanding their lives. They had other things to concentrate on, to make them happy and fulfilled. She was still important to them, but she wasn't—and shouldn't be—the center of their lives.

"Sara," Mac said. His hand cupped her cheek.

"Yeah?" She loved that he was here, that he'd scared Chad off, that he had been paying attention and knew this life wasn't where she should be anymore.

"I can't believe I'm saying this, but I mean it. No one will ever take care of you the way I can."

"I know."

"And taking care of you the right way doesn't mean always doing everything you want, every time you want."

"I know."

"It does mean loving you more than anything. Which makes me the perfect candidate."

"I know. And I love you too, more than anything."

"Will you go steady with me?"

She laughed in surprise. "What?"

"I want to date you. But it has to be exclusive."

"Date me?"

"Yes. Let me get to know you. Let me get to know this confident, independent woman you've become."

That made her tear up. "Yes. I'll date you."

He stood, just looking at her, for a long time. Sara loved it. She just looked right back, taking a deep breath. This was real, this was right—

"You smell like cotton candy," she said suddenly.

He grinned. "I know."

She quirked an eyebrow and stepped even closer. She rose on tiptoes and put her nose against the skin at the base of his throat, pulling in a deep breath. Yep, cotton candy. She flicked out her tongue and tasted his neck. Definitely cotton candy.

"Why?"

"It reminds me of you."

"Won't the guys tease you?"

"I've been so pissy lately no one is getting close enough to me to smell anything."

She smiled. "Got it." She licked along his collarbone. "Let's go home."

"Yeah." He sighed. "Okay." His hands dropped to her rear end and squeezed.

"You don't have to sound so excited," she teased.

"Honey, it's pure relief."

She felt her heart melt a little. "Oh. Good." She rose on tiptoe and flicked her tongue just below his ear, relishing his groan of pleasure. "And for the record, from now on home means Oscar."

"I know."

"And you should know I'm starting a business in Oscar, just like I planned," she said.

"When will your classes be done?"

"Oh, I'm not going to massage therapy school," she said.

"Oh?"

"I wanted my own business, something that would contribute, and that was the first thing that seemed to make sense. But it was just convenient. I have a much better business plan now. And I have six clients already."

"Clients? For what?"

"I'm starting a house-cleaning business."

Mac stared down at her. Then he suddenly tipped his head back and laughed. Loud and long and from the gut.

She just waited.

Finally he settled down enough to say, "I think you got the Cinderella story backward. You're supposed to go from cleaning the house to being the princess. You're going the other way."

She grinned up at him. "I guess so."

"Who are your clients?"

"Angie and some of the other gals who hang out at Style. They all work hard. They need someone to help them out like this."

"Angie told me she drove you back here. You got to be pretty good friends, huh?"

She lit up. "Yeah. A friend I made all by myself."

He pulled her close and rubbed his chin against the top of her head. "I might have started hanging out with you because of Sam but I've always liked you because of *you*, princess."

She felt her eyes sting a little. Besides, it had been three months since anyone called her princess. Dooley and Kevin had stopped after Mac told them to in Oscar, and Mac had been nothing but coolly polite over the past months, calling her Sara on the rare occasions where he addressed her directly. She wasn't going to be as much of a princess anymore, but...

Oh, who was she kidding? She was still going to get pedicures, would never know how to change the oil in her car and would *never* tolerate spiders. And she wasn't giving up her primping, or her creams and sprays, or her dresses for anything.

Which reminded her... "Oh, and I got another tattoo."

That made him push her back slightly to look at her. "You did not."

"Oh, yeah. I told you way back in St. Croix that I intended to get your attention. I thought maybe I had to start over."

He moved his hands to cradle her head as he looked into her eyes. "That's the ironic thing. I haven't paid any woman as much attention as I have you over the years and I still missed it."

"Missed what?"

"The fact that you're just my type."

She hugged him, then looked up. "Which means we *are* going to use nipple clamps and wedges and—"

He groaned. "Hell, yeah. As soon as possible."

"We just have to get back to Oscar."

"Or we could go to the toy store and then to your place."

She smiled. "Oh, you are *definitely* my type too."

"What about Italy?" he asked. "You still want to go?"

"I do," she said. "You want to come now?"

He shook his head. "I think you need to go alone. It might kill me, but I think it would be good for both of us."

"It's only for two weeks."

"And we can always have phone sex."

Ooh. "That's my guy."

Mac bent his head to take her lips again and Sara sighed with happiness.

This was exactly how it was supposed to go. Princesses were supposed to live happily ever after with their one true love.

Even the ones with dragons tattooed on their butts.

About the Author

Erin Nicholas has been reading and writing romantic fiction since her mother gave her a romance novel in high school and she discovered happily-ever-after suddenly went a little beyond glass slippers and fairy godmothers! She lives in the Midwest with her husband who only wants to read the sex scenes in her books, her kids who will *never* read the sex scenes in her books, and family and friends who say they're shocked by the sex scenes in her books (yeah, right!).

For more information about Erin and her books, visit:

www.ErinNicholas.com (including Twitter and Facebook links!)

http://ninenaughtynovelists.blogspot.com/

http://groups.yahoo.com/group/ErinNicholas/